About the Author

Henry Cockburn studied Classical Archaeology and Ancient History at St John's College, Oxford before embarking on a career in teaching. He lives in York with his partner, Lucy, and two sons, Joseph and Jonathan.

The Curious Business of Percival Lowe

Henry Cockburn

The Curious Business of Percival Lowe

Olympia Publishers
London

First Published in 2024

Olympia Publishers
Tallis House
2 Tallis Street
London
EC4Y 0AB

Printed in Great Britain

Dedication

For Joseph and Jonathan — a reminder that the only shadow of
which you should be afraid is your own.
For Lucy — who helped me to remember who I am.

Acknowledgements

Enormous thanks go to my brother, for his constant and earnest encouragement of my writing ever since we were boys together and to my sister, who has always believed in me. Thanks also to my grandmother, Celia, whose love of mystery set me off reading the very best sort of novels from a very young age and to the rest of my family who have tolerated my efforts for many years. Special thanks to Lauren, Charlie, Amy and Kaeli who read the book and encouraged me to push forward towards publication. And the greatest thanks of all to Lucy, without whose honesty, patient thoughtfulness and intellectual spark, this manuscript would have languished forever in a state of suspension.

PROLOGUE
DOVER, 1949

I cannot tell whether it is being back in England that has stirred in me a determination to set down this account of my young life. Perhaps it is the sudden simmering of memories encouraged by these familiar yet half-forgotten places that has brought upon me this strange compulsion. All others who might have told their parts of the tale, even those whose memories were imperfect or distorted, are long since gone and it would be the easiest thing in the world for me now to surrender to the sanctuary of oblivion.

And yet, I know the story must be told. Whether as a warning to others or some means of redeeming my own soul — I am certain that I shall shuffle on in this frail body, without rest, until I have set down fully and finally, with pen and ink, those remarkable happenings which, though they took place when I was still a young man, were to set the course of my adult life.

It is not, however, quite so easy as all that. Whenever, in all these long years, I have wrestled with the question of whether to make public this account, I have concluded time and again that any good that might come of it would be far outweighed by the consequences of some individual taking this narrative as some form of practical guide — by their attempting to accomplish what I have accomplished — what *he* accomplished. For it may well be that Lowe and I have understood more than anyone of matters concerning the nature of man's existence, and yet, in doing so, perhaps we have lost what it means to be truly human.

11

Lowe.

It feels strange even to write the characters of his name after so long and it is hard to think of him clearly now as he was on the first day I met him — so alive, so quick, so alert. Although I swore against it, I suppose I have become like him in these recent years. Perhaps it is this that drives me to set down my account and to write it, of course, in the presence of my young companion, to whom I owe so much.

To those who would take this volume as instruction, then, I suppose I can do nothing to stop you. I would only caution you that to do so will bring you no joy and urge you instead to return to and value a quieter life, if such a route lies open to you.

With all other witnesses long dead and buried, it has fallen to me, and to me alone, to relate my own extraordinary exploits and to furnish some attempt at an explanation of what must be considered the most curious business of Percival Lowe.

CHAPTER ONE
LONDON, 1900

The lettering above the drab window of Percival Lowe's office was so faded and so damaged by long exposure to the elements, that I should never have found it at all had I not been looking for it with the utmost care. The day was a dull, wet one and the rain poured from the heavens in great soaking sheets which were buffeted this way and that by the chill March wind. My overcoat and hat had been thoroughly drenched during the morning's fruitless search of the backstreets and narrower alleyways of Victoria. I had almost given up the whole affair as a bad lot when I stumbled across the place quite by accident.

I had paused beneath a shop canopy for a few moments to check my bearings and to make completely sure that I was not doubling back upon myself, when I happened to catch sight of the building standing directly opposite, the name of the proprietor still just discernible. I crossed the road and pushed against the door, only to find it locked. Moving to the window I found that the glass was so old and so dirty that it made it quite impossible to gain any sort of impression of what lay within. Curious as to what sort of an establishment it might be — for I can swear upon all that is sacred to me that at that moment I had no idea — I put my hand to my eyes and peered hopelessly into the blackness beyond.

"Can I help you, sir?"

The voice to my right came so suddenly and so unexpectedly

that I jumped back from the window in alarm and would have lost my balance and fallen headlong into the gutter had I not put out my good arm to steady myself.

"Can I be of any assistance?"

The voice was not unkind, but there was a degree of haughtiness in it; the tone was clipped and precise. Once I had entirely regained my balance and was fully sure of my footing, I looked up to see an elderly gentleman of medium height whose gaunt face was festooned with the most marvellous pair of bright white moustaches I had ever seen. He was looking at me appraisingly through the perfectly circular lenses of his spectacles and seemed utterly oblivious to the persistent rain.

"I am looking for the office of Percival Lowe," I said. For some reason I was unable to articulate in my mind, I found myself suddenly nervous.

"Then you have found it, sir," said the man with that same, strange tone that was at once both kind and peculiarly aloof. I noticed that he had a habit of tensing the muscles beneath his eyes every few seconds in such a way that you thought he might be about to smile, though the mouth never followed suit, remaining a fixed, mirthless line behind the hairy curtains of his moustaches.

"I was sent here," I stammered. I cursed myself for not having thought this out earlier on and for the clumsiness of my words. I was not much of a speaker at the best of times and the shiver brought on by the wind and rain was rendering matters considerably worse. "I was sent here by Henry Stubbs. He's a friend of Mr Lowe — he said that Mr Lowe might have an opening for me?" I had made every effort to try to mask my desperation, but it had tumbled out with those last few syllables all the same.

"I am not sure I know this Henry Stubbs," said the man, an air of suspicion in his voice, but not so much as to unsettle his blank, business-like attitude.

"He is a doctor, sir," I said, trying not to sound as if I were protesting. "He's in Cape Town. I was in the war, you see." I brandished my arm and the place where my hand ought to have been. The man recoiled from it at once; the stump was not yet fully healed and there was a good deal of dried blood upon it. For a moment I thought he might retreat and slam the door in my face, but he did not go back inside. Instead he regarded me thoughtfully.

"You have been in the war?" he asked, slowly.

"Yes, sir," I nodded. The weather had worsened — though I should not have thought this possible — and a steady stream of water was now pouring from the brim of my hat and from the tip of my nose. "Henry seemed to think that Mr Lowe would be able to make use of me."

"That remains to be seen," said the man, looking at me for the first time with some apparent interest. He paused for a few moments and seemed to be weighing something up in his mind. "Very well," he said suddenly and in a manner of utmost efficiency. "Would you please care to step inside for a moment, Mr Fairlea?"

I was so eager to get across the threshold and into the warm that the strangeness of his calling me by my name did not immediately strike me. It was only nearly a minute later, when I reflected upon his invitation, that I realised that I had not yet offered it to him. It was in that moment, as I turned to ask him how he had come by this information, I noticed that, although I had entered the shop, he had not. He had, instead, remained in the street looking slowly and thoughtfully up it and down it once, twice, three times, before finally satisfying himself, apparently, in his enquiry and stepping back inside, closing the door firmly behind him.

"My apologies, Mr Fairlea," he said, seating himself at an expansive wooden desk which seemed to occupy almost the entirety of that front room, stacked with ream after ream of papers. "This business is rather a peculiar and a particular enterprise and I am afraid one cannot be too careful." I nodded as if I understood what he meant, but the truth of the matter was, of course, that I hadn't the slightest idea.

"Now," he said, pulling a piece of paper toward him from a position near the bottom of one of the piles. "I shall need to take a few particulars from you before we may proceed. Mr Lowe likes to be thorough in these matters."

"Oh," said I, in surprise. "Then *you* are not Mr Lowe?"

"Correct." The muscles in his face twitched again, but there was no further response. He produced a pen and dipped it neatly into the ink. "Now," he said, "let us begin with your full name, if you please."

"George Fairlea," I said at once.

He looked up at me, sharply. "No middle initial?"

I shook my head. "No, sir, I came to my parents late in their lives and my mother—"

"Just so," he interrupted, scratching away with the pen on the paper. "Might I also trouble you for your date of birth?"

"The sixteenth of November," I said. "Eighteen seventy-eight."

"Just so." The pen flicked and the muscles twitched.

"My father's name," I began, assuming that the ordinary personal history was required and presuming to take the initiative.

16

"Is of precisely no consequence," said he, the tips of those great moustaches almost touching the page as he wrote. "Do I take it that you enlisted last year?"

"Yes, sir," I said. "I served five months before they took my hand."

At this he looked up again, those bright, careful eyes searching my face. "Why did you enlist?" he asked.

I was taken aback. It seems foolish to say it, but I had never given the matter very much thought. "I suppose," I said, slowly, "I perceived that I was becoming a burden to my mother and I imagine I wanted to do something for my country."

His eyes did not leave my face as I said all this, watching me and analysing. "You are sure," he said, at length, "that you were not merely seeking out danger for its own sake?"

"I don't understand," I said.

"Forgive me," said the man, "but it is important I clarify something with you. Did you envision in the war an opportunity for adventure and glory and honour?"

I felt the colour rising in my checks. I had encountered much of this sort of thing since my return to London and I found myself growing heartily sick of it.

"It is not that sort of a war," I said curtly. "There's no honour to be had fighting the Boers. You can go there yourself if you don't believe me. Go watch the men dying from their wounds in that infernal heat."

"Just so," said the peculiar man and attended once again to the document in front of him. His blank, emotionless response was utterly infuriating and I would have been inclined to speak further on the subject had it not been for a curious noise that began, at that moment, to fill the room. It was a soft, creaking, crackling sort of a sound which seemed to be emanating from the windows.

"Forgive the glass, Mr Fairlea," said the man, without looking up. "It is prone to complaint when there is a change in the temperature."

Until this point, I had not noticed any such thing, but now that he mentioned it, the air had indeed begun to feel a little cooler.

"It is easily remedied," he said, rising to his feet and attending to a small fire that had slumped low in its grate at the other side of the room. His seat vacated, I had a clear view through the doorway immediately behind the desk and down into the corridor beyond. Though it had appeared cramped when viewed from the other side of the street, the building was not insubstantial and stretched back some considerable way. I could just make out a staircase at the corridor's end and was trying to imagine the possible number of floors above when a silhouette slipped suddenly from one side of that passage to the other and was then gone. It might have been a trick of the light, or the flash of one of my eyelids, but I was certain that a person had moved between rooms.

"That is better," said the man and returned to his seat, obscuring my view once again.

"Is Mr Lowe at home?" I enquired, still trying to peer beyond the shoulder of my interviewer in hopes of glimpsing that shadow again, and perhaps the outline of my prospective employer. The man turned himself slowly in his chair and followed my gaze up the corridor. Then he looked back at me with an expression of deep curiosity on his face. I felt as if he wanted to ask me something, but the moment passed, and he returned to his former manner.

"Regrettably, not at present," he said, brusquely. "Though I

18

do expect him imminently. He has been called away on business."

"May I ask what sort of business it is in which Mr Lowe engages himself?"

The old man flashed his eyes up at me with just the merest hint of a warning in them.

"Mr Fairlea, we have limited time at our disposal. If you are interested in taking up a position here, then may I suggest we proceed with more important matters?"

Privately, I considered that understanding what sort of an operation it was with which I was becoming involved was, in point of fact, among the more important matters in need of attention. But I said nothing of this and allowed him to continue.

"Are you married, Mr Fairlea?"

"I am not."

"Betrothed?"

"No, sir."

"Are you engaged in any courtship at present?"

"I fail to see that that is any of your concern."

Once again, his sharp eyes, framed by those precise spectacles flashed up from the page which had now been half-filled with a neat cursive hand. "Everything is my concern, Mr Fairlea."

"Is this government work?" I asked, suddenly. I had heard that, for certain military operations, ex-soldiers and even civilians were being trained up as spies. "Is this Salisbury? If it is — I'll have none of it." I stood up from the desk and turned towards the door.

The man removed his spectacles and rubbed at his eyes with his hands. "Mr Fairlea," he said, "please allow me to assure you that Mr Lowe's operations are quite independent of the British government. Please do have the kindness to sit down, I have only a very few questions remaining."

There was nothing particularly imperious in his tone, yet I found I did as I was bid. In doing so, however, I allowed myself to risk another glimpse down that long, gloomy corridor, and for the second time, I thought I saw someone move from one side to the other, but the day being as dull and grey as it was, it was impossible to say for certain.

"Are you engaged in courtship at present, Mr Fairlea?" he repeated.

I shook my head and grimaced in the direction of what remained of my right hand.

"Just so."

For perhaps half an hour or more this process was repeated over and over — the man framing questions that probed my personal life and habits. Where had I been stationed during the war? Which engagements I had fought in? What feelings had I experienced when I had lost my hand? But also included apparently random information for which I could find no rationale. Thus, when the interview neared its conclusion, I had been required to reveal nothing of my paltry experiences of education but had been asked repeatedly to indicate whether or not I had visited Finchley. Though part of me was still keen to object and demand an explanation of the logic behind the process, the larger part of me was governed by the calm authority of my interrogator. At length, I sensed that our discussion was nearly at an end. The pen wriggled and twitched in his hand as he made a further note, then he looked up again, his face still twitching.

"Whom should I record as your next of kin?"

"That would be my mother, sir."

"Just so. No brothers or sisters?"

I shook my head. "My parents thought they were never to have children, then I came along when they no longer wanted them."

"Just so."

"Will you be wanting my mother's address?"

"That will not be necessary."

I was puzzled as to how the information would be of any use to Mr Lowe if no address were offered alongside it but had no intention of interrupting the clerk again. He appeared to have reached the end of his questions and the pen was feverishly working its way across the page. For some minutes there was no sound in the room save for the squeaky scratch of the nib on the paper. At last, he put down the pen, picked up the document, blew upon it heavily twice and then stacked it neatly on one of the piles.

"Well," I said, "what now?"

"Subject to the final approval of Mr Lowe, which is a mere formality, I assure you, I am pleased to offer you the position of assistant at the salary of three hundred pounds per year."

I let out a raucous laugh. The sum was impossibly vast. Even officers could not dream of such exorbitant amounts.

"Something amuses you, Mr Fairlea?"

"You are trying to make a fool of me. Nobody pays three hundred pounds a year for a man in my condition!"

"I assure you, sir, these are the terms I have been instructed to offer."

I stopped laughing.

"There are some conditions," said the man, looking not at me but into the depths of his inkwell. "Failure to comply with any one of them, at any time, will render this agreement null and void and your employment terminated."

I nodded. "What are these conditions?"

The man reached for a document that lay on the top of another pile, and having adjusted his glasses to better make out the fine print, he began to read. "The appointment is conferred subject to the following conditions: the person appointed must reside permanently in the business premises so long as he occupies his position."

This did not trouble me in the least. I had slept two nights in one of the rougher sorts of boarding houses recently and my small savings had been almost exhausted.

"Agreed," I said. "I assume that rent will be deducted against my salary?"

"There is no question of rent," said the man, matter-of-factly and continued reading before I had had any opportunity to express my astonishment. "The appointed person shall obey, without question or pause, the instructions and precepts of Mr Percival Lowe in all matters pertaining to his business."

"But I do not yet know what that business may be," I said. "And I have yet to meet Mr Lowe. What if I should find that the business is not to my taste?"

"Then you should be free to leave his employment at once."

The sum of three hundred pounds per year was now a dominant force in my mind; it interposed itself between the joints of my reason with rigid obstinacy. What, I considered, stood I to lose from this agreement? If all went well, I should find myself a man of considerable means. If not, then I would certainly be no worse off than presently. In any case, the following of orders I found personally distasteful would be nothing new to me.

I nodded slowly. "Very well."

The gentleman had just opened his mouth to form what

promised to be another 'just so' when a rogue draught gusted into the room from the corridor and displaced one of the piles of papers so that the pair of us were obliged to occupy some minutes in retrieving them from the floor, during which time that unusual creaking sound arose once again and much more virulently from the windows. The man attended to the fire once more and I collected up the remaining papers and handed them to him when he had returned to the desk.

"How clumsy of me," he said, with a shake of his head. "I do apologise. I must take greater care with my arms."

"But it was not your fault," I said, in some astonishment. "You never touched that pile! It was a draught from that door."

"I thank you for your kindness," said he, the muscles under his eyes pulsating wildly. "But I think, yes, I am quite certain I knocked them with my elbow."

I had no wish to contradict the old man nor to perpetuate a tedious conversation, so I did not insist upon the matter. Yet something in me thought it very strange indeed that he should have been so adamant on an occurrence of such little consequence.

"There is one final condition of your employment of which I must make you aware, Mr Fairlea," he said, returning to his scrutiny of the tiny lettering on the contract. "If you should, at any time, leave the employment of Mr Lowe either voluntarily or under less agreeable circumstances, you undertake to keep in confidence all that you have learned of the nature of his business, both general and specific until such a time as either Mr Lowe has deceased or until you yourself have quit this life."

"That's a very long time," I said.

"Perhaps," said the old man, with the smallest hint of a smile, "and then again, perhaps not." It was a black joke, and I didn't much like it. I considered the matter for a moment, and of course, my mind began to race through the possible implications of this clause. Mr Lowe was evidently a man who valued discretion and yet the nature of my interview gave me no cause to think that his enterprise was criminal in any way. Perhaps it was foreign trading or electioneering or something of that nature. Whatever it was, I thought, it sounded exciting and the cheerful ring of three hundred pounds a year and the warm thought of permanent board and lodging rendered it even more so. I agreed without further hesitation.

"Splendid," said the man, and he pushed the paper in my direction and indicated the place at which I should inscribe my signature. "Though I should add," he said, "that the offer is still contingent on Mr Lowe's personal approval, but I foresee no problem."

I put down the pen and sat back in my seat. The purpose of our meeting now achieved, an awkwardness sprang up. It was evident that the clerk wished to return to his work, but that my presence across the desk from him was a powerful impediment to his ability to do so. I was just on the brink of suggesting that I should go away and occupy myself in town and return later to meet with my new employer, when there was the rattling sound of a key turning in the lock. A few seconds later, the door opened, and bringing with him a spray of rain and a strong gust of that indomitable wind, in strode the remarkable personage of Percival Lowe.

He was not at all as I had imagined him. In my mind's eye the fabric of Percival Lowe had become indistinguishable from the fabric of his establishment and thus I had imagined him to be elderly and run-down, perhaps with a thinning crop of grey hair, his face lined and marred by the ravages of old age. I was therefore, quite surprised and delighted to discover, upon meeting him, that he was barely ten years older than I and probably two or three times livelier. Tall, though not to the point that he appeared gaunt or lanky, the character of his appearance was enhanced significantly by a jolly mop of red hair that sat merrily atop his head and which quivered and shook whenever he spoke quite in spite of the rainwater it had absorbed. His eyes were bright and quick and his mouth was very slightly turned upwards at the edges as if always on the brink of one of his famously expansive smiles. Though the inclement weather had dampened and bedraggled his appearance considerably, it was clear to me even at our first meeting that Percival Lowe was a man of taste and an avid follower of fashion. His apparel — stylishly tailored, no doubt at some considerable cost — was at complete odds with the chamber in which he now stood and yet he seemed entirely at home.

"Filthy weather," he announced, as he turned and shut the door behind him. "I have been out since nine this morning and I declare that, in all that time, I have been dry less than half an hour." He engaged himself for a few moments in wringing out his scarf and tapping the water from his hat with the end of his cane. Then he turned with the thought of addressing, I suppose, the elderly gentleman, but in observing my presence arrested this process at once.

"But this must be Mr Fairlea," he declared with a smile. "My dear fellow! How glad I am to meet you at last. I trust Crane here has made you comfortable."

"He has been most attentive," I said, truthfully.

"And what do we make of him, Mr Crane?" asked Lowe with a grin. "Does he pass muster for our purposes?"

"That is entirely your decision Mr Lowe," said Mr Crane and

he handed Lowe both the document upon which he had noted down my responses to his questions and the contract upon which I had scrawled my signature.

"Yes, yes," said my prospective employer no longer paying attention to the conversation but rather scrutinising both papers carefully. "My decision — my decision indeed — quite right, quite right." He lost himself for a moment in reading. I watched his lips move along with the words as he digested them. In doing so he took one of his long, elegant fingers and tapped it thoughtfully upon the end of his nose. There was silence for some minutes, during which Crane twitched uncomfortably.

"I beg your pardon, Mr Lowe," said Crane deferentially, "but in your absence this morning I received an urgent message from Mrs Finn."

"Finn?" enquired Lowe in great excitement, tossing the papers aside and fixing his quick clever eyes upon the old gentleman. "The widow in Knightsbridge, you mean?"

"The same, sir — she has requested that you call upon her at your earliest convenience and the messenger was keen to impart that the woman is in a state of some considerable distress." He rooted about in one of the drawers of the desk and produced from it a small envelope which was inscribed in what was undoubtedly a woman's hand. Lowe snatched it from him impatiently and tore it open. There were two sheets of paper inside, both of them covered in an immaculate, tiny script. He dispensed with the first quickly, dropping it onto the desk where it lay atop my contract and particulars, but his attention was caught by the second and his breathing slowed audibly as he read on, pausing only to murmur words such as 'untenable' and 'isolated' and accompanying these fragments with nods and an assortment of noises that might variously have been interpreted as approval or dismay.

At length, however, Lowe clicked his fingers with delight, threw the second sheet aside and then clapped his hands in a mood of decided jollity. "Capital!" he exclaimed. "Another success for our little outfit! I will go at once, of course!" Then he turned to me. "You shall come too, Fairlea!"

"Am I to take up the position?" I said, startled by this sudden turn of events.

"Why of course!" beamed Lowe, clapping his hand upon my shoulder as if the thing had been settled months and months before.

"You have no objections?"

"Mr Crane has none and where Mr Crane leads, I am only too eager to follow."

"I am much obliged, sir," I responded.

Lowe turned a benevolent expression upon me that was all warmth and comfort and spread out his hands wide with a little bow, as if to suggest that there was no mortal creature for whom he would not have been delighted to have performed this service. Then he strode to the door, opened it and hailed a hansom from across the street. Replacing his hat upon his head he gestured for me to follow him out of the door.

"Before you leave, Mr Lowe," said Crane, who seemed suddenly ill at ease. "I should also inform you that there was another caller this morning." He held in his hand another envelope. This one was far less expensive in its appearance and had been clumsily addressed.

"And who was that," said Lowe, still captive to his mood of elation and only half listening as he watched the hansom's progress toward us from the other side of the street.

"Mr Samuel Ivor."

Momentarily Lowe seemed to freeze upon the threshold. His left hand moved to the frame of the door and he supported himself there. He did it as subtly as he could manage, in hopes, I suppose, that I should not observe it, but I marvelled at this strange transformation.

"Mr Crane," he said in what was little more than a hoarse whisper. "I have required you to refuse admission to that gentleman under any circumstance."

"But Mr Lowe, he was most insistent."

Lowe crossed the room, snatched the envelope from the hand of his clerk and thrust it venomously into the fire. He turned to look at Mr Crane with a glare of startling intensity.

"*Any* circumstance, Crane. Have I made myself quite clear?"

"Just so, sir."

The clerk returned to the complicated business of managing those intricate piles of paper on his desk, and without so much as a backward glance, Lowe swept out into the rain and I trailed in his wake.

CHAPTER TWO

The first part of our brisk journey toward Knightsbridge passed in almost complete silence (by this, of course, I mean only that we did not speak — the incessant drumming of the raindrops upon the roof of the hansom and the occasional expostulations of passers-by who were splattered by the cab's passage through burgeoning pools of filthy rainwater perforated the peace), but my newly acquired employer retained upon his face an expression of deep vexation. Being only recently acquainted with the man, I did not like to trouble him. After a very few minutes, however, when the grime of Victoria was well behind us, he was more at ease, and little by little, seemed to return to the more genial self he had presented beforehand.

At length he said, "I suppose you must be wondering what sort of a business you have entered upon, Mr Fairlea?"

"Indeed no, sir," I replied, and it was almost the truth. "To be frank, I am rather pleased to be entering into any sort of business at all."

He gave a little snort of a laugh and peered out past the horses into the downpour. "Yes," he said, thoughtfully, "it can't be easy for a man in your position to find work."

"It's very generous of you to take me on, sir," I said, awkwardly and after something of a pregnant pause, for I detested feeling as if I were some curious object to be pitied. My sense of obligation, however, forced me to acknowledge his charity.

"Don't mistake me for a philanthropist!" he shot back, almost at once. At first, I thought the remark was made in jest or borne out of some modesty, but the singular, earnest look on his face was enough to convince me otherwise. "My employing you is not some act of Christian goodness. Of that I can assure you beyond any doubt." His words were sharply spoken and intended, I knew, to show the uncompromising side of his nature, but I could not help feeling a little pleased by them all the same. To have found work at all was fortunate, but to have entered upon it on account of merit rather than by virtue of my absent forelimb gave all the more cause for inward celebration.

"Mine is a peculiar trade," he went on. "And one that is sometimes rather dangerous. It is not, regrettably, one that is easily explained and I have no real talent for articulation in any case. Thus, I advertised among the camp surgeons for a suitable man. A veteran, I specified, and wounded too, though it was imperative that he still be in a state of peak fitness. When Stubbs wrote to me about that business with the Boer in your tent, I knew you were my man."

This came as a shock; I had had no idea that Stubbs had written to Lowe on my behalf, or that, if he had done so, he should have done more than offer a basic introduction. I was not a little appalled that he had chosen to narrate the details of that singularly terrifying ordeal. It had been public knowledge in the camp, of course, but on home soil I considered it a deeply private matter. My throat dried up and I said nothing. The emotion of it clouded my judgement and prevented me from the single most important consideration that ought to have occupied my thoughts: what had so attracted Lowe to the man contained within the account? If I had only asked him then I might have spared us all, but hindsight is an old man's torture and I shall leave this matter for later pages.

"Anyway," said Lowe, ignorant of my discomfort and now knocking his fist against the roof of the cab to alert the driver that we were closing upon our destination, "we must turn our minds to the task in hand. Do not be surprised to find that our present client — the lady of the house — is in a state of some considerable mental anguish. It is essential that, however our conversation develops, you do not ask her the cause. Is that absolutely understood?"

"Of course," I said, regaining myself.

"The particulars of the case are these," he went on, reading from a small black notebook that he had produced from the inside pocket of his coat. "Mr Finn departed this world little more than a year ago. It was a most unfortunate thing: bit of brisket lodged in the throat. Not a fitting end, Fairlea."

I mumbled some form of agreement.

"Well, in any case his wife — Mrs Finn — was utterly distraught about the whole thing as you can imagine."

"I suppose it's very hard for any wife to lose her husband."

The look Lowe turned on me was one of such extraordinary disdain that I felt as if I must be a raving lunatic.

"Don't be ridiculous," he snapped.

"I don't understand."

"Mrs Finn wasn't struck down with *grief,* man! It was guilt! Guilt! That most powerful of beasts. Of course, you can understand why."

"I'm afraid I don't, Mr Lowe."

He looked at me with a pained expression as if to say that he felt I really was being rather slow and awkward about the whole matter.

"Well then," he sighed. "Let us just say that the piece of

31

brisket might not have lodged quite so permanently and quite so tragically had Mrs Finn put down her own knife and fork and gone to her husband's aid." Lowe raised his eyebrows at me in a knowing sort of way.

"So, she just *let* him die?" I said, in shock.

"She was distracted," said Lowe. "I believe she was reading a most entertaining book at the time. Once she'd finished the chapter and looked up, the poor fellow had gone to meet his maker."

I opened my mouth to speak again, but Lowe gave me no opportunity.

"Suffice it to say that since his decease," he pressed on, "she has been subject to the most awful attacks of conscience and — well, we shall discover what else when we go inside. I have been of some use to her in recent months in my attempts to soothe her guilty soul. Your presence today, however, will be an enormous help and will, I think, allow me to bring matters to a swift and successful conclusion."

I nodded, though I could not help feeling a little confused. The comforting of widows seemed an occupation less stimulating and certainly less dangerous than the process of my recruitment had led me to suspect. How my presence was calculated to do any good I couldn't guess — less still could I fathom what Lowe might have meant by the phrase 'swift and successful conclusion'. Nonetheless, there was the question of the three hundred pounds to be considered, and if it were to be earned by such straightforward means as this, then it seemed beyond churlish to think of complaining.

"You are nodding and yet I have not yet told you what I require of you," said Lowe, a slight note of irritation creeping into his voice. "Do *please* try to pay attention. It is absolutely critical that you act in a most hostile manner towards Mrs Finn from the moment we arrive. You are to present yourself as my friend and partner and whatever mechanisms of assistance I proffer, whatever suggestions I make for the improvement of her situation, you are to counsel strongly against them. A time will come when I shall make an offer of seemingly impossible beneficence. At that moment you must tell me in no uncertain terms that, if I proceed, our friendship and relationship shall be, at once, terminated. I will then ask you to leave, which you must do in as dramatic a manner as you can manage. Then return to the cab and wait for me here."

I was so taken aback by these peculiar orders that, for a few moments, I gave him no response at all, but sat, staring at him rather dumbfounded.

"You are not nodding now," he said wryly.

I smiled and indicated that I had indeed understood him.

"Good," he said and hopped down nimbly into the street, giving orders for the cabbie to await our return. We crossed the cobbles as quickly as was decent and passed through the exquisitely fashioned iron-work gates of Mrs Finn's private residence. Having ascended a short flight of steps, Lowe rapped sharply upon the door. It was opened by a footman, but the fellow was in such a state of physical ill health that I almost started when I saw him. The skin on his face was stretched tight across it, so that the hollows of his cheeks stood out bleak and gaunt; his eyes were ringed by great pools of blackness so that one might have thought he had not slept for a month. His hand shook as he closed the door behind us, and without the support of its solid wood frame, he positively swayed from side to side as he spoke to us in a hoarse, croak of a voice.

"Mrs Finn will receive you in the library, sir."

"Capstone, my dear fellow!" exclaimed Lowe in a voice imbued with the deepest levels of concern and sympathy. "Whatever has happened to you?"

"I must apologise for my appearance, sir. I have had trouble sleeping since… since the unpleasantness."

"But it is all behind you, Capstone! It is finished! Forgotten! You must release yourself from its terror!"

"I fear that may be easier said than done," said the unfortunate footman and then he looked at me with a slight hint of unease. Lowe followed his gaze.

"This is my associate and advisor, Mr Fairlea, Capstone."

The footman looked me up and down and attempted to conceal the evident contempt he felt for my dishevelled appearance. Lowe sensed the man's discomfort and immediately clapped me hard upon the back, grasping my shoulder firmly as he did so. "I do believe Capstone thinks you're some vagrant I've dragged in from the street, Fairlea — and all on account of those clothes of mine I made you borrow!"

I let out what I hoped was a knowing chuckle and quietly hoped that Lowe knew what he was doing. I needn't have been concerned. "Dreadful circumstance!" Lowe confided to Capstone. "Fairlea here was half drowned by a cab just outside my place; his outfit entirely sodden. What was I to do but lend him something of my own?"

He had played Capstone well and the footman accepted the story without question — not pausing to ask whether it was really feasible that a gentleman such as Lowe should not have possessed, in what I imagined was a fairly extensive wardrobe, something, anything, more suitable for a house call.

"Now," said Lowe, "before I go in to see your mistress, let us turn our attention to you, Capstone. I insist that you go to see

34

my doctor in Harley Street. I shall make an appointment for you."

If possible, Capstone seemed to grow still whiter. "It is most kind of you, sir, but I doubt that I should be able to leave Mrs Finn, even for the briefest of moments."

"I understand," murmured Lowe, drawing the man close to him. "If it's a question of money, then I shall be more than happy to meet any expense that might be incurred."

It was at this moment that I became aware of a sharp pressure on the toes of my left foot. Looking down I saw that Lowe's heel was planted squarely upon it. I was about to alert him to this painful circumstance when I realised its significance.

"Mr Lowe," I mumbled, my mind racing to fix the words in the sentence before they tumbled from my mouth. "I really must object to this profligate use of your resources."

"I will hear no objection on this matter, Fairlea," said Lowe. The foot was instantly removed from my own. "Capstone has served his mistress with diligence and care and has been through far more in recent months than you or I could care to imagine."

"You have already been more than generous to this household, Mr Lowe," said Capstone.

"My sentiments precisely," I cried, rounding on the footman. Lowe's retort and Capstone's interjection had given me the few seconds I needed to gather my thoughts and I was eager to impress. "If you are to loosen your purse strings for every diligent servant in London, then you will be dining in the gutter within the week."

"I have said I will not hear it, Fairlea," said Lowe indignantly. "He is obviously in need of medical attention, and I am of a mind to ensure that he receives it."

"Your generosity has turned to foolhardiness," said I, now rather enjoying my role. "Listen to me," I implored, daring even to clasp him by the shoulders. "Your generous spirit has always been your greatest fault, my friend. It is fortunate for you that I have been here to prevent you frittering away your fortune on those who are less than deserving."

I had not intended to make this unpleasant swipe at Capstone, but I found my words tending in that direction and I had been rather upset by his reaction to my appearance. Whence came this sudden enthusiasm for the dramatic I knew not. Perhaps it was the raw risk of the situation, perhaps it was my elation at having found employment, but I found that I took to my task with quite unexpected enjoyment. Fortunately, Capstone was so taken aback by the remark that he murmured something about attending to the fires (and I was glad of this, for it was interminably cold in that house) and departed from our presence forthwith.

As soon as he was out of sight, Lowe turned on me with a glare. "Don't do that again," he said firmly. "You must follow my instructions precisely at all times — do you understand? I must know that I can rely on you! If I hadn't stamped on your shoe, I dare say I'd be defraying the medical expenses of half the staff by now!"

I stammered out an apology, but he waved it away with a dismissive gesture of his hand. "Nonetheless," he went on, "that was a nice touch at the end there with Capstone; for a moment I thought he was never going to let us over the threshold." Leaving me no time to absorb this compliment he crossed the hall to the door which, I presumed, lead into the library and beckoned for me to follow. We were about to go in when he suddenly put his arm out to stop me.

"You don't happen to have a pen and paper on you, I suppose?"

I plunged my hand into my pocket — I have no idea why for I knew I possessed neither of these items — and was astonished to discover that there was indeed something papery within. Drawing it out I saw, with surprise so great I almost cried out, that it was a brown envelope with the address of Lowe's office scrawled clumsily upon it. I knew, at a glance, that it was the very same envelope I had seen thrown into the fireplace not an hour before, but I could not for the life of me explain how it now came to be in my pocket. I quickly placed it back there — for I recalled the effect that its first appearance had had upon my employer and I had no intention of antagonising him. If I had gleaned anything of his character thus far, it was that he was subject to quite drastic changes of mood. I replied, apologetically, that I had not.

"Well ensure that you do from now on," he said. "It does us no harm to have a written record of these conversations for later analysis." With that, he pushed back the heavy wooden door and we entered the library.

The room was plagued with the grim aroma that is the perpetual comrade of chronic illness, not a direct unpleasantness in itself, but an indicator that there is something wrong. It was also, I noticed, extremely cold. The hallway had been uncomfortable, but the library was untenable. In fact, I noticed that here and there, where small pools of water had collected on the dark wooden floor (these indeed defied my capacity to account, for there seemed to be no obvious leak that I could perceive), their surfaces were laced with a fringe of fragile ice. At first, I thought that we must be alone for I could discern no figure in the room save that of Lowe, whose breath spouted from his mouth like regular bursts of steam from a kettle. It had not been an unusually cold March, and in the end, I attributed the extraordinary drop in temperature to the fact that the library was

37

possessed of one, very slim but tall window on the east side whose vista was chiefly occupied by the hard stone of the neighbouring property. I saw that a fire was burning in the hearth and crossed to it, but even the hearty blaze afforded little comfort.

"Percy?" the voice was so timid and frail that it sounded like the cracking of ice underfoot and it might have gone entirely unnoticed had we not anticipated a greeting. It sounded to me like the voice of an elderly woman much plagued by fits of nervous exhaustion and thus it was that I recoiled in some state of shock upon turning to discover that the creature propped up so pathetically on the chaise longue opposite the chimney-piece was not only a young lady, but a great beauty at that. Her hair, a rich chestnut brown, hung in opulent ringlets over her shoulders and her blue eyes might well have sparkled with delight and other mischief had they not been ringed by the same great circles of worry and tiredness that had been visible upon the face of Capstone.

"My dear lady," cried Lowe in delight, crossing the room at once and making an extravagant bow before taking her hand in his and kissing it enthusiastically. "How well you look! Indeed, I am astonished by the pace of your recovery! Do you not think so Fairlea? This is my friend, Mr Fairlea, madam, he is lately returned from Africa, and I do so value his opinion on all matters. What say you Fairlea?"

"Mrs Finn does indeed look well," I lied. It was a gamble for I could not tell whether it was Lowe's intention that my planned contrariness should begin at once, but something told me that my complicity in this particular untruth was essential to his scheme.

"It is a pleasure to make your acquaintance," said Mrs Finn, stretching out her dainty white hand for me to kiss. "Though it saddens me to find that you seem to be quite as deluded as Percy here about the state of my health — for I am not well, Mr Fairlea."

"On the contrary, madam," said I. "There is colour in your cheeks and the light of laughter in your eyes. I am pleased to find you a good deal better disposed than my friend had led me to expect."

"And what exactly had he led you to expect?" Those beautiful ruby lips formed the question with expert cleverness, and she began to pull herself up a little more on her pillows. Lowe, who stood behind the chaise longue now and out of sight of Mrs Finn, shot me a warning glance.

"Only," I ventured, "that you have suffered much in your grief, but I am pleased to see that your health, at least seems to be returning to you."

"It is not," she said, defiantly. "I wonder, Mr Fairlea, whether you know what it is to be without sleep for days on end, or if you have ever been so cold that even the most obstinate fire does little more than take the edge of the chill?"

I considered for a moment. The provenance Lowe had provided on my behalf did not seem to allow for my time at war — when I had indeed experienced both these things with agonising regularity. I settled on an ambiguous approach and extended the stump of my absent arm. "We have all had our share of suffering, madam," I said, rather bluntly.

"And yours is at an end!" exclaimed Lowe, springing round to kneel before the relict and seizing her hand. "I assure you that the measures I have taken are absolute. There will be no recurrence of your torment! You are free!" On these three last syllables he shook the young woman's hands imploringly.

"Percy," she said, gently. "I am resolved. I must sell the house."

Lowe rose to his feet in a manner of deepest dejection. He strode to the mantelpiece and stood there, passing a vexed hand across the crumpled lines of his forehead. In the few moments of silence that followed my ears detected a familiar sound: that same tiny creaking, crackling I had heard in Lowe's office. It was the glass, Crane had said, responding to a change in the temperature. I cast my eyes towards that long thin window and saw to my astonishment that the bottom panes were now coated in a thin covering of frost that certainly had not been there when I had last looked.

"Then," Lowe said at length, "I am afraid I have failed you, Mrs Finn."

"Not at all!" I exclaimed. I had, of course, no idea of what it was that the pair of them were discussing, but I felt that to play the part that Lowe required of me, I must remain relevant to the conversation. I stole another glance toward the window and saw that the strange frost had now expanded to cover half its entire length.

"I have no doubt, Percy," said Mrs Finn, "that you have indeed rid me of that force." She gave a cringe of a shiver as she said the word. "But I fear that this house will be forever tainted with memory — for me, and for the servants too."

Lowe turned to her and cocked his head to one side.

"How so?"

"Well for one thing, we find ourselves seeing shadows and silhouettes in the darkness — a feeble trick of the mind, Percy, I know, but we *all* see them nonetheless and darkness has become an abhorrence to us. Nights are spent in wakeful vigilance and the days slip by so fast that sometimes I barely notice them."

"Then I shall buy you lamps, I shall buy you candles! We shall illuminate every crevice in this house from top to bottom."

A thin trace of a smile crossed her lips. "You are kind, Percy," she said.

"Too kind," I muttered audibly. "Far too kind if you ask me — more kindness than sense." Percy dismissed my admonitions with a wave of his hand, but Mrs Finn cut him off before he could remonstrate with me. "Then there is the cold — we all feel it — don't you feel it, Percy?"

"Madam?"

"Do you not see the ice on the window? Can you not perceive the clouds of your own breath?"

Percy looked hard at the window as if he were straining to see something. He strolled right up to it and observed it at close quarters before taking several steps back and considering its full length. Then, he held a hand in front of his face and blew out several strong, experimental breaths, each of which produced a cascading column of vapour, which rose up and quickly vanished above him. Each time, he strained his eyes once more as if he could see nothing at all. In fact, so compelling was his performance that after some minutes I began to wonder whether he really was blind to the piercing chill of the room.

"Eliza," he said, shaking his head and drooping his shoulders. "I am afraid that the room presents itself to me as warmly and comfortably as is to be expected."

"I know, I know," she said, bitterly, her teeth biting hard on her lower lip. "It is all a fancy of mine — and who could blame me for it, knowing what I have endured."

"And you have endured *so much*," said Mr Lowe, crouching beside her and placing an arm about her shoulders.

"I fear that if I do not rid myself of this house, then I shall not rid myself of these delusions."

There was a long pause during which Lowe seemed to

contemplate the predicament. After some twenty seconds had passed he began to nod, slowly and resolutely. "Very well," he said. "If you must go, then I shall assist you in finding new premises, and of course, with the sale of this house."

"Sale?" I said, not quite able to mask my surprise at the apparent riches of the late Mr Finn. "Is the property not rented, then Mrs Finn?"

"My husband was a wealthy man," said the widow, drily. "In life, this place was security and warmth to us. In death it has become something quite other."

"I'm sure matters can be managed swiftly," said Percy.

"Oh Percy," she said in elation, sitting up even further and twisting round to look him full in the face, her eyes sparkling with sudden hope. "I have already found a perfect darling little place — it's in the countryside, not far from the city. Do you really mean you'll help me?"

"Of course!"

"Percy," I murmured in a tone of avuncular disgruntlement.

"I shall make all the necessary arrangements."

"Percy," I repeated, with greater force.

He seemed to pause and catch himself. A frown spread across his face and rippled over that smooth forehead. "Of course, the sale of this property will be quite a difficult proposition."

Her face fell and my heart went out to this glorious beauty whom I felt sure we were somehow on the verge of swindling, though I could not yet see how.

"What makes you say that?"

Lowe affected an uneasy air. "Well there has been *talk* — in certain society circles."

"You don't mean to say that word has got out of what has

happened here?"

"I am afraid I do and it has. I have of course, ridiculed all suggestion of anything of *that* particular nature but," and here he cast a cutting glance in the direction of the hallway, "servants do talk."

Her glassy blue eyes filled with tears which began to flow freely down her cheeks.

"Then I am trapped, Percy!" she cried. "I am trapped here in this horror! If I cannot sell, then I shall be forced to remain!"

"Have you no other means," I enquired innocently. Lowe instantly shot me a filthy look that I did not understand.

"None!" she sobbed.

He rose up to his full height and stood before her, cutting a remarkably heroic figure.

"I can't stand to see you reduced to this," he said, tearing at his hair with his hands. "It was bad enough that you should have suffered that terrible ordeal, but to think that for all my power and authority in that sphere I can do nothing to soothe your present discomfort is a great pain to me, madam."

"You have already done a great service to Mrs Finn," said I, though cautiously, for I was on uncertain ground. Not knowing what had passed between them I trod the path of ambiguity as best I could as a mask for my role as interloper.

"It is true," she acknowledged — much to my relief. "You have put more than your life on the line for me Percy, and more than once! Do not feel that you are responsible for my perpetual well-being!"

"And yet," said her erstwhile saviour, crossing the room in the direction of the window whose panes, I noted, were now so completely covered in ice that the view of the outside world was wholly occluded, as if one were looking at it through a very thin sheet of paper. "And yet — in your hour of need you have sent for me — and what have I to offer you? Nothing but discouragement and fuel for your despondency."

"You have brought me company," said Mrs Finn, a little sadly. In her face I thought I could see the skeletal remains of that striking, flirtatious charm which must have been the cause of so much distress for her late husband; now it hung about her pale skin, fractured and lifeless. "I can see I have upset you Percy," she said.

"You have not upset me in the least, Eliza," said he, returning to her side. "It is only that I am upset on your behalf."

"But I did not intend that you should be either!" she went on. "You should leave this place — there is no room for joy here any more. Come back in the summer and you may find me in a brighter mood." She smiled weakly, unconvincingly. Percy looked as if he intended to protest, but she laid a finger on her lips. "I am tired," she said. "I beg your leave, Percy — I should not have troubled you."

It was now that I began to grow concerned — but not, as I perhaps should have done, for the ailing condition of the young widow. Rather I worried, with a churning sensation in the pit of my stomach, that I had not fulfilled my obligations to Mr Lowe. I had waited, as he had instructed, for him to make some astonishingly generous offer, but that moment had not arrived — neither had my promised expulsion, though we were now, it seemed, on the very verge of departure.

Lowe stood up and dusted off his trousers. He made another little bow to our hostess and then, nodding at me, turned and walked towards the door of that peculiarly cold room. Only when his fingers had clasped themselves over the doorknob and only when his nose was almost against the wood did he suddenly halt and turn.

The abrupt silence caught Mrs Finn's attention and she pulled herself up to see what had arrested Lowe's progress.

"What is it, Percy?"

"It's so straightforward I don't know why it's taken even my simple brain so long to think of it." Lowe spoke in the manner of one in receipt of an epiphany.

"What is?"

"Isn't it obvious? The solution to all of your problems is staring us straight in the face."

"Is it?" A thrill of excitement lit up the young woman's features and she brought herself near vertical in her eagerness to hear these wonderful tidings.

"I shall buy your house."

There was a pronounced pause.

"You would really do that for me?"

I knew that this was the moment at which I must intercede, but the shock of what Lowe was suggesting had set me reeling. I had no conception of the value of houses, but I felt relatively sure that an establishment as grand as this was certainly worth no less than two thousand pounds. Lowe surely could not be serious? The extraordinary salary I was to receive was proof that he was not without means, but surely a man of his standing could not possibly be in a position to make such a purchase! Then of course — and almost too late — I remembered my duty. Fortunately, my stunned silence only lent verisimilitude to the character I had put on for the occasion.

"Don't be ridiculous, Percy," I said. "Paying for doctors for common servants is one thing, but to offer to buy this house? Why the very offer itself is reckless!"

The woman, I noticed, was ignoring me entirely. Offered a way out of that ice-cold existence, she was ready to grasp at any hint of light.

"What is the price that has been set upon your little place in the country?" asked Lowe.

"This is preposterous," I shouted and strode towards him

45

menacingly. "You are fooling around with money as if it were some child's plaything and what's more," I added, not quite knowing what I was going to say next, "you are leading this woman to believe that you can help her when you simply cannot."

"What value has been set upon it?" insisted Lowe, oblivious to my pretended outrage.

"Eight hundred pounds," she breathed. She was, I could see, a woman who was not daring to permit herself the joy of hope.

"I think I could manage — and pray forgive my vulgarity, but the situation demands it — I think I could manage to give you a thousand."

"Do you really mean it?"

"Enough!" I said, slamming my fist down on a table that stood adjacent to the door and dislodging from it an ornamental glass lantern, which shattered obligingly upon that cold, hard, floor. "I think I have heard quite enough. The pair of you are as mad as each other — if you wish to fritter away your meagre fortune Percy then you're a damned fool! And you, madam, if you are so foolish as to want to join him in his fantasies, then I say you need more help than anyone I know is able to afford you! I implore you, Percy, let us be gone from here at once and let us never speak of this business again."

Lowe had his back to me at this point and was crouching down beside the young lady once again, having clasped her hand earnestly at the moment of making that ludicrously small offer. As I spoke, however, he stiffened, rose to his feet and then turned slowly to look upon me, his face full of venom.

"The problem with London," he spat, "is that it is full of people like *you*." He jabbed a finger at me and began to cross the room. "You are a disgusting representation of our race," he continued. "All of your sort! You make your meals from the suffering of those less fortunate than yourselves and you boil it

46

in a broth of hypocrisy! I will remember your advice this day, Mr Fairlea — oh yes, I shall! — and pray that you are never brought low in this world and pray you never have cause to throw yourself upon my mercy! For as surely as I intend to bring my resources to bear to assist in the ills of Mrs Finn, I swear to you that I shall never be persuaded to part with so much as a penny in your direction."

The young woman was regarding the oration in stunned ecstasy. Her eyes flitted wildly between us, drinking in the rage and its effects upon me. Under pressure to perform, I stammered out several abortive protestations and even once proffered a hand of friendship, but this was cruelly swept away by the inexorable torrent of Lowe's rage.

"Percy," I implored. "I am only encouraging you to see good sense! You can't plunge into a scheme like this without considering the matter in the cold light of day. How can I show you that I'm trying to help you? What must I do?"

Lowe leapt on the opportunity I had presented to him in an instant. "You must *leave*, sir!" he commanded in an impressively imperious tone. "You must go — from this house and from my acquaintance. Any understanding between us is terminated; our friendship — annulled."

I nodded, gravely, turned, and having twisted that icy doorknob, stepped through the library doors, crossed the hallway, and without stopping even to acknowledge Capstone's astonished expression (it would not do, I supposed, to resign my character until I was completely gone from that house and protected by the anonymity of the street), proceeded through the front door. Several minutes later I found myself back in the hansom, which was waiting for me — the driver having been as good as his word.

Lowe reached me after less than a quarter of an hour, quivering in jubilation and positively exuding delight. He leapt up into the hansom, and having given the driver the signal to move on, turned to me, grinning from ear to ear and shook me warmly by the hand.

"Seven hundred, Mr Fairlea!" he exulted. "She has agreed to sell it me for seven hundred pounds!"

CHAPTER THREE

Lowe's elation showed no signs of abatement as we wound our progress back across the river to Victoria. At times he would hum to himself in jaunty merriment and at others he would simply sit back, shake his head and murmur the words, "Seven hundred!" over and over, mingling apparent disbelief with evident pride at his own achievement. So positive was his demeanour and so absolute his satisfaction that it was some ten or fifteen minutes before I summoned the confidence to ask the question preying most urgently upon my mind.

"Mr Lowe," I ventured, hesitantly. "May I ask the precise nature of the service you had previously rendered to Mrs Finn?"

"You may ask," he said, turning his beaming face upon me so that I was dazzled by its full brilliance, "but I am not inclined to respond at present."

"I only thought," I pressed, "that were you to impart something to me of your business, I might be of greater use to you."

"But you have already been of enormous use," said Lowe cheerily. "At present it pleases me to keep you in a state of ignorance; it suits my purposes."

For a while there was no sound, save for the wheels of the hansom clacking over the cobbles and throwing up spray from the pools of water that had gathered between the stones and which were, even now, being replenished by a fresh and vigorous downpour.

"May I speak plainly, sir," I asked.

"Always," said my employer, though he was looking out absent-mindedly at the passing buildings.

"I fear that I have become complicit in an act of fraud."

I said it as confidently as I could, but the powerful presence of Lowe made my voice shake and the fragile promise of three hundred pounds hung around my throat like a heavy hemp noose. Lowe, however, threw back his head and laughed heartily.

"Fraud!" he exclaimed. "Is that all you're worried about? You need have no fears on that score. All has been conducted quite above board, I assure you. Mrs Finn's house will pass into my possession and the sum of seven hundred pounds will pass into hers."

"But that is a mere fraction of what the house is actually worth! It doesn't come close to its true value — you must know that!"

"Worth and value," tutted Lowe, impatiently. "These are relative and elastic concepts, Mr Fairlea — not the grandiose concrete structures that you have built them up to be in your mind. To Mrs Finn the house was worth only what it would cost her to be rid of it for good."

"But you made her believe you were doing her a great kindness," I said.

"I *was* doing her a great kindness," he insisted, his impatience growing. "Seven hundred pounds is not an insignificant sum and it will certainly be enough to secure her future."

I had been going to say that she might have had such a quantity — and indeed might have had significantly more too — from another buyer, when I was interrupted by a sudden lurch of the carriage. The horse, apparently disturbed by something in the road, had reared up onto its hind legs and thrown us violently backwards. Then it had retreated several steps and continued to shake and quiver in a state of some evident distress, bucking and neighing at regular intervals. The driver, who had, by some miracle, retained his lofty perch, jumped down from the vehicle and after several attempts, finally succeeded in taking the animal by its harness and quieting it. An eerie, unnatural sort of silence descended and I found myself shivering in the shock of it all. Lowe, however, had sprung from his seat and down into the road as soon as it was practicable to do so and was, even now, standing on the street examining, with some care, the place at which the animal had lost control of its senses. As soon as I had regained my composure, I too dropped down out of the cab and joined him.

"This won't do," Lowe was muttering to himself a tongue of anger flickering around the edge of each word. "This won't do at all." I followed his gaze and saw that it was fixed upon a large puddle a few paces ahead of him. To my astonishment I saw that it was no ordinary pool of water but a solid sheet of ice, reflecting the cold grey sheen of the sky. Far from showing any sign of vulnerability to the rain, which continued to fall heavily all this while, it seemed to have the strangest effect on the droplets as they descended, transforming them, when they came within three or four feet of its surface, into feathered flakes of snow which tumbled gently onto it with a sort of childish impudence. The sight of it, for reasons I could not explain, occasioned in me some absurd impulse to laughter which I only held in check by a Samson-like force of will.

"We shall see about this," said Lowe in a voice so low and dangerous that it might have been a growl. "It must not be tolerated — I will not stand for it, do you hear? I will not stand for it!" He declared these last phrases into the gloom of the late afternoon, but not to any audience that I could detect — and certainly not to me. In fact, he seemed entirely oblivious to my presence for several minutes. Then, turning abruptly to face me, he said, "I'm so sorry you have been discomfited in this manner, Mr Fairlea." It was a strange thing to say — as if some dog of his had slipped its leash while walking in the park and yapped at me.

"I do not understand," I replied. "What has happened?"

"Disobedience," said Lowe, in a tone of resigned pragmatism. "It is nothing more than simple disobedience." For a moment he lost himself in thought but then suddenly rallied, clapping his hands together, as he was in the habit of doing whenever an idea crystallised in his mind. He seemed rejuvenated and excited — captivated by that same exuberance which had overwhelmed him at the prospect of a visit to Mrs Finn's house. "Do you enjoy the theatre, Mr Fairlea?"

The question arose so completely unexpectedly and without warning that I was quite unable to respond for several seconds. Even when I did eventually reply, it was only to confess, in a stuttering, stumbling sort of way, that I had never been.

"Never been?" Lowe was incredulous. "Never been to the theatre? My dear fellow! Well we must do something about that — and at once!" The curious behaviour of the horse and the peculiar puddle of ice appeared to be all forgotten now. He hailed another hansom, having amply rewarded the driver of the first and expressed, both repeatedly and forcefully that he did not blame him at all for what had happened and would be glad if he would be kind enough to wait outside his premises tomorrow. Then, when we were installed in the new vehicle, we set off again in the direction of Victoria.

"I have a few matters to attend to," he said. "Crane must be informed of the arrangements I have made with regard to Mrs

Finn and then there are one or two other things that demand my consideration. In the meantime, you really shall borrow some of my clothes. You must be chilled to the core in that get-up and it certainly will not do for a visit to the theatre this evening. No, do not protest, sir! I insist and there's an end of it."

Lowe was always infectious in his jollity and by the time we drew up alongside the grimy windows and faded lettering of his establishment I was in high spirits and relishing the prospect of the evening ahead. The circumstances in which Mrs Finn had been relieved of her property no longer concerned me. This, I reasoned, was business after all and Lowe had only done what was necessary to realise a profit. There had been no deliberate lie, no conscious omission of fact — indeed, when I thought about it I realised that my part in the affair had provided the young widow with every opportunity to turn down the proposition. With the benefit of old age and wisdom I reflect it is a sad commentary on the human condition that morality and conscience flee so readily before the might of security and prosperity.

Crane greeted us on our return and Lowe told him eagerly of what had passed — dwelling most flatteringly on my role and making of it much more than was necessary. He instructed Crane that the money for the sale must be raised immediately and gave him the name of Mrs Finn's solicitor.

"It must be done as soon as is humanly possible," he repeated. "The woman is quite deranged, Mr Crane, quite out of her wits and I do not like to think of her experiencing a change of heart. We must give her no opportunity to prevaricate."

"Just so, sir," nodded the clerk.

"And when you have relayed my instructions, you may write at once to Mr Whitton and tell him that I am now in a position to be able to offer him a house for the season at the rent we discussed."

This then, in my naïveté, I assumed to be the business of Percival Lowe. He was, I imagined, a man of property, buying from those in desperate circumstances and renting to the wealthy who were keen to go in for fashion. No wonder he was coy about his trade. Yet I could not help wondering what purpose I was to serve in all this and why on earth I had been recommended for the task. Surely there was not a great quantity of mad widows in London upon whom this same charade was to be practised? Nonetheless, I did not dwell on the matter. My conscience had been assuaged for the present and I had no desire to unbalance it again in idle speculation.

His discussions with Crane complete and with the latter now engaged in the drawing up of several complicated letters and documents, Lowe led me on through that strange front office and into the corridor beyond. I recalled that when I had first set foot inside the premises that morning I had seen a figure in this corridor which I had taken to be that of Lowe himself, though it could not have been, I recalled, for he had been out on errands all morning.

"These are my quarters," said he, standing before a large red door. As he spoke, I could not help but notice that it bore upon its surface several rather peculiar looking gouges and scratches — as if it has been buffeted by some feral animal. "Should you ever need me in the night, do not hesitate to come and knock here," he went on. "I am a poor sleeper and you will usually find me at my work." He took out a key and led us through. Within, there lay a further narrow corridor with three further doors. Two of these stood slightly ajar and I could see that the first led into a bedroom and the second into a sort of a study. The last door, however, was painted such a deep shade of black that no light could escape it and was set about with several severe looking locks and chains.

"You will find me here in my study if you need me," said Lowe, gesturing toward the second door. "I am seldom in my bed nowadays."

"What is behind the black door?" I asked. My curiosity bordered on rudeness, I knew, but the door had imposed itself upon my thoughts, almost to the exclusion of all else. Lowe looked at me thoughtfully.

"Something of which you will come to know in time — when you are ready." It was such a decisive response that I felt I should have been unable to pursue the matter any further even had I wanted to. "Now," he went on, "let us see what we can do about finding you some clothes." He darted into the bedroom and opened a large wooden wardrobe which positively overflowed with a wealth of finely tailored costumes. Attending to his task with precision, he withdrew first a tailcoat, then a shirt and cravat, a waistcoat, a pair of formal trousers and then, from the floor of the wardrobe, he extracted a pair of shoes and a hat box.

"I fancy we are not dissimilar in build," he said, looking me up and down. "The shoes may be an ill fit, but I daresay you can make do for the evening. Tomorrow we shall see what we can do about having you outfitted more appropriately."

I ought to have been more grateful to him both for the loan of these items and indeed for the generous offer to furnish me with clothes of my own on the following morning, but no matter how hard I tried to pay attention to what he was saying, my thoughts were dragged, by some intractable force, to that peculiar, chained door in the hallway. Though not a clever man, I have never wanted for imagination and in the absence of facts to calm my mind, fantasy began to run riot — at least a dozen possible scenarios presented themselves to me as Lowe delivered instruction on how best I ought to tie the cravat, and it was only with the greatest difficulty that I was able to remain attentive through the fog of my own thoughts.

"Now," he said at last, producing a key from his pocket and handing it to me. "You will find your own quarters along the hall from here. I have one or two private matters I should like to attend to. Once you have finished dressing, perhaps you will have the goodness to wait for me in my study?" I agreed readily, glad to have the opportunity to free myself of the oppressive influence of that black paint and those curious chains. I stepped out again into the corridor, and a few paces further on, found another door on the opposite wall. Applying the key to the lock I opened it and discovered, on passing through, that I had been very handsomely catered for indeed, for my own quarters were the mirror image of Lowe's. There was a small, plainly furnished study — with a green leather high-backed chair drawn up by a fireplace and second chair adjacent to a bureau which stood near the window. In the bedroom I found a more than reasonably capacious bed and a wardrobe, which while, it was not quite of the same gigantic proportions as Lowe's own, was, nonetheless quite sufficient to contain all the clothes I could ever imagine owning.

It did not take me long to change and I cannot express here how grateful I was for the new clothes whose warmth and dryness cheered my spirits no end; those who have not suffered the perils of near-destitution will never, I fear, truly appreciate the simple comforts of warmth and shelter. My own damp things I hung across the back of the small wooden chair, and as I did so, something fell from the pocket of my trousers onto the floor. It was that curious envelope — the one which I thought I had seen

Lowe throw into the fire at our first meeting that afternoon. I bent down, and taking it up gently between my thumb and forefinger, examined it carefully. The rough, angular handwriting on the front gave nothing away, only Lowe's name and the address of his establishment. For a moment I refused to give way to my curiosity. After all, the correspondence within was not intended for me and I had seen quite clearly the effect that the letter had produced upon Lowe, but in the end this was what weakened my resolve. The man was so energetic, so convinced of his own actions. I had to know what it was that had undermined that effortless confidence. I turned the envelope over and began to break the seal with a silver letter-opener that I had noticed lying upon the bureau.

As I did so, I became conscious of that strange sound once again — the same noise that had interrupted my interview with Crane and which I had also heard at the house of Mrs Finn. It was a gentle, delicate, crackling sound — as if someone were twisting a bundle of twigs. Looking about me, I saw, in wonder, that one of the panes of glass in the small window which sat high in the wall, had entirely frosted over. I began to shiver and I could not tell if it was because the room had suddenly grown extraordinarily cold or because I was in anticipation of some further unnatural happening. Nonetheless, I pressed on with my task and slipped out the letter from its envelope, examining it as best I could by the lamp, for the window, small and high up as it was, would have produced little natural light on the sunniest of days let alone on a dull and dreary one such as this. The text was not difficult to make out, for although the hand was inexpert and rough, the author had taken the trouble to print each letter for the sake of clarity. The address at the head of the page was the first thing that piqued my interest, for it purported to have come from a gentleman who lived in Dollis Brock in Finchley. At first, I could not recall why this had any special significance until I remembered that Crane had asked me, during that most peculiar interrogation, whether I had ever visited Finchley myself. I read on, eagerly.

To Mr Lowe,

I write once again most humbly to beg your assistance, for I have been informed by all to whom I dare to speak of my experience that you are my sole hope of salvation. Words cannot convey the depths of my despair. I am quite lost to a terror that is beyond my power to express. Matters cannot continue as they are. I cannot stand it; I will not stand it! You may name your fee, Mr Lowe and I swear that I shall find some way to pay it — only please come quickly and render to me the service for which you have gained such a reputation.

I await your response,
Samuel Ivor

I read the letter over several times, dwelling on individual words and phrases to see if I might extract from the page some further clue to the source of Mr Ivor's apparent distress or, indeed, what had made Lowe so reluctant even to open his correspondence. But the writing remained impervious to my investigation, and defeated by it, I placed the letter carefully into a drawer of the bureau. I had just pushed it shut when I was startled by the sound of raised voices from further down the corridor. Though I could not make out the words, I was certain that it was Lowe's voice and it seemed to be in a state of some agitation. For a moment or two I was unsure how to proceed, after all, I had no wish to interrupt an altercation with Mr Crane of the kind that had followed the production of the letter earlier on that day. In listening carefully, however, I did not think I could make out a second party in the conversation and the structure and rhythm of the voice was not suited to an argument between two people. In fact, Lowe seemed simply to be repeating the same phrase over and over. I went to the door and opened it a crack the better to hear what was going on. As I did so, the conversation — if that was what it was — entered into a new phase.

"The terms of our arrangement are clear," Lowe was crying out at the top of his voice. "My conditions have not changed. Disobedience will not be tolerated — do you hear me?" I passed out through the door of my room and began to edge quietly along the corridor. "Do as I say," Lowe continued, "or I will be forced to reconsider our contract." Then there was a sudden noise that was all at the same time like wind and fire and rain and it was followed instantaneously by that sound of crackling ice which was fast becoming familiar to me. There followed an abrupt and sudden silence.

I was gripped now by a strange sense of terror and wished that my own breath, which seemed to rattle out in horribly audible gasps, would stop its obvious intrusion into the muted landscape about me.

Then I was startled by a new noise from behind. It was the sound of wood moving over wood. At first I wondered if it might not be the sound of that wooden chair being dragged across the floor, but it did not seem loud enough for that. I took one or two paces back along the corridor toward my own room but then stopped dead in my tracks. The door, which I had taken the precaution of closing behind me, was swinging slowly open and the light from the gas lantern within was spilling out into the dimness of the corridor. This, in itself, might not have been enough to disquiet me, but for the fact that I saw, as clearly as I had seen anything before in my life, painted out in shadow on the floor, the silhouette of a person. I drew myself in hard against the wall, my heart racing. I tried to tell myself that my fear was irrational, after all, I had never enquired into Lowe's domestic arrangements. Might it not be that the dark shape before me was some servant to whom I had not yet been introduced? Might they not have slipped into my room to set the fire or perform some other perfectly ordinary task just after I had left it? But logic was not enough to combat the terror firmly lodged beneath my breast and I stood there for some moments, my eyes transfixed by the combination of light and darkness on the floor.

Then, just as I was resolved to call out and challenge the figure, it moved back into the room and the shadow was gone. Though every instinct railed against it, I found myself walking forward to the open door. Inwardly I chastised myself — after all, what was the substance of this fear? I told myself that at any moment I should feel foolish, that a rational and logical explanation would present itself and the one that was currently in orbit around my rampant imagination would be shown to be false and childish in the extreme. I took another step forward, dreading that at any moment, the distorted rectangle of light which lay across the floor and halfway up the adjacent wall would be once more occluded by the outline of a figure.

Another step.

I was close now, less than a foot away from the moment at which I would have to confront whatever lay within. A sense of nausea rose up within me alongside the panic and I felt I might be violently sick at any moment, and such was my irrationality, that my chief concern was how I might explain the matter to Lowe. I stretched out my hand and took hold of the handle of the open door which was now all that lay between me and the moment of discovery. I drew in my breath and stepped forward.

Nothing.

The room was empty and quite as I had left it except for one small detail. Casting my eyes to the bureau I noticed that the drawer I had closed stood open once more and upon its top sat that peculiar letter, placed there quite deliberately. The only other discernible difference was that the room was now as cold as the library in Mrs Finn's house and the window covered entirely with that thin coating of frost, just as hers had been. In writing them down, these two effects do not seem significant enough to have triggered the abject horror that consumed me in that moment, but until you have undergone an experience of this kind for yourself, you cannot know the dread that may be induced by such subtle alterations.

"Have you found everything you need, Fairlea?" Lowe's sudden and unexpected arrival caught me quite off guard and the shock of it caused me to clutch at the door frame. "I say, dear fellow," he went on, noticing my distress and taking me by the arm. "Are you quite all right?"

I looked up at him and noticed that his features were oddly changed. Some of that seemingly inexhaustible energy, that lust for life, which had characterised my experiences of him that day, appeared to have drained from him. Lines of care had formed at the sides of his eyes and across his forehead and his hair — which had been so meticulously arranged not twenty minutes before — was now in a state of total disarray. His cravat was askew and he appeared to have something like chalk dust on his jacket. He was scrutinising me intently, then the light seemed to dawn in his eyes, and turning from me, he examined the room, his gaze roving around as if in search of something. It did not take him

61

long to locate his object, and crossing the floor in a few strides, he took up the letter in his hand, and without any expression of surprise, or shock or anger, tore it into tiny pieces which he then proceeded to throw into the grate. He stood there watching them for some minutes as if he thought that they might somehow defy the laws of nature, reconstitute themselves and return to the desk. When they did not, he gave a sigh of satisfaction and turned to me apologetically.

"You must think me quite unfeeling," he said, in tones of deepest sympathy. "That business with the cab will have shaken you up something terrible, I'm sure and I've offered you nothing to steady your nerves. Follow me. I shall find us both some brandy. That ought to warm us up."

I wanted to speak of what I had seen — to protest that my time at war had prepared me for far greater misfortunes than an upset carriage — but then it occurred to me: how could I tell him? How could I explain the cause and centre of my terror when I was not even certain of it myself? I could offer him nothing but shadows and an open drawer and he would conclude either that I was out of my wits or I was practising some deliberate deception. Neither explanation was likely to result in the continuation of my employment and I needed the money badly. Thus it was that, forsaking my true concerns, I nodded gratefully and followed him from the room back toward his own quarters.

As we turned in from the corridor I noticed that the black door, which had been so securely chained before, was now standing ajar. Lowe saw my curiosity, but said nothing, he only stepped forward, closed it and refastened the chains.

"What's in there?" I asked.

"Nothing of any value," he said testily — though I did not think his irritation was aimed at me. We proceeded to his study where he opened a cabinet at the top of the bureau and withdrew a bottle of brandy and two glasses into which he poured a generous portion for each of us. Raising his and nodding slightly he tipped back his head and poured the liquid down his throat. Then, having drained the glass, he smacked his lips and gasped, shaking his head vigorously from side to side.

"It isn't *easy*, you know, Fairlea," he said. "It isn't *easy* what I do. People think it is — but it isn't."

"What is it that you do, sir?"

Lowe laid a finger alongside his nose and gave a secretive smile. "All in good time, dear fellow! All in good time."

Another man might perhaps have grown impatient with Lowe's unwillingness to part with information, but here I was warm, dry, well dressed and equipped with a very fine glass of brandy and I have observed that it is difficult to remember the harder times in life when one emerges into those that are better, even if the latter follow hard upon the heels of the former. He gestured for me to sit down in one of the chairs. He took the other and we spent some moments in silent contemplation. I searched for a subject that might prove fertile for conversation but my thoughts kept returning to that letter and to the question of the figure in the doorway and it seemed sensible to mention neither. In the end I settled on a mundane question which I thought might yield the information I desired.

"Other than Mr Crane and yourself," I asked cautiously, "am I to be the only other resident here?"

"Crane?" Lowe raised his eyebrows in surprise. "You don't think he *lives* here do you? Not that miser — not for any money." He closed his eyes and exhaled loudly and sharply through his nose. "Crane live here? I should say not; I should say not!"

"He has his own lodgings?"

"I assume so," said Lowe, airily. "I've never asked him. He comes in and does his job — does it well, mark you! I have no complaints on that score. There never was a closer scrutiniser of contracts and deeds and other documents as old Crane."

"Then it is only you and I living here — there is no housekeeper?"

"Ludicrous expense," snorted Lowe. "An utter nonsense — fancy having someone live with you to do all the chores one ought to be perfectly capable of doing one's self and to pay them *and* give them board and lodgings into the bargain?"

"I suppose it does seem rather foolish put like that," I replied.

"You're a military man, are you not," said Lowe, leaning forward in his chair and addressing me earnestly. I nodded. "Then you will know," he went on, "that there is little greater satisfaction than that which is to be gained from attending to one's own affairs, regulating one's own routine and so forth."

I agreed readily — I had drawn great comfort in Africa from that minor level of control in my own little sphere. Helpless to contest the military dictats that governed the grander narrative of my life, I had busied myself instead with lower-level matters: my tent had been kept in immaculate order, my face had been clean shaven; every inch of time that was my own from morning to evening was meticulously planned and executed according to a precise schedule.

"Besides," said Lowe, sinking back into the chair once more and staring rather disconsolately at the floor, "those sorts of people aren't to be trusted, Fairlea. They talk, for a start. Rumours and tittle-tattle would be all over half of London if I were to take on a housekeeper and if they gained even half an idea of the sorts of things that went on here…" He trailed off and looked up at me shrewdly. "And yet you do not yet know what *does* go on here, do you?"

I was being tested. I could sense it. He had all but instructed me to ask no further questions about his business and he was watching to see if I would obey. I bit back my curiosity; I would not be so easily faulted.

"Did you say, Mr Lowe, that we are to attend the theatre?" said I, changing the subject.

"That is indeed my intention," he said, pouring a second, but more modest glass of brandy. "And if I am not much mistaken, that noise you can hear is Crane working his way down the corridor to bring us our invitation."

There was a gentle knock at the door.

"Come," said Lowe, without looking up from his glass.

"A messenger has arrived from Mr Stefano Gatti, sir. He and his brother are the proprietors of the Vaudeville theatre on the Strand," said the old man. "They come to you upon the recommendation of one of their patrons — Mr Garson. I think you will remember him, sir. It appears that they are experiencing something of a disturbance at the theatre and would be grateful if you felt able to attend upon them at your earliest possible convenience."

CHAPTER FOUR

It was not five o'clock when we set out from Victoria in the cab. Though Lowe's regular driver was standing by to take us, I was pleased to find that my employer, having sent him home once again with a hefty tip and instructions to rest himself and his horse and return in two days, selected another to bear us to the Strand. That feverish excitement that I had seen in him following our visit to Mrs Finn was, once again, easily discernible upon his features, and prior to our departure, he had spent a good deal of time repairing his appearance from the slightly ruffled state in which I had found him that afternoon.

"May I enquire," I asked, "what assistance you desire of me on this occasion? Am I to play your counsellor as I did at the house of Mrs Finn?"

Lowe thought for a minute and rubbed the tips of his fingernails together, surveying the darkening streets as we rumbled onward. Though the sun had not yet set, those ominous rain clouds hung in the sky like a cloak and the warmth and light had long since surrendered to their rule. Every so often one of the gaslamps, ignited by some diligent lamplighter, shone out as an island in the smothering darkness.

"No," he said. "I think that would not be sensible on this occasion. I will need you to be my assistant in this instance — and my support should things turn sour."

"Then I am to simply do as you bid me?"

"Precisely," he said.

"Do you permit me to enquire what that may be?"

"That," said Lowe, with a sigh of resignation, "will be largely determined by the manner of the problem we find when we reach the Vaudeville." With that, he clapped his palms together gently and tapped his nose with the tip of his finger — a signal that our conversation was over.

I was surprised by the willingness with which I accepted my instructions from Lowe. It was not — I flatter myself — simply a case of the promise of generous rewards for so doing, but rather the fact that the man possessed a natural authority. There was a calmness about him and a confidence that left one in no doubt that his course of action was the most appropriate in any circumstance; there was almost a paternal quality to it. Had an employment of such an irregular nature emerged from the mouth of any other man I feel I might have recoiled against it or at least made regular protests, but such thoughts never entered my head in his company.

The cabbie dropped us off at the entrance to the theatre at which place various billboards advertised the success of *French Maid*, the incumbent musical comedy. I confess that I felt some small degree of disappointment. When Lowe had mentioned that we should attend the theatre, I had jumped to the conclusion that we should be seeing a performance, not undertaking some peculiar task.

Stefano Gatti was waiting for us anxiously on the steps leading up to the foyer. Behind him stood a thinner, sour-faced man who did not look remotely pleased to see us. Lowe strode towards the former and extended his hand.

"Percival Lowe," he said. "Very much at your service, sir." Then he made a sweeping gesture in my direction. "This is my assistant in all matters, Mr Fairlea."

"Mr Lowe!" exclaimed Gatti with a broad grin of relief and delight. "We had just begun to give up hope of your coming — it really is so very good of you to attend upon us at such short notice."

"Not at all," said Mr Lowe.

"This is my brother," went on the theatre owner, indicating the gaunt man loitering in the shadows. "Agostino, this is Mr Lowe, our saviour."

"We don't need a saviour," said Agostino, drily. "We need a plumber."

Gatti gave us an embarrassed smile and turned on his brother with a barely suppressed rage and hissed at him venomously. "You have not been there, Agostino — you have not heard it!"

"I do not need to have heard it," replied Agostino bitingly. "Any fool can tell you that it's the pipes rattling that is all. Your explanation is quite absurd."

"Absurd!" exclaimed Gatti. "It is you who are absurd! Half the cast refuses to go on stage and you would have me call for a plumber! No, brother, you have this quite wrong. Only Mr Lowe can help us in this circumstance."

"That remains to be seen," said Agostino, coldly. Then he turned to Lowe. "And what exactly is the going rate for a saviour nowadays? I suppose you'll want paying."

"I require nothing so vulgar," said Lowe, meekly and with the faintest hint of offence. "My gift is for the benefit of all those in need and it would be wrong of me to employ it for personal gain."

"Very well," said Agostino. "But I still say it's the pipes."

"Perhaps it might be more productive if you took me to the precise scene of your distress gentlemen?" asked Lowe. "Or perhaps you would prefer us all to grow damper by the minute

68

under this infernal rain."

"Of course, of course," said Mr Gatti, apologetically. "Please do follow me."

He led us up the steps and into the foyer. Producing a mighty bunch of keys from his pocket he sorted them expertly until he found the one that he needed and applied it to the lock of the central doors that led into the auditorium. His brother followed us at a distance with an evident attitude of deep scepticism.

I do not know why, but I had prepared myself for a great shock when those doors swung open, but there was nothing to dread. The interior of the theatre, with its red seats, golden rails and impressive chandelier seemed entirely ordinary. Lowe too, seemed surprised.

"I do not understand, gentlemen," he said. "I see nothing out of place here."

Gatti said nothing but simply pointed towards the stage. We proceeded towards it, but as we did so, I could still see nothing that was remotely unusual. The curtains were drawn beneath the proscenium and, other than the fact that they seemed rather faded toward the bottom, there was nothing about them that appeared remotely worthy of note.

"There," said Gatti, suddenly. He pointed at the rail that prevented the audience from tumbling into the orchestra pit and I gave a little start of surprise.

"Is that ice?" I asked in astonishment. Gatti nodded.

Like some festive Christmas fringe, there hung, right the way along the length of the rail, a glittering trail of icicles. I looked ahead of me to the stage and saw that the curtains were not faded as I had imagined, but rather, coated for two or three feet above the floor surface, with a layer of frost.

"You see?" demanded Gatti, turning on his brother. "This

happens and you want to call a plumber?"

"I still say it's the pipes," said Agostino. "There's sure to be some perfectly logical scientific explanation."

"There is," said Lowe, speaking for the first time since we had entered the auditorium, his voice dripping with wisdom and authority. "You are quite wrong, sir, to imagine that my work is unscientific. It is, in fact, more precise and methodological than that of any chemical or physical practitioner you may choose to name."

Agostino looked surprised, but still not impressed.

"Do not expect me to produce the usual tools of fantasy," Lowe went on, and I gained the distinct impression that this was a patter he had employed previously. "I shall not affect the demeanour of some great sorcerer or enchanter or, and perhaps worst of all, cloak my methods under the shroud of religion — no sir! I shall not banish you from proceedings as others might that they may better perpetrate some fraud. No! You shall observe me at my post, gentlemen. You shall see what I do and then you will judge whether you have exhibited some disrespect by means of your prejudice."

The brothers were taken aback by this powerful oration and said nothing.

"Now," said Lowe, taking off his jacket and rolling up his shirt-sleeves. "I assume that you would like me to rid you of your — *problem* — and if that is the case then I shall require certain materials."

"Naturally," said Mr Gatti, eager to be of any help. "If there is any other way in which we may aid the exorcism, please do inform us and we will be only too happy to oblige you."

"First and foremost," said Lowe, "this is not an exorcism. Such things are imprecise and unscientific. What you have

70

experienced here, gentleman is an intrusion by the world of death into the world of the living. Fairlea, pass me that handkerchief from your top pocket."

The manner in which Lowe had made this pronouncement made the whole concept, in the moment, seem perfectly ordinary. I therefore handed over the article without reservation. Lowe took it up in his hands and presented it to the two men. "There is a barrier," he said, "between our world and the hereafter — whatever that may be. This barrier usually prevents crossings over from one realm to the other. But," he said, dropping his voice lower so that his revelation might be rendered all the more dramatic. "There are times when the barrier is not as thick or as impenetrable as it ought to be."

"And why is that?" asked Agostino. He was no longer hostile, but he had not yet relinquished his scepticism altogether.

Lowe smiled and shook his head. "We do not know for certain," he said. "I have my theories, of course. Perhaps it happens in places where there has been significant death — where the barrier has been weakened by the passage of too many souls from this world to the next."

"But that would hardly account for this place," said Agostino, irritably. "There have been no deaths here in recent history. The cast and theatre staff are all very much alive! I should know, I pay them!"

"But there is another possibility," said Lowe. "And here we pass very much into the realms of acute speculation. As a race we have always puzzled over the origins of our most creative thoughts — why did the ancient Greeks, for example, attribute their greatest works of art to the muses?"

"You mean," said Gatti, with breathless credulity, "that our *art* may be responsible?"

71

"It is quite possible," said Lowe, earnestly. The theatre proprietor drew in an exquisite breath in wonder and pride as he considered the implication of the theatre's creative output having been of such profundity as to generate a rift in the very fabric of reality itself.

"At all events," Lowe continued. "The question that stands before us now is how we are to send this spirit back whence it came."

"I suppose you'd like us to leave you to it," said Agostino. "I suppose you'd like us to wait out in the foyer while you sit here and do nothing and then collect your fee. I've never heard such a great load of nonsense in my life — spirits crossing over! Muses indeed! You must think I was born yesterday."

Lowe was angry but restrained. "I have already told you, Mr Gatti, that I require no fee for the work that I do and have indicated that I am perfectly happy for you to observe it. In point of fact I do occasionally ask my clients to leave me to my work alone — not as a facade for some skulduggery, but rather for their own protection. On this occasion, however, I fear I must request that you stay — no, I must now insist upon it in the interests of preserving both my reputation and my dignity. Would you be so good as to take a seat just here, where you will have the best view?"

The brothers sat in the third row of the stalls. Looking up, I was conscious that further faces were staring down from the circle — curious members of the cast and theatre staff, keen to see the cause of all the commotion. I sidled up to Lowe and alerted him to their presence. He gave a small smile.

"Let them watch," he said, quietly. "It's always good for business." Then he turned to the Gatti brothers. "I trust that there is some mechanism somewhere for these curtains?" Stefano

72

nodded. "Could you please arrange for them to be drawn back?" An order was barked out and seconds later the curtains began to part, the ice crackling and falling from their lower portion in the process. Lowe vaulted himself up onto the edge of the stage and took stock of the situation.

"Ice, Mr Fairlea," he said, "and plenty of it."

"Indeed," I said, uncertain how else to respond.

Lowe then did something most unexpected. He sank to his knees centre stage on that frozen surface and, bringing his hands to his face in an attitude of prayer, he started to mumble something over and over to himself. For a few minutes nothing happened, and despite my faith in the strength of his character, even I began to wonder whether he was quite in his right mind.

"Well this is a lot better than the damned farce you've got playing at the moment," chortled Agostino. "If he manages to thaw the place out you should put him on a contract."

But his brother, to whom he was addressing these remarks, was not listening. Instead he was staring at the stage where something quite extraordinary was indeed occurring. Several larger shards of ice had cracked away from the floor and had risen silently into the air around Lowe, who was continuing to intone, apparently oblivious.

"How's he doing that?" snapped Agostino.

"Please, do not distract him," I answered. I had no idea what was happening, but I was convinced, somehow, that it was critical that nobody broke Lowe's concentration. The raised shards, pointing into the centre like daggers, were now beginning to circle around Lowe and then, slowly but surely, they were surrounded by others. Hideous, grating, shifting, squealing noises came from the great sheet of ice as they detached themselves to join in this improbable orbit.

"Fairlea," said Lowe, his eyes now open and resting upon me. "I need you to find some fire, and find it fast." He spoke slowly and in measured tones, but there was a deep-seated urgency.

I did not even consider pause, but ran to the wings of the stage where I fancied I might discover an oil lamp. Finding, to my delight, that there was one and that it was alight, I took it up and stepped to the edge of the stage again. Lowe was now at the centre of a whirlpool of ice, which was rotating about him slowly and menacingly. Looking out into the auditorium I saw that all those who had chosen to watch were enchanted by the spectacle. It *was* mesmerising; there was something hypnotic about the supernatural form of it.

"Fairlea," said Lowe, insistently, and I realised that I too had been arrested by the marvellous sight of those thousands of shards of glass revolving slowly in perfect circular motion about Lowe's head. "Bring me the lamp — slowly, mind."

It was bitter cold beneath the proscenium. The principle effect of the ice had been, of course, a visual one and it had been so stunning that I had not had opportunity to notice how very chill the air in the theatre had become. My breath now rose from my mouth in a plume of steam and the skin beneath my fingernails was a greyish blue.

"Go careful," said Lowe. "You are walking on ice."

I made slow progress towards his position, partly because the lethal ice-satellites were difficult to avoid and their velocity increasing by the minute, and partly because I was aware that the surface underfoot was treacherous.

"Mr Gatti," said Lowe, in a slow measured voice that gave the impression that the vast majority of his concentration was elsewhere. "I wonder if you would have the goodness to

74

extinguish all other lights?"

Gatti obliged at once and barked another order. Then by degrees, in the moments that followed, the auditorium was plunged into an abyss of blackness, the only light being that which I now held in my hand. The shards around me reflected and refracted the brightness of the lamp so that a pattern dance began about me. Now the light would pirouette upon a point and glint brilliantly from the tip, then it would pass through the ice like a glass prism and shatter off into rainbows.

"Bring me the lamp, Fairlea," he said, slowly and calmly. I followed the voice and just when I was beginning to wonder how I would ever reach Lowe at the epicentre of the whole affair, the circling suddenly stopped. The shards hung dead still in the air, their tips still all pointing in towards the centre. There was now a clear path between the two of us. Wasting no time, I hurried forward.

"Careful, you fool!" he hissed, but his warning came far too late. I had misplaced my footing and the next thing I knew I was airborne and so was the lamp. It left my hand and rose upwards into the air where, once having completed a somersault or two, it hung for a moment and then slowly descended toward the stage floor where it finally met its end, an inch beyond the futile reach of my fingers. There, the flame tried valiantly to battle on, but bereft of its fuel which now lay in a pool across the surface of the ice, it lasted only a few seconds. After that we were in absolute darkness.

"What the devil are you playing at?" Lowe's admonition rang out; a hissed whisper in the black. I opened my mouth to apologise, but before I could do so there was a great rushing, roar of a noise that seemed to be coming from all places at once. Instinctively I crawled forward to where I had last seen Lowe, keeping my head down to avoid the vicious edges of the shards which I could only assume still hung in the air. The source of the noise, however, soon became only too readily apparent. Lowe struck a match and held it out to the darkness to discover that the shards were now spinning around us with such great speed and in such great density that they appeared as nothing more than an icy blur.

The match went out and Lowe cursed as he struggled to light another quickly. As soon as he was successful, he held it out again and I saw, to my horror, that we were how faced with a solid wall of ice that seemed to be bearing terrifyingly down upon us.

"Get behind me," said Lowe, earnestly.

"What?" I asked unable to comprehend the instruction.

"I said get behind me," he repeated and he took me firmly by the shoulder and threw me down to the ground. In doing so, of course, he sacrificed the match and we were left, once again in darkness. The wall of ice, however, continued to advance — the sound was now unbearable in volume. It drew nearer and nearer in that unholy night until finally I thought it must surely crush us, but just at the last moment there was an air rending shriek of shattering, as if some clumsy butler had dropped a thousand champagne flutes. Then silence.

Once the relief had subsided, I was gripped by a terrible fear. Suppose that dreadful wall had descended entirely on Lowe? Had he sacrificed himself simply to shield me? Before I could make any further investigation, however, another match was illuminated in the darkness.

"Are you all right?" came Lowe's voice; still calm, still confident.

"I think so," I said. "What must we do?"

There was a long pause. The small portion of Lowe's face

that I could see illuminated in the match light was lost in a furrow of concern. "This is far worse than the other day," he murmured to nobody in particular.

"What must we do?" I repeated, stupidly.

"I fear," said he, "that we must provoke it."

"Provoke it?" I asked, dumbfounded. "Have we not already done so?"

"No indeed," he smiled. "It has only been playing with us thus far."

Prior to setting foot in the Vaudeville I had had no real thoughts on the existence or otherwise of the spiritual realm. Now that it presented itself to me as paralysingly real and thoroughly dangerous, I rather felt that any further provocation was to be avoided, not orchestrated. But my protestations were crystallised too late.

"You do not belong here," said Lowe to the darkness. He had lit another match and he was looking out again into the blackness that surrounded us. "Do you hear me, spirit?" he cried. "Do you know who I am?" There was a dull shivering of ice on the floor. "My name is Percival Lowe and I have been responsible for sending countless numbers of your brethren back into that inferno to which you all belong." There was another uneasy rustle.

"Where is it?" I asked, my voice shaking with terror.

"Close," he said. Then, suddenly, he demanded, "The lights, Mr Gatti — the lights!"

If Stefano Gatti was still in the audience, he made no sound, but one of the braver stage hands was bold enough to relight two of the lamps, so that we existed now in a murky gloom. I strained my eyes into the darkness and saw Lowe's face, but this was quite a shock. All the confidence and authority had drained from it —

neither was there any colour left. He was staring instead at something just up stage from us. At first I dared not look, but then I convinced myself that if I did not look now I should always regret it for the rest of my life and spend every night in sleepless wondering.

It was a figure. A figure formed entirely of ice. It looked to be a female figure, but how old I could not guess, for she was revealed to us in rough outline only. Whatever she was, she was very much alive, but she looked as if she were animated by some terrifying infernal force. Her movements were stiff and uncomfortable, but she was moving jerkily and unevenly towards us.

"Is that the spirit?" I asked, breathlessly, but Lowe did not respond. He simply stood, staring at the creature as it came on.

"Is that the ghost?" I pressed. But there was still nothing from him. She was close upon us now, like some animate tailor's dummy, bereft of face or expression.

"Lowe!" I exclaimed. "You must do something!"

This final imprecation seemed to have the desired effect for he sprang into action. Plunging a hand into his pocket he removed a stone not larger than a child's fist. Drawing back his arm he hurled it at the ice spectre as hard as he could with the simple imperative, "Be gone!" I feared that this might be a futile gesture, for the creature looked solidly built and I imagined that the stone, even with the force of Lowe's throw behind it would simply rebound off the frozen surface. In fact, the missile caught the ghoulish creature straight in the centre of its forehead, and at the moment it made contact, the form of the thing transformed into a column of water which cascaded down onto the stage floor.

That the creature — the thing — was gone I had no doubt. Its absence was most obviously felt by the sudden rushing in of warm air and with it comfort and goodness and a sense that the ordeal was over.

"Lights!" bellowed Lowe. "For God's sake would someone light the lamps?"

There was a scramble of activity in the wings and then in the circle, and before long, a good quantity of the lamps had been lit once more and the whole scene was bathed in warmth. The stage was drenched in water which had pooled in all the imperfections of its surface. I looked up to the balcony where I saw the crowd of spectators watching in awed wonder — still too stunned by what they had seen to talk. I looked at Lowe. His hair was unkempt and his face showed signs of the deepest strain, as if the encounter were not over and he were still wrestling with some thought that refused to leave him in peace. He rose to his feet and dusted himself off. Fortunately for him, the water seemed to have accumulated around and about where he was but to have left him utterly dry. I, however, found myself quite wet through for the second time that day.

"Who was she?" I asked. The question seemed natural then, but awkward now as I write it. Unless you had been there and experienced it yourself, you will not know the great personal power of the apparition. It was not some force of nature or physical distortion — it was evident that the visitation had some vestiges of humanity left in it.

"Yes, Mr Lowe," exclaimed Gatti, who had risen from his seat in the auditorium and joined us on the stage. "Have you any idea whose spirit that was?"

Lowe shook his head slowly, he affected a demeanour of confidence, but it was certainly less genuine than before. Though I had known him less than a day I could already discern that something had surprised him; something had not gone as he had

79

planned.

"I really have no idea, Mr Gatti," he said. "But whatever that *thing* was, I promise you that it will not trouble you again."

"Can you be sure?" It was Agostino's voice now that rang out crisp and clear from the back of the theatre. He had risen stiffly to his feet and even from my position on the stage I could see that he was shaking dreadfully. "There will be no more visitations?"

"I am as sure as I can be," said Lowe. "Once I have removed a spectre, I have never known it return."

Agostino nodded gravely. "You must forgive my former impertinence, Mr Lowe," he said, slowly. "I see now that you have rendered us a great service, and you too, Mr Fairlea."

I nodded in acknowledgement, but the truth of it was I could not see what I had done to help at all — except put us in even greater danger. I looked back at Lowe. Was this really his business? Was this how he earned the sort of money to acquire properties as grand as that of Mrs Finn? Had Mrs Finn too suffered from an apparition of this kind — had he helped her in the same way? The questions jostled for position in vain, for I dared not trouble Lowe with them until we had left the theatre. I was brought out of my reverie by a series of shouted orders from Gatti who was making ready to clear the water from the stage. It was evident that he had anticipated needing to cancel the performance but now, with the spectre vanquished, he was not going to let an evening's takings slip through his fingers quite so easily.

We were removed to the brothers' office which was a small but comfortably furnished room which sat somewhere within the labyrinth of passages that constituted the backstage portion of the theatre. There we were supplied with brandy and American cigars. The former was most welcome, but having only smoked the occasional cigarette to be social during my time in Africa, I had no use for the cigar. Lowe, however, lit his enthusiastically and allowed — through repeated, almost greedy inhalation — colour and confidence to return to his features.

"I do believe," said Gatti, "that we have witnessed something really quite unique this evening."

"Not at all," said Lowe, blowing smoke from the corner of his mouth. "It's all in a day's work."

"You mean to tell me," said Agostino, "that you routinely encounter such forces?"

"Of course," said Lowe.

Agostino let out a noise of disbelief. "You are a braver man than I," he said.

"I fear not," said Lowe, with a smile. "It's perfectly scientific you see — what I do. I may sensibly rest assured that as long as I follow my procedures to the letter then there is very little that might go wrong."

"And your hand, Mr Fairlea," said Agostino, turning to me and observing my stump. "Was that a little something going wrong?"

There was an awkward pause as I struggled to frame a response, but then Lowe laughed. "You would need to go a long way in this life gentlemen to find a force that is equal to the evil of man; Fairlea was in the hands of the Boers, out in Africa."

"A veteran?" Agostino looked impressed. I shrugged as modestly as I could manage.

"Now," said Gatti. "Let us talk of recompense — no don't wave me off like that, Mr Lowe, you have gone to a great deal of trouble on our account and I want to give you something in return."

"That is absolutely not necessary," said Lowe, sternly.

Gatti looked exasperated. "There must be something we can do for you to show our gratitude?"

Lowe assured him that there was nothing and then indicated to me that we should be going. He shook the hands of the men heartily and informed them that he would be at their service should the trouble recur (though he gave them — particularly Agostino — every assurance that it would not). At the door of the office, however, he turned and seemed to remember something.

"Oh there is one thing," he said. "It's a small thing and may be impossible for you to manage — but my colleague and I were hoping to catch *The French Maid* at some point. Might there be any tickets left for this evening's performance do you suppose?"

"*Might* there?" exclaimed Gatti, looking to his brother in joy and delight at the opportunity to repay the debt with such ease. "My dear Mr Lowe you shall have more than that, sir! You shall have our finest box and you shall have it as often as you desire! No, pray! Say no more on the subject, sir! The thing is done!"

CHAPTER FIVE

Lowe had not enjoyed the play. It had been a rough, bawdy sort of comedy which was a pleasurable enough experience from my perspective, but evidently tedious to him. I sensed, also, that he had not yet fully recovered from the earlier experience. That queer anxiety still danced behind his eyes as we rolled our way into Victoria. I wanted, of course, to give voice to a tirade of questions, but Lowe's downcast manner precluded that course of action and I had no wish to make myself appear impudent on what was — now that I reflected on it — still only my first day of employment, and indeed, acquaintance with the man.

"I am very tired, Fairlea," he said as he rummaged in his pocket for the key to his establishment. "I do not expect you shall see me tomorrow. I shall need to recuperate." His voice was a dull monotone and I was conscious of the contrast with the vigour and enthusiasm which had been so effervescently apparent in his character that morning. "Here," he said, suddenly, "take these — you've done well today." He thrust a pile of banknotes against my chest and I found myself taking hold of them, too stunned to protest. He did not look at me, but made his way past Crane's unattended desk and into the corridor beyond.

"Is there any duty you would have me perform for you tomorrow, sir?" I asked.

He paused and looked back.

"No," he said. "Take the day for yourself — only I shall take the liberty of booking you an appointment with my tailor in

Gracechurch Street at eleven. You can't continue to borrow my clothes indefinitely. Have him run a few things up for you and bring back the bill of sale. Crane will deal with that, just leave it on his desk; he can't abide a loose sheet."

I began to thank him, but he had already slipped away into the cloaking darkness of that corridor. I looked at the notes in my hand. The total amounted to more than a hundred pounds — more than a third of my proposed salary.

"One more thing," he said, his head emerging from the darkness without warning and causing me to start suddenly. "There is a ball tomorrow night at Claridges. I have an invitation, but I will be in no state to attend. Would you do me the courtesy of going as my proxy?"

"Of course," I said. I had never attended a society ball, but I could not imagine it was far removed from a military one and of those I had naturally seen plenty.

"Keep an ear out for gossip, business, opportunities, that sort of thing?"

I remarked that I should find it a good deal easier to keep a watch out for possible business opportunities if I fully understood the precise nature of his business.

"You will know them when you see them," he said. "You do not have a young lady to take with you, I suppose?" I shook my head. "Pity," he said. "Women are often the best at ferreting out precisely the sort of information we need. Well, it can't be helped. Goodnight."

He retreated again and this time I listened out for the sound of his exiting the corridor into his suite. I heard him lock the door behind him then waited for a few moments in silence. Perhaps it is a damning indictment of my morality that the principle emotion I felt was a paralysing sense of excitement. Here was I

— I who had been, that very morning, awash with despair and dejection — employed by a person of apparently limitless means and whose occupation, though still shrouded in unfathomable depths of mystery, seemed at the very least to be rife with drama and challenge. Such was my elation at my new circumstances that both the horrors of the early evening and the peculiar events of earlier that afternoon were entirely absent from my thoughts as I lay myself down on my bed that night and slept in perfect peace.

I awoke around six the following morning and became aware, by means of a powerful aroma of bacon, that my breakfast had arrived. Stepping out into my study I discovered a full plate upon which I set to work with voracious energy. As I fell to it with great relish, I realised that I had not eaten anything at all the previous day — not since my arrival in Victoria at least. As I sated my hunger with grateful vigour, my rationality began, by degrees, to return to me. The questions I yearned to ask about the activities of my employer rose up in great waves in my mind and refused to be quieted by the simple comfort of nourishment. Nonetheless, my curiosity, I realised with sinking resignation, was entirely futile. Lowe had made it quite clear that he would not be available that day and so I turned my mind to other matters.

I would have been more successful in this endeavour if, at the completion of my breakfast, I had not picked up the tray and discovered something completely extraordinary on the desk beneath. There, slightly charred and tattered, but immaculately arranged so that the original inscription remained easily legible, lay the fragments of the letter that I had now witnessed Lowe convincingly commit to destruction on two separate occasions. I read the text again but could find nothing odd in it. Why should he have been so determined to destroy it and how, despite everything, did it come to be back upon my desk? The situation was rendered even more peculiar by the fact that the fragments lay adjacent to a small pool of water which had dripped off the desk and onto the floor, presumably at some late hour of the night. I gave the matter deep consideration for some time but could find no logic in it whatsoever. If the letter was written in some carefully conceived code, then it would require a finer man than I to decipher it.

As to how it had found its way onto my desk again, I had no idea. To my knowledge the only people with access to this room were Lowe and myself, the former having presumably entered to deliver the breakfast — which raised another question: had he cooked it himself? Ultimately I was so at a loss in my efforts to explain any single one of these conundrums that I gave the whole thing up and resigned myself to living in ignorance until such a time as Lowe consented to give me a little more information. Having dressed in my own clothes (which had dried quite admirably in front of the fire) I stepped through into the office in which I was surprised to find Crane already at his desk and hard at work, though it was not yet eight.

"You keep a very long day, Mr Crane," I exclaimed.

"Just so, sir," said he allowing his neutral expression to crack into one of slight remorse. I sensed that there was an opportunity here to press my advantage — after all, Crane must know something of Lowe's routine.

"Have you been working for Mr Lowe very long?"

"For eight years, sir," said Crane, not looking up.

"How did you meet?" I asked, eagerly and ignoring the deliberate abruptness of the previous response.

"Mr Lowe placed an advertisement, sir, and I responded. That is, I believe, the usual manner of such things."

I was clearly going to achieve nothing by subtlety and thus decided to take a more direct approach.

"Mr Crane," I said, boldly interposing my hand between his gaze and the document before him. "I must ask you this question and I hope you will do me the honour of responding as honestly as you may." He looked up at me, startled, but said nothing. "Mr Crane — do you know exactly how it is that Mr Lowe makes his money? That is, do you know what it is that he does?"

"Why should that trouble me, Mr Fairlea?" he asked with genuine incredulity. "My position requires me only to manage Mr Lowe's financial affairs, his contracts and so forth. What he does with his days is his own concern. He does not pay me to worry about his personal business, in fact, he pays me so that he can make that business his own and his exclusive concern."

"But you must wonder?"

Crane smiled. "Wonder and curiosity are the playthings of children," he said. "I have long since put them away, and if you are wise, you shall do likewise."

Then he removed my hand gently from the page in front of him and returned to his work, pausing only to inform me that he had already arranged the appointment with Lowe's man in Gracechurch Street. Taking advantage of a free moment and the proximity of paper and pen, I scrawled a quick epistle to my mother informing her that I was safe and well in London and that I had secured a well-salaried position. I then enquired of Mr Crane whether it might be possible for him to forward a part of that generous salary to the ageing widow on a regular basis. He noted down her particulars and assured me that it would be seen to. He also kindly agreed to post the letter on my behalf along with Mr Lowe's not inconsiderable correspondence.

That done, I decided that I should prefer to walk to Gracechurch Street. When I made it known to Crane that this was my intention, he gestured through the window and reminded me that the heavens were still very much open. When I insisted that I was used to the wet and that the walk would do me good (the truth being, of course, that I had become somewhat claustrophobic and wanted to lose myself and my thoughts in the general milieu of city life), he insisted that, at the very least, I should take with me Lowe's umbrella. To this demand I assented and withdrew that item from the hat-stand by the door. I wished Crane a hasty goodbye — to which his only response, as he bent low over the papers, was a raised hand of acknowledgement — and stepped out into the street.

I had not been walking more than twenty minutes before I noticed, with some irritation, that I was being followed. Though the loss of my hand had incapacitated me significantly, I was not an insubstantial man and certainly not timid. Even now, though slowed and weighed down by old age, I like to think that I could still hold my own in a brawl. I was not in the least afraid of this slight figure pursuing me, darting from awning to shop doorway to barrow and then to awning again. In fact, had I not been so intent on clearing my head of all things peculiar, it might rather have amused me. But the constant intrusion of this person into my thoughts drew me constantly back down into the reality of my confusion and thus I resolved to put a stop to it. Deviating slightly from my route, I took a sharp left down a narrow street and then, having proceeded only a few steps, I waited.

I did not have to wait long. I heard the hurried footsteps and drew myself up to my full height so as to be ready when their author appeared around the corner. Before that moment came, however, the sound of the footsteps faltered and there was a definite sound of a scuffle. Someone or something fell heavily and there was a grunt of pain. I had just made up my mind to investigate and had taken a few steps forward when I collided with another person rounding the bend at that exact moment.

To my surprise I found that it was a woman, and a young woman too. She was primly dressed, with her thin brown hair drawn up tight into a bun beneath her hat, although several strands were out of place and there were one or two tears in the hem of her skirt which was damp with gutter water. She carried an umbrella, and though I could not be sure, it looked very much as if she had been employing it as a weapon moments before.

"Good morning," I said, cheerily, not quite knowing what else to say.

"Beastly man," she muttered, sheepishly, inspecting the umbrella carefully with a pair of startlingly blue eyes. "Well, he won't be trying that on again, will he?"

"Are you all right?"

She leaned the umbrella up against a wall and began replacing the wayward strands of hair into their neat arrangement. "Oh yes," she said. "Quite all right, thank you — it's not the first time and I doubt it will be the last. One of these days I'll—" She had looked up at me for the first time and her eyes widened. "You!" she exclaimed, in what I took for delight. "It's you — isn't it? From the Vaudeville?" She quite forgot her hair now and stepped towards me with her palms towards my face as if I were some Christmas ornament and she a curious child.

It was then that I realised where I had seen her before.

"You were at the theatre," I said. "Last night — before the performance — you were watching from the circle when Lowe—

89

" I stopped, for I realised I had no means of easily explaining what Lowe had actually done, mostly because I really didn't understand it myself. I allowed the silence to persist, hopeful that she would infer my meaning.

"Yes!" she said excitedly and at once. "Yes — I was so *hoping* to run into one or other of you."

"Well," said I, "you've got your wish"

She blushed. "Are you going somewhere now?" she asked, excitedly. "Is there another — another *problem* for you to sort out?" She began to look around and about me almost comically. "Is the other man here with you?"

"Lowe? No — he's resting," I said, feeling slightly dejected. "I'm afraid you catch me on rather an ordinary journey actually. I'm going to the tailor on Gracechurch Street."

"Oh," she echoed, her face falling a little.

I felt rather a disappointment and desperately wracked my brain for something to say that might make it up to her. "Look," I said, after what had seemed an interminable age of silence, "if you're going that way, we could walk together." I eyed the umbrella. "It might prevent you having to use that again?"

She blushed a little and laughed, then she looked at her watch — a little golden affair on her left wrist. "I'm supposed to be back before lunch," she said hesitantly, more to herself than to me, but then she seemed to make up her mind. "I'd like that very much. You may escort me to Gracechurch Street."

There was a charm about her brazenness. She was a peculiar little thing and I confess she appealed to me. I agreed readily on condition that she should at least afford me her name.

"Molly," she said. "What's yours?"

"George," I replied. "But most people call me by my surname — Fairlea."

"Why?" she asked.

"I confess I've never really given the matter much thought," I said, slightly embarrassed. "A military thing, I suppose."

"Do you like it?"

"Not especially."

"Well, I shall call you George," she said. Then, leaning in under my umbrella, she whispered, barely containing her laughter, "But don't worry, I'll go straight back to Fairlea if there's anyone important about."

So we proceeded toward Gracechurch Street under one umbrella (two having become thoroughly and hilariously inconvenient at an early stage in the expedition) conversing as old friends. It is a curious thing that an unplanned meeting in peculiar circumstances can so often yield a more instantly natural relationship than the clunky rigours of a formal introduction. She, it seemed, worked for the Gatti brothers at the theatre in some vague sort of secretarial role (though she was none too happy about it and it seemed to me from the very few details she gave that she was rather ill-used by the two men). When she had finished narrating her provenance, she began to ask questions about mine and I filled in the dull details as honestly as I could. There was something so refreshingly open about her that one instinctively wanted to bestow trust upon those extraordinary eyes. Before I knew it I was divulging to her something of my experiences at Lowe's establishment, but then I quickly caught myself, mindful of the contract I had signed.

"But how do you think he does it?"

"Does what?"

"Expels the ghosts or exorcises them or whatever it is you call it? I saw it last night — watched the whole thing! It was so very extraordinary I can't get it out of my mind. I feel I must know how it was done or I'll go mad! I swear I'll never tell another soul!" She looked so desperate that, had I been possessed of the information she sought, it would have taken all my powers of restraint not to divulge to her everything I knew. Fortunately, I was as much in ignorance as she was.

"I confess I do not know. I cannot even say for certain whether we are dealing with ghosts or demons or spirits or parlour tricks. Please do bear in mind that I only came into his employment yesterday morning."

"Yes," she frowned, attempting to mask her bitter disappointment. "I was forgetting that."

She slipped her arm around mine, but either ignorant or forgetful of the absent hand it simply slipped through and returned to her side. "Oh I'm sorry," she said. "That was foolish of me."

"Please don't apologise," I replied. "It was a mistake, that's all."

Nonetheless, a sudden awkwardness now hung in the air between us and I was heartily glad when first the signs for Gracechurch Street and then the name of Lowe's tailor came into view.

"Well," I said, "thank you for the walk. I have much enjoyed your company."

"The pleasure has been mine, George," she said, and she dropped a little curtsey. I smiled and a sudden thought occurred to me. It was such an utterly ridiculous thing to suggest on the back of a chance meeting and yet — I reflected — so much of my life these last few weeks had been determined entirely by chance that I saw no harm in rolling the dice once more.

"I say, you're not at work this evening, are you?"

She looked at me, curiously. "No. It's my night off — why

do you ask? Is Lowe going out on business again?" Her tone was suddenly eager and excited.

"No," I said. "It's nothing as dramatic as all that, I'm afraid. Look, this is very forward of me and I'd like you to understand that I've no motive at all here, there's nothing implied."

She began to laugh.

"Look," I said, trying to master my painful embarrassment, "I've been invited to a ball at Claridge's and I was wondering if you would do me the honour of accompanying me? I am without a dance partner, you see."

Her face lit up in wild delight and I won't deny that I took some pleasure in it; until this point, I had feared that the promise of my company had only been attractive as a means of experiencing Lowe indirectly.

"I would be delighted," she said, beaming. "I shall try to borrow a gown from a friend."

"Can you get to Lowe's place for seven o'clock?" I asked, giving her the address.

"Yes," she nodded, with alacrity. "Yes, I'll be there!" Then she kissed me lightly on the cheek, turned and scurried off into the crowd and I trudged on towards the tailor.

I have never been particularly fond of tailors, not, it must be said, that I have had much cause to deal with them. I have generally found them to be over-fussy types who give the impression that their understanding of what is pleasing to the eye or fashionable or comfortable (that last usually being strictly incompatible with the former) is far superior to that of their customer. I was pleased to discover that Lowe's gentleman in Gracechurch Street was none of these things. I'm not sure why I was surprised by this. If I had learned anything of Percival Lowe in my time with him it was that he did not suffer fools gladly. The

93

very notion of his tolerating some simpering idiot fussing about him with tape measures and pins was impossible to conceive.

In fact, I was in Mr Crowloft's shop for less than an hour. The man was quite extraordinary. Old as the earth itself, and as I thought, actually already exhibiting the symptoms of the earliest stages of decay, he stooped over his desk and consulted a number of books, all the while muttering to himself. He took no measurements, but simply spent a good deal of time looking me up and down and requiring that I turn to this side or that so that he might observe me from all angles. "Bigger than Webster," he murmured to himself at times. Or, "Not so full as Corkley." Then without so much as consulting me on the colour or nature of the fabric he intended to use or even as to the sorts of clothes I might require, he drew up the bill of sale and informed me that I could call in to collect the garments on Thursday week if that was quite convenient. Neither knowing Lowe's immediate plans for me nor what I might be doing on Thursday week, I simply agreed, resting on the supposition that Crane would deal with any irregularities that might arise. The old man grunted, handed me the paperwork and then retired into the private backrooms of the shop, leaving me quite alone in the foyer.

It being just about noon when I stepped out again onto Gracechurch Street, I found my way to a nearby inn where I took lunch. This lunch was, to my mind, quite extravagant. Partly this was as a means of compensating for the meals I had missed the previous day and partly it was a test of my new means, for though I knew I carried a pocketful of notes, their value seemed vague and ephemeral to me. It was such an improbable sum that I felt I should not feel the full worth of it until I had spent some of it. Unfortunately, as I went to pay for my food, and indeed for the two pints of ale I had enjoyed (considering that I had easily earned these by my experiences in Lowe's employ thus far and that there was plenty of time for me to sober up in advance of the evening's duties), I made the grave mistake of producing the whole wad of notes from my pocket in full view of the other patrons.

My carelessness in this matter was rewarded some fifteen minutes later when, for the second time that day, I had the very clear impression of being followed. This time, however, it was not the slim figure of Molly, but a broad man in naval uniform whom I had previously observed watching me as I ate. Once again, I took a sharp left, and waited for my pursuer to join me in a narrow alley off the main thoroughfare. On this occasion, however, there was no jocular conversation. The man, perceiving my injury, had imagined, I think, that I might be easily overpowered and so set upon me the moment our eyes made contact.

I have heard that when a man goes blind his other senses grow stronger as a means of compensating for that weakness. I do not know if there is any truth in this nor whether the same logic can be applied to arms and hands, but I have found that my one good arm is now far more powerful than I had known it previously, and that my legs too, seem to have become tougher in the months since losing my hand. Thus it was that, although my assailant appeared to have made some progress with his first foray, he quickly found himself on a losing footing. I caught him a strong blow to the temple and he staggered back a few paces, striking his shoulder against the wall. Pressing home my advantage, I cuffed him twice in the stomach before cutting his feet out from under him with a well-aimed kick to the left knee, where I perceived he was resting the vast majority of his weight. The man collapsed into the stinking mud of the gutter and held up his hand to indicate his capitulation. The fury was now upon me, however. The greed of the man and his assumption that my weakness made me an easy target had ignited a furnace in my head and all reason and sense fled before the flames. I took up Lowe's umbrella which I had thrown aside at his first advance, and having collapsed it, raised it above my head and beat it hard across the fellow's chest and then cracked it three of four times upon the arm he had raised in protection until he screamed in agony clutching at the fractured limb.

The piercing noise of the scream and the pooling red liquid that mingled itself with the mud and rainwater quickly brought me back to sanity and I looked down in some horror at what I had done, at the pathetic figure who lay now cowering in the grime. I tried to justify my act by believing that his intention had been to do the same to me and leave me unconscious, if not dead, once he had extracted the notes from my pocket. Nonetheless, I could not assuage the sweeping feeling of guilt that now filled the vacuum where the fury had been only a few seconds before.

"I'm sorry," I said. Though the words felt false and shallow and my voice cracked as I spoke them. For the first time in minutes I became conscious of the rain dripping from my hair and clothes and found that I was trembling either with shock or cold. I reached down into my pocket and withdrew the money that had been the object of his assault. I took from the sheaf of notes about twenty pounds — a ludicrous sum —, and crumpling the papers up, pressed them into his hands, murmuring something ineffectual about finding a good doctor. Then I stepped away from him. I couldn't look any more. Finding myself at the end of the alleyway, I brushed myself down and used water from a puddle to cleanse the spots of blood from my clothes. The shame was not so easily dealt with, however, and as I joined the thronging crowd of umbrellas once again, I felt as if each of them were watching me, judging me, silently aware of what I had done.

I do not recall much of the walk back towards Victoria, my mind being occupied by a grim reconstruction of my recent altercation — and of other past events whose memories presented themselves painfully and inextinguishably in grim sequence, but as soon as I approached the entrance to Lowe's office I became dimly aware that something out of the ordinary was occurring. A slight looking man, prematurely grey and clearly of a nervous disposition, was picking up stones from the street and hurling them at the windows, pausing between each throw to shout at the top of his voice words which at first I was too far away to clearly distinguish from the general hubbub. Quite a crowd of onlookers had gathered, and by the time I came upon the scene, one or two public-spirited people were trying to reason with the fellow. They appeared to be enjoying some success for a time, but then he broke away from them again and picked up another stone which struck and shattered one of the panes.

"You can't hide in there forever, Lowe!" the man shouted. "I'll speak with you, whether you like it or not — do you hear me!"

"What's going on?" I asked one of the onlookers.

"The fellow's out of his mind," he replied. "He keeps on saying something about a ghost or being haunted or some such nonsense. He claims that there's a gentleman inside who refuses to help him."

I gave a sympathetic roll of the eyes and turned my attention back to the incandescent figure of the man who had scored another successful hit on the window.

"It's money you want isn't it, Mr Lowe — well name your price and you shall have it — do you hear me? Name your price!"

The last of these three syllables he punctuated by throwing three smaller stones toward the glass.

"Samuel," came a voice from the crowd and I saw that a man in a bowler hat was barging his way to the front. "Samuel, this won't help. Good heaven's man, what's got into you? Come away with me — come with me now before you do something else you regret."

"Regret!" clamoured Samuel at the top of his voice. "Don't talk to me about regret — I could fill up whole oceans with the stuff! What's your price, Lowe?" he demanded, turning once again to the window. "What tariff do you put on a man's sanity? How much will it cost me to be able to sleep at night?" But his friend, having at last reached his side, took hold of him by the arm and managed, by a series of reasoned entreaties to drag him back into the crowd, and within a few moments, the spectacle was over and the street was restored to its normal order save for the fragments of broken glass that lay on the road outside the front of Lowe's office.

I had just put my hand to the door to knock upon it when it opened and a terrified-looking Crane poked out his head. At first, he was startled by the proximity of my face, but his anxiety was soon replaced with evident relief.

"Come in, come in, Mr Fairlea," he said, and having ushered me inside and performed his ritual of looking up and down the street, came in himself and shut the door behind him.

"Who was that?" I asked, when we were both safely inside.

"I'm sorry you had to see that, Mr Fairlea," said Crane, who was busying himself in performing a makeshift repair to the damaged window. "I'm afraid that people are never as civilised as they pretend to be. Dear me, what a depth society appears to be sinking to. O Tempora! O Mores!"

"But that man knew Lowe," I said. "Or at least he had an idea of what he does." Then a connection that was so obvious that I felt ridiculous for having missed it before occurred to me. "That was Samuel Ivor, wasn't it?"

Crane looked up at me sharply, but said nothing.

"What is the history between him and Lowe?" I asked in a tone that I hoped might overcome the secretary's reticence.

"You would do better not to ask about that," said Crane and continued to busy himself with the repair. From somewhere in the room, that peculiar crackling noise was beginning to sound again. "Oh dear," he said, halting his labour. "I'd better attend to the fire again."

"Why is Lowe so afraid of Samuel Ivor?" I persisted.

"That is a question you will need to ask Mr Lowe himself," said Crane as he bent low over the grate. "I am not at liberty to discuss such things."

"Mr Crane!" I cried venting my frustration. "It strikes me that we are in very real danger here — that man was clearly not in his right mind! If I am to risk my life by working here I think I at least have the right to know the reason why!"

The crisp, cracking noise which had been building all this while rose in a crescendo and suddenly, without warning, the fire was extinguished and a great sheet of frost shot out from the hearth across the floor, up the wall and over the window, where it filled the empty panes with ice at least an inch thick. Then the noise stopped and the two of us stood there in dumbfounded silence.

"Well," said Crane at length, "that will serve nicely until a glazier can be found."

CHAPTER SIX

"He works with Percival Lowe," said Molly, completing my introduction for what seemed to be the thousandth time that evening. For all the champagne and chandeliers, the ball seemed to be turning into a very tedious affair. Not however, I reflected, quite as tedious as the hours of waiting that had preceded it. Crane's exclusively pragmatic approach to the visit of Samuel Ivor and the extraordinary happening in the office had precluded the possibility of any further meaningful discussion on the matter. Several of his precious documents had been damaged by the melting ice sheet and their rescue and restoration had occupied a vast proportion of his time. Each time I did attempt to raise a query or at least cause him to engage in discussion of what we had just experienced, he either waived me away with some feeble remark about the intemperate nature of British weather or reminded me that Mr Lowe would not like us to discourse on such matters. Finally, dejected and infuriated, I had returned to my rooms where I had divided my time equally by thinking matters through to dead ends, pacing about a good deal and in attempting to read one or two of the dusty tomes that sat upon the shelf above the desk. These were almost exclusively translations of great Latin classics including the *Eclogues* of Virgil and one or two volumes of Livy's *History of Rome*. None of these titles was particularly scintillating, the translations having been forged in such a stuffy and academic manner that the English text was rendered quite as impenetrable to me as the Latin original.

The hours passed remarkably slowly, and when my mind lacked stimulation, my thoughts returned again and again to the unfortunate brawl of the morning and to the damage I had done to the sailor. It was with some relief, then, that I heard the little clock in the front office striking six — permitting me decently, I felt, to begin the process of getting changed. Lowe, whom I had not seen at all that day, had been kind enough to lay out some appropriate attire for me and I took great pains to ensure that I was as presentable as possible. Partly to pass the time and partly — though I should never have admitted this myself — because I wished to impress Molly. At the time I did not subject this desire to win her affection to deep scrutiny, but with hindsight it seems to me that I was less desirous to have her admiration for its own sake than to extract myself from the eclipsing personality of Lowe.

Molly. She was a saving grace all that evening — the only thing making the boredom bearable. She had arrived at seven as promised, dispensing with that tedious notion of fashionable lateness. I shall not hesitate to say that she looked beautiful in the gown she had borrowed. The prim little bun of the morning had been released and her hair was now plaited so that it wreathed her head, the individual strands having been interwoven with a fine silver ribbon.

"Will I do?" she asked, when she arrived.

"You look marvellous," I said.

Crane had looked up in some surprise at Molly's arrival but had said nothing at all. I explained — though I need not have done — that Lowe had suggested I take a young lady with me in the interests of business. Crane had accepted this with a shrug and a, "Just so, sir", but had continued to eye Molly with peculiar interest until our carriage arrived.

Neither of us had known quite what to expect from the event — neither of us having attended such a function before, but Molly's confidence allowed her to fit in seamlessly with the crowd. She talked with lords and ladies as if they were her familiars and they were more than happy to reciprocate her delicate and precise conversation, which substituted neatly for inherent nobility. Meanwhile I stood awkwardly by, patiently awaiting her introduction.

"Lowe, eh?" said one important-looking gentleman. "He's the railway man, isn't he?"

"I think not, sir," I responded, but once again I felt the insecurity of the ground beneath me. Who knew what Lowe's interests really were?

"What line is he in?" asked another guest, joining the conversation.

"Property," I said, loosely. Nonetheless, the ambiguous response appeared to do the trick and conversation moved on to other topics in which I had no interest. These were questions of government and taxation and imports and exports and I was neither competent nor articulate enough to offer any form of opinion. Molly, on the other hand, revelled in the opportunity to state hers and I was rather impressed to see her holding her own with, and indeed scoring points off, men whom I had imagined to be superior to her in both wisdom and experience.

Then the conversation moved on to the war and I found it increasingly difficult to remember my position. One or two of the older gentlemen were insisting that the British army of twenty or thirty years previously would never have suffered the sort of routs that the Boers appeared to be inflicting upon us with crushing regularity. Then they turned themselves to an inexpert analysis of the conflict criticising, by turns, everything from incompetence of the generals to the inexperience and cowardice of the men on the ground. This last disparagement was too much for me and I was unable to restrain myself.

"I have been 'on the ground' in Africa, sirs," I said suddenly and with a sort of petty youthful impudence for which I cursed myself, "And I saw all manner of things — but certainly not cowardice." I felt my ears growing red and my face flushing and I wished above all else that I had just some small portion of Molly's confidence.

"Is that so," remarked one of the men, drily, but without interest. His companions regarded me for a moment or two and then drifted away to continue their conversation on the other side of the room, away, I thought, from the distractions of reality. There is nothing, I have often observed, that spoils the excitement of criticism and speculation so much as an injection of incontrovertible fact.

For an hour or perhaps two after that, I held my silence as a series of gentlemen tested their wits against Molly's as if she were some sort of fairground attraction. None prevailed — but Molly never allowed her eloquence to transform into complacency or arrogance and her brilliantly formed responses were phrased in the most deferential terms. Thus it was that, as they fell from the conversation, the men would turn to me and make remarks such as, "You've picked yourself a winner there, my boy!" or, "She'll give you a run for your money, you mark my words."

Though I enjoyed observing Molly's progress, I was growing increasingly conscious that Lowe had sent me to the ball for the purposes of business and that, thus far, I had achieved little. When there was a lull in conversation, I drew close to Molly and pulled her into the corner.

"What is it?" she said, brightly. "Aren't you having a good time?"

"Listen," I said, ignoring her question to which my answer would have been an emphatic negative. "Lowe sent me here tonight to see if I could pick up anything that might be useful for him from a *business* perspective."

"What sort of thing," she said in breathless excitement and once again I winced inwardly at the powerful effect Lowe's name seemed to have on her.

"I'm not sure," I replied. "He said I would know it when I saw it."

"And have you?"

"Have I what?"

"Have you seen it?" she asked, as if I were quite mad.

"No," I said, in frustration. "That's just the point. I've heard a good deal of rot here tonight but nothing that would interest Lowe in the slightest."

"Oh, you're not getting all upset over that talk of the war are you," she asked in surprise. "It's ball talk, George, that's all. Nobody comes here to say what they mean! They just compete to see who can sound the most clever or impressive; there's no truth in any of it."

"Then what's the point?"

"I don't suppose there is one," she said brightly. "But if it's gossip you're after there's only one way to get that."

"And that would be?"

"I shall have to go dancing."

With that she drew me back out from the corner and onto the floor of the ballroom where we joined the perimeter of a circle of waltzing couples. She put her head on my chest and I caught the scent of her hair, sweet and somehow familiar. Even now I can recall it, despite all that has passed. There was the glimmer of the hope of happiness for me in that fleeting instant and it is a memory that is perhaps more precious to me than any other I now possess.

"In a few moments," she said. "I need you to drop me."

"Drop you?" I asked, incredulous.

"Precisely," she said. "Don't worry, I shall do most of the falling. After you do so, however, be sure that you are effusive in your apologies and — and this is the most important part — you must make it clear to everyone that you only have one hand."

"Why the devil would I do that?" I exclaimed, recoiling at the thought of such a public humiliation.

"Because nobody can resist a damsel in distress," she said and before I had a chance to respond she had purposely placed one of her legs behind my own and thrown herself to the floor in the most dramatic fashion causing the nearest group of fellow dancers to turn and look to see what the commotion was all about. For a moment I was too stunned to speak.

"You fool!" exclaimed Molly from the floor, gathering up her skirts and making a great play of checking that her hair was still in immaculate condition. "I thought it was your hand you'd lost, not your mind!" Several women had gathered around her and were helping her to her feet — though I saw she was making this as difficult for them as possible in an effort to extend the spectacle.

"I'm very sorry," I muttered.

"And so you should be! I don't know why I consented to be your partner this evening at all," she bit back. "You dance like an elephant!" This elicited some nervous laughter from the growing crowd of onlookers.

"I'm afraid it's my hand," I said, brandishing the stump for all to see. I felt deeply uncomfortable, but something in the assured manner with which Molly was approaching the whole thing gave me a thin strand of confidence.

"No," she declared with a malicious giggle, pointing at the stump. "It *isn't!*" This caused an eruption of laughter from the throng, and blushing a deep scarlet, I turned away and strode to the side of the room where there was a punch bowl. Dipping a goblet into it I withdrew it and hastily consumed the contents. I am not an habitual drinker, but I knew I needed something to dull the injury to my pride. Turning to look back at the dance-floor, however, I saw with some surprise that Molly's ruse had clearly worked to dazzling effect. She was already in discussion with four men and two others were lingering on the edges in hopes of reserving a dance — each eager to demonstrate both his skill and the fact that he was equipped with a full set of functioning limbs.

I turned back to the punch and filled another goblet. I had just raised it to my mouth to drink it when I was interrupted by an insistent tap on my shoulder.

"Excuse me," said a nervous looking gentleman who was holding a handkerchief to his face and looking about him, his eyes darting fretfully back and forth. "But did I hear you say that you are an associate of Mr Lowe?"

I nodded.

"Mr *Percival* Lowe?" he asked, becoming even more nervous so that the feeble piece of cloth which he pinned against his nose shook like a flag in a storm. "Forgive me," he went on when I had once again indicated that he was correct. "the same Percival Lowe who is the proprietor of the office in Victoria?"

"Indeed, sir. I do not know it to be a particularly common name," I replied in puzzlement.

"But it is a far from common occupation," he whispered.

Then, seeing my surprise, he drew back and those eyes widened in terror. "I should not have said anything," he whimpered. "You obviously do not *know*; you have not *heard*."

"For the sake of argument," said I, calmly, "let us assume I *have* heard and that I *do* know." He seemed very much relieved at this and even consented, for a very few moments, to drop the shroud from his features. He was not an old man — indeed, he could not yet have seen his thirtieth birthday — but his face was unnaturally aged by lines of worry that sprang out like tentacles from his eyes and grappled with his rather ill-defined temples. It was a rounded, soft sort of a face that might, in other circumstances, have imparted warmth and friendship, but on this encounter it was strained and much vexed. So much so, in fact, that I was forced to wonder whether it could ever conceivably return to a state of lesser distress.

"How can I be of assistance, sir?" I asked. At last, I felt, I was on the trail of an opportunity that might interest Lowe and I wished to be as proactive as I could. Lowe was the sort of person that one wanted always to impress, and I was still conscious of being under some form of probation.

"I heard what happened at the Vaudeville," said the man, quietly. "I heard what he — that is, what you and he — did for the Gatti brothers."

"I see," said I. "I had hoped that Stefano and Agostino would honour Mr Lowe's request to speak to no one of what we undertook that evening." Lowe had been emphatic on the point — scandalous gossip must not be permitted to spread; rumours must not be put about.

"Oh don't be angry at them," said the man, the handkerchief rising once more to his face so that only the beseeching eyes were now visible. "Don't chastise them on my behalf! You must understand that I have the honour of being in the very innermost circle of their acquaintance and they have urged me to be quite clandestine in my own dealings, but when they saw what Lowe could do they were put in mind of my own predicament."

"Your own predicament?"

The eyes became suddenly those of someone to whom I had given some terrible offence, then they softened slightly. "I'm so sorry," he said, with saccharine politeness. "I should have introduced myself — my name is Edgar Carstairs." He announced this final piece of information as if it were the critical element I needed to make all others fall into place, but I looked back at him blankly.

"George Fairlea," I said, extending my good hand. The man took it absent-mindedly and I realised that he was busily fighting an internal battle. He could not, I assumed, allow his disappointment that I did not already know of his 'predicament' to show without revealing himself to have been indiscreet and yet he did not wish to lessen its seriousness by presenting it as a private matter between he and I.

"Perhaps you would like to explain your predicament?" I ventured, deciding to put him out of his misery. "Once you have detailed the matter to me, I shall relay it to Mr Lowe and we shall see what may be managed." I felt ridiculously grand saying this. What was I really? Nothing but Lowe's lackey! Yet nonetheless, the sensation that Carstairs was now obliged to court me as proxy was a particularly pleasant one.

"I am tormented, Mr Fairlea," he said, drawing closer to me and tugging on my arm so that we sat together on one of the couches at the edge of the room. Pleased though I was to have found a business opportunity I deemed worthy of my attention, I could not prevent my gaze from drifting out to the dancers where

I saw Molly whirling merrily with a young gentleman while three others stood off to the side, remonstrating with each other in equal measure — presumably in competition for her favour. I caught myself envying them and with a great effort, quickly dragged my consciousness back to my new companion.

The story Carstairs told — or what small amount of it I could make out between the muffled sobbing and whimpering sounds that intruded on the narrative from beyond the handkerchief — certainly did seem to be a peculiar one. He was currently renting a room near the centre of town. He was rather vague about the address, but was troubled on a nightly basis by what seemed to be an apparition or visitation. He described, in painful detail, how the figure of an elderly man who resembled his father, appeared to him each evening, at a few minutes after midnight, and stood motionless at the foot of his bed, dressed in rags and wearing a set of heavy-looking chains on his hands and feet. The eyes of the man, according to Carstairs, had burned with the fury of hell and there had been a strong smell of what he had been fairly sure was sulphur in the room after each appearance.

"And does he say anything to you?"

"Who?"

"Your father — if that's who it is?"

Carstairs screwed up his eyes as if the experience were too painful to fully recreate in his memory. "Oh yes," he said at length. "Yes!"

"And what did he say?" For someone so eager to impart his problems, it seemed to be taking an undue length of time for me to tease out the particulars from him.

"Terrible, terrible things," said he, shaking his head mournfully. "Scandalous things!"

"Such as?"

"You surely do not expect me to discourse on these matters in an open forum such as this, Mr Fairlea? If I am to speak in greater detail, then I shall expect a private interview with Mr Lowe himself!"

I frowned. I had a hunch that Lowe was not a man for private interviews and an even more compelling one that he was not the sort of man who would tolerate men like Carstairs, whatever the weather. By the same token, I had no desire to return to Lowe empty-handed or, worse still, only with information that Molly had energetically extracted from her growing crowd of admirers.

"I'm afraid that will not do, Mr Carstairs," I said, rising from my chair. "Mr Lowe trusts me implicitly and places great authority on my judgement; if I do not know the details then I cannot very well make the case to Mr Lowe. If I cannot make the case to Mr Lowe then your predicament is and shall continue to be, very much your own."

Faced with the prospect of suffering in solitude, Carstairs gave a start and sprang up at once. "Forgive me, Mr Fairlea — or George, if I may presume so far — you must understand that all of this is new to me. I am, you see, a man of habitual discretion and sobriety." I didn't doubt this. The man was a pathetic specimen and it seemed to me that this ball was probably the most exciting thing he had done in months.

Lowering the handkerchief, he brought his face near to my ear and whispered into it. "The spirit informs me that my father was cruelly murdered before his time."

"Indeed?" said I, intrigued, for this really did feel like the sort of thing that might interest any man, Lowe included.

"Indeed," said he, and then he raised both his hands so that he formed a tunnel between his mouth and my ear, all the while looking furtively about him to ensure that nobody was listening.

"He says that it was done by poison — and by my own uncle."

This really did shock me and I began to see the rationale for Carstairs' nervous disposition. "Did he give any idea of motive for this act?" I asked.

"Alas," said he, tragically, "as in so many cases I fear that love of Mammon has been the root of all this evil. My father was a wealthy man but his brother had fallen on hard times. He and my mother had what I would describe now as an unnaturally close relationship at the time of my father's death, and not two years following that dreadful event, they married."

"You suspect your mother was complicit in the action?"

"I have no doubt," he said, throwing the back of his hand across his forehead in an affected manner. "What is more, the moment I came of age I was cast out from house and home on a meagre allowance and reduced to my present state, while he and she enjoy the fatted calf together."

"That sounds most outrageous," I said, though I was inclined to take the casting out story with a pinch of salt; Carstairs was hardly destitution personified.

"Then you see," said he, clasping my hand in his, "why I am so desperately in need of Mr Lowe's assistance in this matter."

I nodded gravely and gave him assurances that I should pass on everything he had told me. Ultimately, I was only able to extricate myself from his company (which had of course begun as a pleasing and fulfilling antidote to my shame) after he had plied me with such blandishments and flatteries as to make me blush and wish I were somewhere entirely other.

"Who was that?" asked a bright-eyed Molly, putting her hand lightly on my shoulder as Carstairs retreated from the hall.

"A possible business opportunity," I said, somewhat coldly. For all her performance on the floor had been play-acting I could not but find myself hurt by the comments she had made.

"Really?" she asked, her face abounding with excitement. "Tell me!"

"I'd rather get Lowe's opinion on it first," I said in an aloof sort of a way and I gave her what I thought to be a condescending smile.

She stepped away from me a little and looked me up and down with a suspicious smile on her own face. "You're not upset about that business before, are you?" she asked, after a few moment's pause. "Good heavens you *are*! Didn't you see that was all a ruse? Didn't you understand that I never meant a word of it?"

"Did it work?" I asked, ignoring the question.

"Did it work? I've been danced off my feet for what feels like hours by half the eligible young men in London. I've heard more stories of bravado and wealth and riches than I care to recount. They all want to impress, you know; it's quite pathetic. They go on and on and on about things they think I'll admire when really all a woman like me wants is intelligent conversation. The only time I got close to that was this one fellow — Pitt, I think was his name — who was in such a fervour about his recently acquired collection of neo-impressionist paintings that I think he'd pretty well forgotten I was there by the end of the conversation."

"Did you learn anything that might be useful?"

"Not one thing," she sighed, flopping down onto a couch in defeat. "I mean I learned a good deal about the finer points of art dealerships and how not to be swindled. I think my Mr Pitt has had his hands burned rather badly. I wouldn't be surprised if he weren't in a bit of a tight spot financially — but I've had no luck at all with the spiritual realm. People just don't want to talk about it."

"You don't mean to say that you asked them openly?" I exclaimed in horror. The notion of a forward young woman going about asking people whether or not they had been haunted was one of which I was sure Lowe would not approve in the slightest.

"Of course I did," she replied as if it were the most obvious thing in the world. "How else was I to do any real digging?"

"You bring the conversation around to it by degrees," I said in astonishment. "You drop in subtle hints — did you hear about the business at the Vaudeville? That sort of thing."

"Oh well," said she, without a care in the world, "it didn't seem to do any harm."

The rest of the evening passed pleasantly. Resting in the sure knowledge that I had succeeded in my mission, I decided to take my ease. I seated myself on the couch beside Molly and we spent the night watching the various characters chart their ungainly courses (some most grotesquely when it came to the dance floor) and making predictions about their movements and generally conversing in that free and unencumbered manner that turns hours into minutes and minutes into seconds.

When our carriage arrived, she insisted that I be dropped at Lowe's office first declaring repeatedly that this was in acknowledgement of convenience over etiquette, but I knew that it was secretly because she hoped she might gain a glimpse of the man himself. I agreed — I hadn't the energy to contest. So it was that we made our gentle progress through the city, reviewing the more amusing and intriguing moments we had experienced together. For all her confidence and abruptness of manner there was something rather extraordinary about her and when she went on to recall the essay she had received on the technicalities of pointillism and divisionism from her art-loving dance partner, it dawned on me that she was possessed of an exceptional intellect. When I could no longer keep pace with her, for her other chief characteristic was a persistent and unquenchable energy, I allowed the conversation to lapse into silence and contented myself with the comfort of her company.

"I meant to say," said she, suddenly as we crossed the river. "That you've turned out rather well, Mr Fairlea." She blushed as she said it and I felt that my own face reddened in the hearing.

"And you are none too shabby a specimen yourself, Molly," I replied as confidently as I could, but this sudden turn in the conversation had caught me off balance. I had not, until this moment, realised that I was beginning to develop an attachment to this girl and since it was thrown into the great whirlpool of the newness of everything else, I was not yet sure how I felt about it.

"Shall we meet again often, do you suppose?"

"Should you like that?" I asked, hesitantly.

"I should like that very much indeed." Her long lashes quivered in the low light and her eyes danced in the sparkle of the gaslamps. The coach was slowing now, we had almost reached the place which I realised I must now call home. Just as the wheels ceased turning, she leant forward from her seat and would, I believe, have kissed me earnestly on the lips had it not been for the intervention of a loud and unwelcome rapping on the carriage window.

"Mr Fairlea!" came a muffled and familiar voice. "Mr Fairlea!"

Pulling back instantly from Molly's pursed lips I opened the door of the carriage to discover the author of the commotion.

"Oh Mr Fairlea," said Crane, for it was he, still dressed in his sober suit, but clutching at his small black bag. "I am so glad you have returned. Mr Lowe gave instruction for me to wait up for you."

"Why on earth would he want you to do that?"

"It is not my place to question," began Crane.

"I know, I know," I interjected, irritably. "You don't question the orders of your master."

"Just so, sir."

"Well, I am returned now, Mr Crane, so I think you may safely take your leave."

"Absolutely, sir, and thank you," said he with relief in his voice. He began to walk away from the carriage when a sudden thought struck him, seemingly with the force of a blow to the head. It caused him to stop in his tracks, cry out, spin around on the spot and walk purposefully back in my direction.

"It is the lateness of the hour," he said, by way of explanation. "I had quite forgotten that Mr Lowe required me to tell you to attend upon him directly in his study — he would like to review the evening's activities with you."

"Now?" I asked in amazement.

"Just so, sir," said Crane with a congratulatory smile. Then, with no more farewell than a tip of his hat, he strode off into the night.

"I'm sorry," I said to Molly. "I think you'd better go too."

She nodded, sadly. "But we will see each other again soon?"

"You may depend upon it. I know where I may find you."

She smiled at that. I closed the carriage door and gave the driver his instruction. She waved until the darkness separated us and I, only then realising that it was still raining and that I had already grown cold, dashed hurriedly across the threshold, straight through Crane's little antechamber and along the corridor to the place in which I knew Lowe would be waiting for me.

He was sat before a fire that was burning so energetically that I could only assume it had been the object of his constant attention prior to my coming. He did not look up as I entered, but continued to stare into the flames, pressing the tips of his fingers together and releasing them in a metronomic sequence. He wore an expression that is not easily described. It contained within it elements of displeasure, of curiosity, of confidence and of impatience, but each of these emotions flitted and fitted so quickly that it was impossible to tell which was truly in command.

"A productive evening, Mr Fairlea?" he asked, but he did not appear as if he were really interested in my feelings on the matter. His eyes remained fixed on the fire.

"I believe so, sir," I said.

His eyebrows rose in apparent interest and he removed his gaze from the hearth, briefly allowing it to alight on my face. Unsure how to respond, I smiled and nodded.

"Have you been struck mute?" he asked, with more carelessness than malevolence; it was as if the gentility in his character had been somehow stretched too far in recent days.

"I beg your pardon, sir," I stuttered. "I only thought that the hour might be a little late for discussions of business."

He made a movement somewhere between a laugh and a shrug and turned his attention back to the fire. "Would that it were so," he murmured quietly, and by a gesture of his hand, he gave me to understand that I should proceed.

"I met a gentleman," I began, cautiously, "who told me a very strange tale indeed. He claims that he is haunted, sir, by the ghost of his father." I let my trump card fall early in hopes of regaining his confidence and interest which I somehow — through no fault of my own that I could discern — appeared to have lost. But my employer continued to stare blankly ahead, as if I had uttered nothing more exciting than a description of the

116

weather. A minute or two passed during which neither of us spoke and the distant noise of the rain falling into an already over-full gutter was clearly audible in the stillness of the room. Unable to bear the tension any longer and suddenly filled with fear — as one is so easily in the small hours of the morning — I pressed on with the story.

"He claims, you see, that the ghost has information pertaining to the murder of his father."

A smile began to play upon the lips of Lowe, nothing obvious, but a subtle upturning of the corners of his mouth. I should have read the warning signs and stopped myself, but I plunged on like a fool. "He is convinced that he was murdered by his uncle."

"Indeed?" asked Lowe in what began to sound like interest. "Tell me, he didn't happen to suggest that his mother was complicit in this conspiracy? Or that the deed was effected by means of poison?"

"Yes!" I exclaimed in some elation. "That is exactly what he proposes! However did you guess?"

"When you have been in the business as long as I, one gains a certain intuition for this sort of thing. Tell me, did the fellow happen to give you his name?"

"Yes," I began, excited at last to have proven myself worthy of his trust.

"Wait," he interrupted. "Let me see if I can guess that too." He paused for a moment and made a great show of straining his mental faculties. "Something foreign, I think," he said. "And something noble too." I knew of course that Carstairs was neither of these two things, but I did not wish to interrupt his processes; I was fascinated to know how he was making these deductions. At length he seemed to hit upon it. Looking me square in the face he said, "Good heavens, Mr Fairlea, what exalted circles you do move in. I had no idea you should have been in the presence of royalty this evening!"

I was lost for words — was Carstairs better connected than he let on or was Lowe on the wrong track altogether? I tried to stammer out some sort of a response, indicating that I had not thought I was in discussion with such an elevated person, but he pressed on.

"Indeed, Mr Fairlea, you have been in conversation — it seems — with the Prince of Denmark, Hamlet himself!"

I did not need Lowe's prolonged bout of cruel laughter to make me feel a fool. How could I not have seen what any half-educated idiot might have spotted at first glance? The knowledge that Lowe was mocking me was nothing — insignificant — next to the dawning realisation that somewhere across London the pathetic author of the tale was presumably rocking back and forth clutching at his sides, howling at his own cleverness.

"I sent you to the ball," said Lowe, becoming suddenly serious, "to look out for business opportunities, did I not?"

"You did, sir," I replied quickly. "And I thought—"

"You did not *think* at all," he said, irritably. "Did you really imagine I meant you to go about looking for fantasists and confidence tricksters? To waste time listening to fiction dreamed up all in the hopes of gaining attention? You might as well have gone about openly asking people if they had been haunted and setting out a list of my services with prices attached."

In that moment I resolved not to tell Lowe about Molly. His estimation of me appeared to have fallen to a nadir and I dreaded to think what might happen if he learned that she had done almost precisely that which he had described.

"Our purpose is not to seek out apparitions and hauntings," said Lowe. "Perhaps I should have been clearer in my instructions to you. You know very little of this business, but let me ask you to think something through in a logical sequence for me." He got up and strode to the fireplace where he warmed his

118

hands and cast his eyes up to heaven in what I read as an urgent prayer for strength and patience. "Let us imagine," he went on, "that you have suffered a haunting. Your nights are terrifying and your days are merely disjointed collections of hours before the night comes again. Do you follow?"

I nodded, although I was not entirely sure I did.

"Put yourself, please, in that situation. In this dire circumstance, is your first impulse to attend a society ball?"

"No, sir," I admitted.

"Even supposing you did agree to such an event — perhaps forced into so doing by concerned friends and relations — do you find yourself inclined to discuss your predicament even with your most intimate circle of acquaintance?" He did not wait for my response. "Of course you do not! How much less so, then, will you be disposed to disclose the whole affair to a man you have never met before, whose discretion cannot be guaranteed and whose social standing is infinitely inferior to your own?"

The logic of what he said was all too plain to see.

"Furthermore," he added, "I have good reason for supposing that I am already aware of any such supernatural occurrences in this city. When I send you out on an errand such as I did this evening, I expect you to be on the lookout for *business* opportunities as you might for any other investor. Leave the rest to me, do you understand?"

Again, he did not wait for me to respond, but ploughed on with his oration. Incredulity had turned to anger and he almost shook in his fury. "I have employed you on the basis that you are a man of good sense, Mr Fairlea," he went on. "A man of intelligence and good judgement."

"I am very sorry, Mr Lowe," I said.

"And so you should be," he went on, but he seemed to soften slightly. "The evening appears to have been entirely wasted."

I hung my head in shame. Now that it had been expressed in

such clear terms I could not imagine how I had been so foolish in the way I had construed what was expected of me. There was a long and uncomfortable silence.

"Did you glean anything else that might be of use to a man of business?" said Lowe, at last.

I racked my brain for something, anything that might serve my purpose, but nothing was forthcoming. "I'm afraid not, sir," I said. Lowe dropped down into his chair and passed a hand over his forehead. "The war was the chief topic of conversation — unless you happened to be interested in neo-impressionist paintings."

"What was that?" he asked sharply.

"What was what?"

"What did you say about paintings?"

I strained my mind, trying to dredge up the details of what Molly had told me. "Only that there was a young man — Mr Pitt — who has recently acquired a set of these paintings for an extraordinary sum. He appears to be very much on the back foot on their account."

Lowe paused and I could see that fine mind whirring away busily in contemplation. At length he clapped his hands together, as was his habit, and sprang up again from his chair. "Mr Fairlea," he said. "I have done you an injustice. The evening has not been wasted at all."

I looked up at him in dazed astonishment.

"Mr Pitt, you say?"

"Yes," I replied, mystified by his sudden interest in this apparently insignificant detail. "Do you know him?"

"Not yet," said Lowe, "but I have a feeling that the poor fellow may soon be in need of our services."

CHAPTER SEVEN

It was four days before a message arrived, via Crane of course, that Mr Reginald Pitt had requested Mr Lowe to attend upon him at his residence in Battersea. How Lowe had known that this would come to pass remained a mystery to me. I felt that I had lost all rights to curiosity by my foolishness over the Carstairs affair. This matter, far from being forgotten, or passed over was frequently brought back to the forefront of my mind by Lowe's keen and regular jibes. He insisted on referring to me as Horatio at every opportunity, and whenever there was a knock at the door or a visitor, he would say that it was Rosencrantz or Guildenstern or perhaps Ophelia or indeed any other of the *dramatis personae* from what he carefully alluded to as Shakespeare's *best known* tragedy. He insisted also on referring to Crane as Polonius and on frequently warning him not to stand behind the arras when I was in the vicinity. Crane himself, seemed to take this in good part and even partook in the humour himself (though I am convinced that he had no conception of the context) going so far, when he informed me that arrangements had been made for my mother to receive a percentage of my salary, as to offer me a stern admonition to be neither a borrower, nor a lender. All of this I took in good spirit, counting myself fortunate that my error had yielded only mockery and no more serious consequence and that the salary upon which I had hung the hope of prospect, remained intact.

Lowe himself appeared to be extremely busy most of the

time and spent many hours behind that peculiar door in his suite of rooms from which he would always emerge looking bizarrely shaken and weak. Again, I dared not ask him how he was occupying himself, reasoning that he would tell me when he was ready. All this while, however, one comment he had made that evening when I had returned from the ball played upon my mind. I could not quite see what he had meant by it and the possibilities tormented me. *I have good reason for supposing that I am already aware of any such supernatural occurrences in this city.* Did he have employees other than myself of whom I was not aware? Did he have some other mechanism for discovering spiritual disturbances — was this what lurked behind that sinister black door? I lost myself in contemplation of these mysteries, but naturally, got nowhere with them.

Time continued to pass with tedious slowness. There was little for me to do at the office on these days. On occasion I was sent out to transfer papers or collect contracts like some common errand boy (many of which pertained to the sale of the Finn property — which seemed to be proceeding smoothly), but I did not object to these mundane tasks which at least took me out of the dreary surroundings of Lowe's office and also offered me opportunities to meet with Molly.

These liaisons, while undeniably pleasant, were marred somewhat by the spectre of Lowe hanging at all times over our exchanges. Mindful of my contract and also keen not to make a spectacle of my own reprimand in front of that young woman, I said little or nothing of business affairs and instead restricted my conversation to other matters. I was fortunate in that the Gatti brothers appeared, despite my former impression of them, to be really very liberal in their treatment of Molly. She, who had complained so acerbically of the burdens they placed upon her, seemed to be able to get away from the theatre at a moment's notice to join me for lunch or an afternoon walk or a tour of a gallery or museum. Though she masked it well, she was deeply frustrated at my unwillingness to discuss Lowe. She tried every possible tack to squeeze information from me but found herself resisted gently, but firmly, on every occasion.

These encounters seldom lasted more than an hour, and for the vast majority of my time, I was faced with the prospect either of remaining in my rooms and reading the dry texts that languished on the shelf in my study (among which, I noticed, Lowe had amused himself by placing several copies of *Hamlet*), or aimlessly wandering the city. The latter option might have been a more attractive one had it not been for the fact that, with the exception of a very few minutes, the clouds had continued their merciless assault on the already sodden ground. Thus it was that I tended to remain inside more often than not and mark out the floor plan of Lowe's establishment with futile pacing.

Beside the gentle mockery I received at the hands of Crane and Lowe, however, I found that I was uncomfortable in my lodgings for other reasons. Although there was no recurrence of the strange experience of the shadow in the doorway, I found that I was beginning to be constantly aware of some sort of presence lingering just beyond the field of my perception. Sometimes, for example, when I was in the office with Crane, it would seem to me that I would see a small figure crossing the corridor behind him or, just as I was going to sleep, I could swear that I had seen a shadow flit through the door where there was no sound other than that perennial noise of crackling ice. When I had become confident that my experiences were now so regular as to preclude a trick of the light or the fantasy of the mind, I resolved to ask Crane about the matter once more, but he only answered that he was not aware of anything of the like and that if I really were concerned I should raise the matter with Mr Lowe. Since I knew I could not do this without at best risking his irritation and at worst incurring his wrath, I continued to suffer in silence and allow the hours to trudge by in an eternal tedium.

My astonishment when the messenger arrived from Reginald Pitt, was therefore balanced, by no inconsiderable level of relief that matters were at last emerging from a state of stagnation. Lowe seemed to be almost electrified by the missive and for several minutes did nothing but read it over and over and clap me on the back and congratulate me for my insight. Then, having left the note on Crane's desk, he strode back toward his rooms and indicated that I should follow him.

"The question is," he said, once we were safely inside, "how are we to play it?"

"I'm not sure I follow."

"How shall we do the thing? What form shall it take?" He was, I thought, like a child planning a practical joke for a governess. I continued to look blank and then, after several moments, he clapped his hand to his head and unleashed a gale of laughter.

"But you couldn't know," he said. "How could you!" Without a further word of explanation he jumped up from his chair, darted out of the room and returned several seconds later with Pitt's letter which he began at once to read aloud. "Dear Mr Lowe — and so on and so forth there is a lot of flattery here and a strained attempt at a familial connection, but it's all rot — ah! Here we are:

I am writing to you on a most pressing matter that has, of late, occupied all my thoughts to the exclusion of everything else. To put it bluntly, sir, I believe that I have fallen prey to some malign force and that my house, once, as I considered it a haven from all ills.

And so on and so forth, there is some pointless description of the residence here and a tedious account of its descent through a string of ancestors — ah! Now we come to the rub of it, Fairlea!

I have heard that you offer a service to men and women afflicted in this manner and though I admit to having considered such matters pure poppycock.

Poppycock! Did you hear that Fairlea! Poppycock!

I must concede that on this occasion I am open to help from whatsoever avenue may prevail. Please do call upon me at any time, day or night, that is convenient to you. I am very much obliged to you, Reginald Pitt "

"Reginald Pitt," I exclaimed. "What an extraordinary coincidence that he of all people should require your services!"

"Yes," said Lowe, blandly. "Quite improbable isn't it? Nonetheless, one mustn't look a gift horse in the mouth, eh Fairlea? Now, we must be very clear on what is to be done here from the very start. This will be a coup for us if we can only pull it off. A coup of princely proportions! We must, at all times, bear in mind our object."

"Which, is," said I, hoping to show myself to be attentive and alert, "to rid his house of whatever presence seems to be lurking there?"

Lowe looked at me as if I had gone mad, furrowed his brow

125

sternly and said, "Not at all, Fairlea! Our business is to extract from Mr Pitt a good selection of his excellent paintings — very fine and very lucrative no doubt."

"You cannot intend to steal from him?" I exclaimed in outrage, rising from my chair.

"Oh dear me," said Lowe. "You really are very dull, Fairlea — and altogether too black and white. Do sit down, there's a good fellow."

"Then what exactly is your meaning?"

"We shall, of course, rid Mr Pitt of the troubling presence in his house, but that is a nothing, a mere click of the fingers, almost, and it is done."

"It seemed to require more than a click of the fingers at the Vaudeville," I said.

Lowe laughed a low, pointed chuckle. "Dear me," he said. "I'm obviously getting far more polished than I realised. It's a trick, Fairlea — it's a game!"

"There was no spirit?"

Lowe's face darkened. "Oh there was a spirit," he said gravely, "Just as there will most certainly be a spirit at Reginald Pitt's house later today, but in both cases the remedy is so simplistic a child could manage it."

"And what is it then?" I asked, leaning in, eagerly.

"That," said Lowe, laying a finger aside his nose and allowing the joy of secrecy to dance behind his eyes, "would be telling. Suffice it to say that it is not difficult and can be managed at a moment's notice."

I sat back in my chair and allowed my disgruntlement to show in my face. I had been in his employ less than a week and had not yet earned the right to the inner truths of his business, but nonetheless it irked me to be treated thus and to be treated thus so often.

"No," he went on. "The art of it comes in putting on a show — making it a spectacle. Do you realise that I might have dealt with that business at the Vaudeville in a matter of seconds had I chosen to? But no! The skill lies in drawing it out and in giving the impression that one has exerted oneself for the cause."

"But why," I asked. "Why not do it as quickly and efficiently as can be managed and get out?"

"Where would be the fun in that?" asked Lowe. "Where — more to the point — would be the profit? If I had just clicked my fingers for Mrs Finn, I would not now be in possession of her former dwelling. Had I simply whistled for the Gattis, I should not have the right to a box at the Vaudeville on any evening of my choosing!"

"Do you not," said I, hesitantly, "consider it at all immoral?"

Lowe sighed and shook his head as if I were a petulant child. "I am an artist, like a sculptor or a pianist or a painter or a poet. Let us take the latter as our paradigm here. Imagine if Homer, upon being commissioned to commemorate the Trojan war, had sat down and trotted out a single stanza in which he had said, succinctly and concisely, that there had been a war, it had been woefully long and pretty unpleasant too but that Greece had emerged victorious from the fray and it had taken Odysseus an intolerably long time to get back to Ithaca. Do you suppose for a moment that he would have been remembered as the poet of an age? More crucially perhaps, do you suppose that anyone would have paid him so much as a — whatever the Greek equivalent of a ha'penny was — to hear it?"

"I'm sure you're right," I said, slowly. "But I do not see how it justifies what you are doing?"

"I *am* the poet!" declared Lowe. "I *am* the artist! People

127

expect a show; they expect passion and drama and they expect me to expend every ounce of my energy in their cause. If I did not, they would never believe the matter concluded. They would insist that the job had not been done and I should certainly not be in a position to employ half-wit assistants at three hundred pounds a year."

I had no answer to this. For all my unease, the security of my position was a powerful force within me. There was, I reasoned, no actual harm being done here, no one was being made to suffer unduly. It was artistic licence, that was all, just as Lowe had said and if people wanted to reward him for the service he had rendered them, then why should they not? Had he not done what they had asked of him? The end justified the flamboyant means.

"Now," said he, returning to a more pensive attitude, "how best to frame the situation at Pitt's?"

"I presume," I said, "that it will depend very much on the nature of the apparition that awaits us."

"That will have very little bearing on the matter. You will find, as you work with me, that one haunting will come to resemble another very closely. I doubt there will be much at Pitt's house that differs from the sort of thing we encountered at the Vaudeville: the cold temperatures and the ice and so forth."

"The same thing I noticed at Mrs Finn's?" I said suddenly.

Lowe looked up at me and for the first time I had a feeling of his genuinely having been impressed by a leap in my reasoning.

"That's why you pretended there was nothing out of the ordinary," I went on. "That's why you pretended not to see when the window froze like that — the place was still haunted wasn't it! She was still at the mercy of her husband."

"Don't get yourself all worked up," said Lowe waving a

hand at me irritably. "First of all, I knew beyond all shadow of a doubt that the spirit in question would do her no harm. The symptoms of mental and physical degeneration you saw were the products of her own guilt at the way she had treated her husband."

"How can you possibly know," said I, incensed.

"I know," said Lowe. "That should be enough for you."

"Then when did you end it?"

"The same day you and I visited her. Once I had got her to agree to the sale of the house and felt that an apparent improvement in her environment might easily be attributed to her having rid her mind of the burden of the property itself. She is far happier now and has written to me three times to thank me in the most profuse fashion for all I have done."

"But she might have been both happy and wealthy," said I.

"Perhaps — but does she desire wealth? No? Is she covetous of property? No. Overall I think I can rest easy. She has her happiness and we have her money."

When written down like this and so baldly stated, I can find nothing to recommend Lowe's arguments and looking back upon myself as I was then, a bilious sense of disgust ploughs through my thoughts. But in that moment when every impulse in me was striving to find some justification for the position I had taken and the monies I had received, I saw in them a twisted sort of logic.

"Thus we return again," he said, sensing his victory won, "to the central question. In what manner shall we demonstrate our worth and skill to Mr Pitt? And how shall we convince him that those paintings are the source of all his misery?"

"Can we not repeat what you did at the Vaudeville?" I asked.

He shook his head. "Repetition breeds familiarity and familiarity breeds contempt. We must be sure that every single incident is handled differently."

I was anxious to prove my worth. Ever since I had entered upon his employ I had been nothing but a profound disappointment. I began to feel at that moment, however, that I had understood what was required and this understanding allowed the gentle formulation of an idea.

"Well," I said slowly. "You were adamant with the Gatti brothers that you were a man of science in your approaches."

"And so I am."

"What if you were not on this occasion? What if you were to take a more religious perspective?"

"Interesting," he replied, pondering the thought. "The idea is certainly not without merit, but I think that it has the potential for causing our client to ask too many questions. It really is far simpler the less they understand about the mechanics of the thing."

What he said made sense. If Lowe developed a sudden devotion to the almighty, he might be forced to alter his personal habits to provide credibility to the illusion. "But," I said, hesitantly, "may we not employ the trappings of religion without making any direct reference?"

"Go on," he said, evidently intrigued.

"Well," said I. "We could use a number of associated properties, a bell, for example, perhaps some candles? A weighty and learned book of some kind? We needn't pray of course, nor recite any verses, but the allusions would be strong enough to strengthen the illusion."

"Bells," he murmured to himself. "A book. Yes! Yes! What an extraordinary fellow you are, Fairlea — yes! We shall send out for the necessary equipment directly. I shall add in a chalice too. I happen to own a rather special silver goblet that will suffice and blood — there ought to be a little blood, but I think I shall

130

take care of that. Yes — that will do the job nicely, Fairlea! Go and get Crane in here at once would you, he can go and get the necessaries, he only sits there reading the same document *ad infinitum* anyway."

I rose from my seat and called down the corridor in the direction of the worthy Crane who, stooping as if the earth held a portion of its gravity in reserve for exclusive use upon his brow, appeared before us.

"What may I do for you, sir?"

"Take this." Lowe had made good use of the intervening minutes to scribble down a list of supplies. "And bring back everything on it. If you cannot find precisely the items I have specified please bring a suitable alternative. You may make arrangements for payment from my account."

"Just so, sir?" Crane looked slightly taken aback by the instruction.

"Is there a problem, old man?" Lowe laced his enquiry with an ounce of contempt.

"Only that I wondered whether Mr Fairlea might not be better equipped to handle such a task."

Lowe stared at him as if he had spat in his face.

"Mr Fairlea is not a common errand boy, Crane," he said, drawing himself up.

"And neither am I, Mr Lowe." Crane's response was firm, but not impudent. Lowe, however, eager to stamp out this first kindling of rebellion, chided him like an infant.

"You certainly shall be, and a great deal of other lesser things should I wish it." He glowered at the secretary, whose stoop seemed to become even further pronounced as he stuttered out his apologies. "I pay you, Crane — and handsomely too — to attend to my business. It is not in your gift to determine which aspects this shall and shall not include. If I asked you to dance for me right here on this floor, I should expect you to do so — do you hear me?"

"Yes, Mr Lowe."

"Do you wish to dance, Crane?" Lowe's face was wild as if something that had, until now been only loosely caged within him, had suddenly been released.

"Indeed no, Mr Lowe."

"And if I commanded you to desire nothing more?"

"Then I should consider it the highest of pleasures," said Crane, so quickly that his moustaches quivered up and down like butterfly wings. "But now, sir, if you will excuse me, I have quite a list here and I imagine you will be wishing to visit Mr Pitt this afternoon, so I shall hurry along if it's all the same to you and Mr Fairlea?"

"Get out you miserable old hobgoblin," sneered Lowe.

"Good afternoon, Mr Crane." I nodded hurriedly toward the departing figure, but the last syllable rebounded off the door that he had closed in his wake. It was always the way with Lowe that whatever was cruel or malicious was set neatly off against something that was enticing or tantalising — just as it was here. I felt for Crane who had done nothing to earn his shameful treatment, and yet I could not fully empathise with him for I was too much absorbed in celebrating my own elevation into Lowe's inner sanctum. The immediate benefit to oneself is always felt more keenly than the suffering of one slightly removed.

"Now," said Lowe, clapping his hands together sharply and arranging a set of objects on the table. "This will do for the goblet I suppose and bring those two candlesticks across will you from the mantelpiece, there's a good chap. Now where the devil did I put my matches?"

"I beg your pardon, sir," I said, "but may I ask what we are doing?"

"Rehearsing, Fairlea!"

And so passed what must rank among the most peculiar and exhilarating hours I had spent in my short life up to that point. For, far from being the bystander I had been at the Vaudeville, it was clear that Lowe intended me to be an active participant in this particular drama. There were lines to be learnt — not just a linear script, following from cue to cue, but a dynamic set of responses that would change in content and tone depending on how the situation unfolded. Lowe was a fantastically quick innovator and his mind, unlike mine, was fixed entirely on the task at hand and thus easily able to recall, at a moment's notice, precisely what was to be said and at what time. I was sluggish and foolish, and such was the pressure and intensity of our rehearsal process, I began to spout lines here and there that bore no relevance to what was unfolding in our imagined scenario.

"Enough," said Lowe, sensing my discomfort. "I think we are tolerably well prepared."

"What if I should make an error?"

"I am sure you will."

"And what will follow?"

"I shall cover for you. The principle object of this exercise was not for you to learn the script, Fairlea, but for me to see exactly the sort of mistakes you are likely to make."

"I shall try not to be too far offended by that, sir."

He laughed. "Do not take me for a bully, Fairlea," he said. "I have reasons for being the way I am — and good ones too. Very soon I shall help you to understand a little more of my philosophy, but until that time I hope I may count upon you to keep your curiosity under control?"

133

I nodded. I might perhaps have asked him to set a date for my induction into the deeper mysteries but for an unusual scraping, clattering and grunting sound from the corridor that indicated the return of Crane with our purchases. Without so much as a word to the old man whom he casually dismissed with an impatient wave, Lowe examined each of the artefacts in turn and uttered little approving noises along with such phrases as, "Well this will serve perfectly well", or occasionally, "He might have selected a finer specimen, but I suppose it will have to do".

Then he asked me to accompany him into his bedroom in which, atop the great dark-wood wardrobe, there sat a large wooden trunk. Having taken this down, we proceeded to pack Crane's purchases into it with enormous care, for Lowe was of the opinion that we should treat each of the items as if it were a holy relic for the sake of realism. When this was accomplished, he returned to his study and took down, from the upper shelf, an extraordinary manuscript, bound at front and back with wooden panels and printed on vellum.

"What is it?" I asked as he opened one or two of the illuminated pages for me to see.

"A bestiary," he said. "And a very old one too. It's eleventh century — or so I'm led to believe. We are fortunate that the illustrator, whoever he was, had evidently never encountered any single one of these creatures and the result is that they all look rather unearthly. Take that bear for example — why the devil did he feel the need to attach udders to its belly, I wonder? Nonetheless, I suspect that this will serve as our learned tome — provided that Mr Pitt is no expert in Medieval Latin or possesses more than an ordinary talent for deciphering the hand of eleventh century monks."

We placed the book in the top of the trunk and Lowe

pronounced it complete. His usual driver was already in the street, his horse, I was relieved to see, looking as calm as one could hope. Two youths were cajoled (for a small sum) into carrying the case out into the street and lifting it up onto the hansom, and once Lowe had informed Crane that we should almost certainly not be back before nine or ten o'clock and that he should therefore go home once he had concluded any outstanding business, the driver was instructed and we set off in the direction of Battersea and to the aid of Mr Reginald Pitt.

CHAPTER EIGHT

"I cannot thank you enough for responding so promptly to my letter, gentlemen," said Pitt for what must have been the fourth or fifth time since our arrival. Upon seeing him, I remembered him at once from the ball. A short, nervous-looking sort of a man who was prematurely bald, but otherwise cursed with that unwanted youth of face which predisposes others to patronise.

"It is no problem at all," said Lowe. "As soon as I noted the address on the epistle I gave instructions that we must depart directly."

"Indeed?" asked Pitt, a little confused. "I had not realised that I was so well known in society circles?"

"Oh, forgive me, Mr Pitt," said Lowe, with a light laugh. "It was not your reputation that drew me here — though I am sure it must be an impressive and far-reaching one quite outside of my meagre acquaintance. No, sir, it was the *address* itself that drew me home."

"Home?"

"Home indeed," said Lowe with a sombre face as he surveyed the opulent surroundings of Pitt's residence. "I grew up not a half a mile from here."

"Did you really?" Pitt's eyes brightened as he sensed a fellow traveller on life's great sojourn. "You will remember my parents, no doubt?"

"Who could forget them? And how are they?"

"They are both dead."

"My condolences," said Lowe, unfazed. "The community is all the poorer for their loss I am sure."

"And I too," said Pitt, remorsefully.

"Of course," said Lowe. "Forgive me for drawing you on the topic."

"Not at all," said Pitt who seemed eager not to give offence.

"I'll tell you who else I remember," said Lowe allowing a broad smile to sweep across his features. "That old dragon of a cook you had working here. Dear me, now, what was her name?"

"Surely you don't mean Mrs Watson?" asked Pitt, incredulous.

"I most certainly do," said Lowe with great enthusiasm. "That woman was the curse of every boy who played on this street."

"How extraordinary," said Pitt, his brow furrowed in consternation. "She was ever so sweet to my sister and me — never gave us a cross word as far as I can recall."

"Nor to me!" said Lowe, patting Pitt hard on the back and grasping his shoulder in a gesture of camaraderie. "We were the good ones, I suppose, you and I, but some of the other fellows who grew up down here. Well, one only has to look at the track record since to see that they were bound to go wrong from the start."

"Well," said Pitt, "you have quite a point there. Gilbert Williams has been up against the magistrate three times this month alone and Albert Finmyle lost everything on the gambling table." It was evident that he was warming to the theme and Lowe was more than ready to capitalise on his receptive attitude.

"Of course," he said. "They didn't have the benefits that you and I had — and your sister too, of course."

"Benefits?"

"Well let's take governesses for a start — we both got rather lucky there, I fancy. We had dear old Nessie and you had that little thing — oh what the deuce was her name? Look at me, not yet past forty and my memory is already falling apart?"

"Elizabeth," said Pitt, with a smile that positively oozed nostalgia. "Elizabeth Blane — yes she was quite magical; Matilda and I were quite under her spell."

"Byegone days," said Lowe with another pat to the back of our host. "And better times, perhaps?" He nodded in agreement and I suppose Lowe must have decided that the relationship had been established in a suitable manner for us to proceed to matters of business.

"But where are my manners," he exclaimed. "This is my colleague, Mr Fairlea — a man well-practised in these arts."

I extended my good hand. "Delighted to make your acquaintance, Mr Pitt." But Pitt was looking at my other arm with some interest. I could tell he remembered me from the ball.

"Do not be distressed by Mr Fairlea's unfortunate condition," said Lowe. "Our business is not always an easy one and sometimes we attempt to deal with situations that are beyond us. I wish there were time for Mr Fairlea to relate to you the story of the manner in which his hand was lost, but I fear that there are more urgent matters to which we must attend."

"I thought you lost it in the war," said Pitt, the slightest traces of scepticism creeping around the edges of his tone. "That's what the young lady told me at the ball the other evening."

Lowe's demeanour did not alter, his eyes did not so much as flit in my direction and yet I felt the towering wave of anger and disappointment teetering above me and ready to crash down upon me at any moment. I had to think fast.

"I'm afraid," I said, as calmly as could be managed, "that the story is not a pleasant one and not suitable for the faint-hearted. Certainly it is not suitable for the ears of female persons — especially those so flighty and ungrateful as my dancing partner that evening. In such circumstances I prefer an easier fabrication to the unwholesome truth."

The cloud of doubt cleared from Pitt's face as he grunted his understanding and I felt Lowe relax a little. I was pleased by my response which made sense and which, I hoped, would give the impression to both Pitt and Lowe that I had severed all connection with Molly in most acrimonious circumstances and had no wish to discuss the subject further.

"Forgive me," said Pitt, apologetically. "I'm afraid that I am very much on edge at present."

"That is absolutely to be understood," said Lowe. "We have already taken up too much of your time. Perhaps you could show us to a suitable room in which we may set up our equipment?"

Pitt nodded and gestured to an impressive pair of doors through which lay a large banqueting hall. I could not suppress a gasp as we entered and he looked pleased. "It's quite spectacular isn't it?" he said. "It used to serve as the magisterial court until recently. Now we only use it for social functions, not," he added, sadly, "that there have been too many of those since my parents passed on."

"This will serve us admirably," said Lowe. "Fairlea, see about bringing in the trunk, would you?" This I did, quickly conscripting two young boys from the street who were pleased to accept a glimpse of the inside of Mr Pitt's house as their payment (until I escorted them outside again and they required further, more tangible remuneration in view of several economic pressures which they were only too keen to enumerate for me). Meanwhile, Lowe occupied himself in walking around the room, periodically closing his eyes and apparently listening for something. I began to unpack the trunk.

"I wonder," said Pitt hesitantly, "if I may ask you a little about what you intend to do?"

"That will depend very much," I said, remembering the rehearsal, "on the sort of spirit we identify. No two hauntings are alike, Mr Pitt. They must be handled in isolation. Without specific details it might be very dangerous to employ an incorrect approach."

"What sort of details?" asked Pitt. His face had washed a garish white and beads of sweat had appeared upon his brow.

"Well," I continued in as business-like a tone as I could manage. "It would help us to know, for example, whether the apparition has taken on a particular form; whether it has appeared at a particular time; in what location it is most prone to dwell and if there have been any environmental effects."

"Environmental effects?" said Pitt, sharply. "What do you mean?"

"Well it's a small thing really, I don't know why I said it — I shouldn't concern yourself with it."

"No," he said earnestly. "Go on, please!"

"Well," I said, feigning hesitation as if I were imparting this information with the greatest of reluctance. "In some very rare cases — *very* rare cases, mind you, Mr Pitt — there are spirits so powerful that they are able to gain a level of control over the elements within a small area. They can cause fire or wind or sheets of ice or rain—"

"Ice?"

"Yes," I said, pretending that this word held no special significance. "But only in very rare cases."

Pitt clutched at a chair and sat down hard upon it. "But that is my experience," he said, looking up at me with hollow eyes. "Ice, great sheets of it that come from nowhere and in the warmest rooms too; that's how I know it's here."

"Are you sure?" I asked in as grave a tone as I could muster. Lowe was still moving slowly around the room, his eyes closed. "I must tell you, Mr Pitt, with the greatest of respect, that exaggeration is not to be attempted in this matter. If we approach the spirit in the wrong manner, we may all be in very grave danger."

"I am quite, quite sure," said Pitt.

"I wonder," I said, "if you would give me a moment to consult with my colleague in private?"

Pitt looked at me dumbstruck as if he had not heard a word I had said. In fact I was obliged to repeat my request.

"Of course," he said shaking his head violently as if by doing so he could rid himself of his torments as a horse dispenses with a gadfly. "I shall wait in the lobby."

The poor man retreated from us and closed the doors behind him.

"We have him where we want him," whispered Lowe. "He trusts us — and he now believes that even we, who have seen so much of this sort of thing, are cowed by the terror he has experienced here."

"Did you really grow up on this road?"

"Of course not, don't be an imbecile. If there is any certainty you may count upon in life that is neither death nor taxes then it is that almost every gentleman living had, at some stage in his youth, a dragon of a cook and an angel of a governess."

"Wasn't that risky?"

"Not at all — if he had denied the existence of these people, I'd simply have said that I was obviously remembering a different house. Now what *is* risky is the store we have set by this ice business. Let us hope he is not a regular patron of the Vaudeville nor a friend of anyone who is."

"He doesn't strike me as the type to enjoy farce," I said.

"No, you're right, there," said Lowe, contemplatively. "In any case, that story will have been long exaggerated by now — the ice will be nothing to the physical apparition that all will swear they saw. But talking of risky, Mr Fairlea, at what stage were you planning to inform me that your connection to Mr Pitt came through Miss Molly Easton?"

"I — I was going to say something," I stammered out, rather pathetically.

"No, you weren't," he said. "Don't make yourself a liar as well as a coward. Well from now on please do not attempt secrecy, it's an insult to both of us — particularly as Crane reports to me on everything he sees or hears."

"Oh," said I. I had assumed this to be the case, but hearing it so baldly stated made me feel the restriction on my privacy very keenly indeed.

"Now don't look at me like that," said Lowe. "You surely don't expect me to part with the sort of money I'm shelling out on you without knowing everything there is to know?"

I supposed it made sense, but it didn't make me feel any more comfortable.

"Now," said Lowe, clapping his hands together as was his habit whenever business loomed. "We must get to work. Are you ready?"

I nodded.

"Absolutely not!" he shouted suddenly in a voice calculated to be clearly audible beyond the closed doors. "You may be willing to risk life and limb — but you will certainly not risk mine."

"I see no reason not to proceed," said I, raising my voice a little too. "We have no evidence to suggest that it is something with which we have not dealt before."

"Ice!" cried Lowe. "Ice! You know what that means as clearly as if it were written on the wall. The most sensible thing we can do is to pack up now, leave and never return to this place?"

"And abandon him?" I asked in a fit of apparent moral outrage. "You know what that would mean! You know what sort of a fate we'd be leaving him to!"

"I like the gentleman," said Lowe, still speaking at just below a shout. "But I do not *know* him and I should like more of a firm foundation than a casual acquaintance before I put my life — indeed my soul upon the line."

At that moment — just, in fact as Lowe had predicted (though we had rehearsed several more lines of dialogue in this vein just in case matters turned out differently), the doors flew open and Pitt burst back into the room, his eyes wide with terror and his body shaking visibly from head to toe.

"Gentlemen," he said, clasping my hand in the manner of a suppliant. "I beg that you help me. You are my only hope of salvation — things cannot go on as they are now. If they do, then I am inclined to think that I may not endure much longer."

I exchanged a meaningful glance with Lowe who tossed his head petulantly and muttered something under his breath. It was at that moment, for the very first time, that I noticed he was holding something clutched in his fist. It was something small, a piece of jewellery, perhaps. I had only a flash of a glimpse at it before he closed his fingers completely. Then he heaved a great sigh. "Very well," he said. "But I cannot guarantee success, is

143

that understood?"

Pitt nodded gratefully. "Thank you," he said, in great earnest, still not relinquishing my hand. "Thank you." I then observed something rather curious. Pitt appeared to be dividing his gaze equally between the two of us and a portrait that hung on the wall at the far end of the room. I had a sudden hunch, and applying the lessons I had learned from my mentor, I decided to exploit it.

"Mr Pitt," I said, dropping my voice almost to a whisper and giving the impression that I did not wish us to be overheard by some malevolent third party. "Do you have any reason to suspect that what you are experiencing could be connected with a person from your past? Perhaps someone recently deceased."

His eyes flitted to the portrait once again and I knew I had him.

"My father," he said, falteringly. There was a fear in him now that had nothing whatsoever to do with the haunting. I hesitated. To push on this door might take us into unpredictable territory and would certainly mark a deviation from the prepared script. Nonetheless, if it worked, then I would win great glory in the eyes of Lowe, and in that moment, this was my utmost desire.

"Forgive me," I said, gently, "but may I ask when he died?"

"It must be over five years ago now," said Pitt. His voice was airy, dreamy — he appeared to have entered into some recollection from which he could not escape. "He always said I would never amount to anything, said I was the weak link in the chain — that I'd lose it all."

"Lose all of what?"

"The money," he said, blankly. "The money, of course. He said I'd throw it away on some damned fool project and it seems he was right."

"Just occasionally," I said, as delicately as I could, "a

144

haunting of this nature can be brought about by a particular action that disturbs the soul of the deceased? Can you think of anything you have done — anything at all that might have upset your father?"

There was a long silence during which Pitt continued to look at the portrait. "No," he said and there was a resolute defiance in his voice. "There is nothing I can think of."

"Are you certain?" asked Lowe. He could see the object at which I was now driving.

Another lengthy pause during which the timidity in Pitt's face as it surveyed the painted features of his parent matured into evident hatred. "I can think of no reason," said Pitt very deliberately, "to justify his anger."

"I am sorry to push the point," said I. "But if we cannot establish the cause of the disturbances, we may not be able to end them. Please think carefully, Mr Pitt. Is there anything at all you can think of that has happened in recent weeks?"

"I am certain that there is nothing," said he.

"Typical," whispered Lowe, drawing himself close to me and murmuring into my ear so that Pitt — whose eyes were still fixed upon the portrait — could not hear us. "This is the moment he chooses to stand up to his father. We shall have to work hard here."

"There is one easy way to test the hypothesis, Mr Pitt," said I strolling over to a table and picking up the largest and most impressive looking of three handbells that I had extracted from the trunk. "We shall attempt to summon your father's spirit."

The young man's face flashed white and he swallowed hard. Insensible of speech he simply nodded uncertainly.

"I shall need your father's first name, if you please."

"Thomas," whispered Pitt who was now in evident dread.

Those two syllables emerged from his mouth only after the application of a significant effort.

"Are you prepared, Mr Lowe?" I asked, allowing a hint of fear to creep into my own voice. This was not difficult since I was in fact terrified of encountering another spirit like that with which we had engaged at the Vaudeville.

"I stand prepared, Mr Fairlea," said Lowe, grimly. I took the bell in my hand and shook it three times so that the noise rang out sharp and crisp and clear and reverberated down the length of that long hall.

"Thomas," I spoke loudly. "If you are here — reveal your presence."

Nothing happened and Pitt seemed visibly to relax. I picked up the bell once more and again rang out three clear chimes, repeating the invocation I had used previously. At first it seemed as if the attempt would fail again, but I was just in time to see Lowe out of the corner of my eye, apparently murmuring something to himself. No sooner had he done so than the room began to shake very gently. The first noise we heard was that of the chandeliers — of which there were two handsome specimens hanging from the ceiling. The individual crystal beads began, ever so gently, to knock together.

"Here it comes," whispered Pitt, turning his eyes from the portrait of his father and looking instead to the assemblage of crystal suspended above us which, as well as swinging pronouncedly from side to side, now appeared to be changing in shape. Some of the larger stones on the lower tier seemed, at first to be melting, then to be growing and all at once I realised that neither was the case. Thin shards of ice, like the sort of icicles one might expect to find on guttering or on window ledges in the depths of the harshest winters, were forming from the bottom of each. Jagged, razor knife edges pointed vindictively downward towards the floor where Pitt and I stood in rapt astonishment. I felt his hand take my arm for support.

It is a curious thing that fear of something is decreased significantly, or at least appears to be, if there is someone present who is patently more terrified than you are. Pitt had become rigid now, as stiff as the ice itself, and was watching the descent of the frosted tendrils with an intractable gaze of wonder and dread. Had I been alone and experienced this phenomenon without the very tangible symptoms of his fear, I should have been reduced to a quivering wreck. But somehow, knowing that there were things I knew about the haunting that he did not and the understanding that Lowe might, at any moment, bring an end to the experience with the click of a finger, gave me an inner strength that I had not previously known.

"Look out," the warning came almost too late. Lost in my contemplation of my emotional response to the haunting, I had not noticed that the now familiar sound of the ice forming had been joined by another; it was a strange noise, a twisting, wrenching squeal that seemed to be coming from all places at once. It was only Pitt's sudden exclamation and a sharp nudge to the small of my back that threw me clear of the chandelier which, dislodged from its rose, clattered to the floor in an explosion of shards and fragments and splintered ice.

"I am no match for this spectre," said Lowe in a half-whisper. "I shall need your aid, Fairlea."

I nodded gravely, and leaving the stunned Pitt to survey the ruins of the ancient chandelier, followed the rehearsed routine to the letter. First I produced the book and leafed through it carefully, making intelligent mutterings to myself as I did so. Then I burned incense in a censor and intoned a nonsense phrase,

147

striding up and down the length of the room as I did so. This ritual complete, I took a piece of chalk from the trunk and drew, with the assistance of a length of cord, a perfect circle on the boards in the centre of the floor. Inside this circle I sprinkled several drops of blood from a silver flask — I am not sure what poor creature suffered to produce it, but Lowe informed me he kept a ready stock of the stuff for occasions such as these. Taking twelve candles, I set them out in the manner of a clock — just as we had agreed and then summoned the spirit once more with a ringing of the bell. The apparition played into my hands superbly well, as I thought, for no sooner had I rung the bell for a third time than it circled around the candles and extinguished each one, before filling the circle itself with a glass-frosting of ice, causing Pitt, who was standing near to the perimeter to stumble backwards and collapse against the wainscoting.

I will confess that I was enjoying myself, dreadful though it is to admit. I had gained, or at least thought I had, some measure of control over this terrible supernatural force and I was able, within parameters, to bend it to my will. I drew a range of symbols on the floor and watched in delight as the ghost traced over them with its trail of ice. I sprinkled what had been described to Pitt as a specially formulated solution, widely over the room and had the satisfaction of seeing the droplets transformed into a twisting blizzard of white which bore down on us in terrifying force, until at my command, it suddenly abated. The script we had designed — embellished at points by myself to add emphasis and verisimilitude (Lowe never deviated from the prescribed lines, he being a stickler for precision) — played out neatly to its conclusion as we consoled, reprimanded and encouraged each other in the quest to vanquish this hell-fiend. In fact, I was so caught up in our charade that I did not notice, until Lowe intimated it to me by a clandestine gesture, that it was grown dark outside and that we must draw our act to a suitable close.

"Mr Pitt," I cried out, panting — for my most recent efforts had involved the practising of several and various ancient gesticulations which had taken a physical toll upon me. "I fear that unless you have other information for us, this visitation you are experiencing may be beyond our craft."

"You cannot stop!" wailed Pitt. "You *must* continue!"

"It is no good," said Lowe, mournfully. "We have attempted every technique I know. It may be that with time and with greater research, our labours may yet prove more fruitful, but at present—"

Lowe was interrupted by the sudden and immediate descent of a silent darkness. The candles and gaslamps that had hitherto lit the great hall were extinguished and with them that confidence and exuberance that had so lately animated me. Here was a scenario we had not rehearsed. In that darkness I felt myself completely alone and dreadfully vulnerable; only now did I begin to wonder about the sense of our approach — had we been controlling the spirit or bating it? Perhaps torturing it, even? Was it now out there, lurking in the darkness like a wounded bear? I prayed that Lowe would have the good sense to do whatever it was he could do to cast it out before any harm befell us.

But the silence persisted.

I wanted to talk, to whisper, to seek reassurance from the others, but I felt myself gripped by something. It was not the ghost — or whatever you want to call it — that held me back, but rather something from inside me, perhaps the pent-up terror that I had ignored by my false bravado of the hour just passed. Iron bands of panic threaded their way subtly along the lines of my ribs and my stomach twisted violently.

"Light," I managed to gasp out, eventually. "We must have light."

The answering silence was perhaps even more terrifying than that which had preceded it. I longed for a hint of a sound. Anything, I thought, would be better than this mute night.

Then a sound did come — and as soon as it did I cursed myself for my wish and would have given anything to return to noiseless solace. It was not the sort of terrible noise one reads about in books. Not the vicious scream or the sobbing of a child or the howling of a banshee, but a soft, subtle sound that seemed, by its very quietness, to fill the rooms so that it was in all places at once. It was the soft, scraping noise of a piece of chalk being drawn across the wooden boards.

The noise went on for some time and the silence resumed, though for a few minutes I held my breath — not wishing to trust it, believing that that terrible sound would come again. Then, with no warning nor any reason, the lights suddenly flared back into life and we saw ourselves, standing ashen faced and shaking on the circumference of the circle I had drawn earlier. It was Lowe's face that frightened me most — in fact I think I felt more anxiety at that moment than I had done in the cloak of the spirit's darkness. The powerful, confident figure was gone and there stood in his place a pale and broken substitute. He looked older, more careworn and his eyes seemed, somehow, to have shrunk back deeper into his face, his jaw hanging slightly open as if from weakness. Although this impression was only fleeting — for one swift toss of his head restored his characteristic vitality — it lodged itself in my mind and I could not help being reminded of it each time I looked at him thereafter; noticing its vestiges upon his features.

"I suggest," he said, his tone now laced with anger, "that you

150

have a good think, Mr Pitt. A very good think indeed. Examine your thoughts and your character and decide for yourself whether you have been truthful with us or whether you have caused us, by your insistence on deceit, to risk ourselves needlessly."

"I — but gentlemen," stammered Pitt in exasperation. "You cannot leave me here."

"Indeed, we cannot stay," said Lowe. "That much is clear." He began gathering up the equipment and placing it back into the trunk.

"I cannot go on like this," said Pitt, staring at the pair of us as we picked up the case and began to haul it to the door together. "I can't do it!" His voice was pitiful, pathetic. Here was a man wrecked with fear.

"When you have decided to be honest," said Lowe, contemptuously, "you will know where we may be found."

"I warned you," I said, turning back to the wretched creature with a shake of my head. "I told you that if we attempted to tackle—" But I stopped dead in my tracks causing the trunk to lurch and almost toppling Lowe off his feet. I stared at the wood panelling at the end of the hall. In the relief of the return to light, I had not thought to look for the result of all that scraping in the darkness, but now I saw it in letters at least five or six feet high chalked upon the oak. The characters were sweeping, shaky and uneven, but there was no mistaking the word they were intended to form.

"Ivor," I read, my mouth forming the sound before I had fully processed the meaning.

Lowe put down the trunk and strode to the wall, making a great pretence of examining it. "It is a crude writing," he declared. "That is often the case when those from the netherworld interact with our own; their control is not precise." His voice was imbued with its typical confidence, but I heard in it the echo of the weakness that had shown itself a few minutes before.

"What does it mean?" asked Pitt in confusion. "Who is this 'Ivor'?"

Lowe picked up the chalk from where it lay on the floor and took a handkerchief from his pocket. He adjusted the writing subtly here and there and rubbed at some of the letters, standing back periodically to examine his handiwork. After a good few minutes of activity, he seemed satisfied.

"There," he said. "I think the message is pretty clear — do not you, Mr Fairlea?"

I nodded gravely, and Lowe having picked up his side of the trunk, we departed leaving Pitt, shaking with fear as he surveyed the single, damning word: 'Liar'.

CHAPTER NINE

"Of course there's a connection," said Molly, who had sat and listened to my story with wide eyes. "That couldn't possibly have been a coincidence!" I was pleased to have confided in her, but at the same time I was growing concerned that I was coming close to contravening the terms of my contract. But it was hardly trade secrets I was giving away, here — I was simply sharing my experiences. "How was he afterwards?" she asked.

"He was fine." The question had irritated me. No matter how carefully I constructed the conversation, no matter how I jaundiced the narrative in my favour, the focus of her attention always drifted back toward Lowe. It was his enigma, I decided, that attracted her. She was enticed by what she did not know or understand; such things were not uncommon to those with pioneering or inquisitive natures. Knowing this, however, did not make it better. "In fact," I went on, "he didn't mention the matter at all, just kept on saying how well he thought it had all gone."

"Didn't you ask him about it?"

"No." I couldn't explain to her why this was because I didn't fully understand it myself. It was the sort of feeling one experiences when there has been a piece of unpleasant news or when a particularly unsavoury task requires attention. The natural response is not to talk about it — not to give it light and warmth and nurture the vexation — but instead to bury it deep down and pretend it has not happened. Besides which, in the cold, hard light of day, the sound of chalk scratching out four letters on wood panelling did not seem quite as terrifying as it had in the actual event.

"*Will* you talk to him about it?" she insisted. Her tenacity, I considered, was among the least attractive of her qualities.

"I don't think so," I said. The truth was that my contact with Lowe had been rather infrequent since our return from Battersea. He had disappeared into his room again, this time without giving any indication of when he might come out. There was no sign of him the following morning, though the breakfast arrived with clockwork efficiency. That afternoon I knocked gently on the door with a mind to enquire about his health, and when there was no response, I had put my ear to the wood to see if I could at least discern movement on the other side. At first, I could not comprehend the noise that emerged dully through the heavy oak, but after a few moments I realised to my astonishment, that it was the noise of a grown man crying. It was not gentle weeping, such as one might expect from a fellow who has lately lost a grandmother or another less than immediate relation, but an aggressive, frustrated howling punctuated by a dull thudding sound which I could only imagine to be the beating of fists on the walls. Frightened by my intrusion into Lowe's personal space, I retreated and occupied my time in reading and contemplation.

Later that afternoon he had appeared at my door, restored to his normal, energetic self and brandishing a note on a piece of paper. Pitt had written to us once more, imploring us to return and confessing the grounds for the displeasure of his late progenitor. He had recently acquired, so he wrote, a set of paintings at great expense — too great an expense. He begged us to return, so return we did, Lowe in his most effervescent temperament.

The pictures, Lowe commands, must be removed from the

house at once. Pitt agrees readily. But I object as per my instructions — are not the artworks tainted now? Will not the next recipient be subject to the same terrors? There is consternation — Lowe appears lost in deep thought; Pitt is in a frenzy. The paintings must go, he acknowledges, but he must recoup some of his investment. We appear to be at a dead end — then a sudden idea from me, dismissed at once by Lowe as an absurdity: we should purchase the paintings. There is much discussion with Lowe warning all the while that this is a foolish notion and I playing the virtuous hero, prepared to make the sacrifice to preserve the dignity and solvency of one of London's foremost families. Lowe reluctantly acquiesces on the basis of his childhood memories of Pitt's parents and various invented members of the domestic staff. A deal is struck and within the hour, the ghost has been exorcised (this time with only a minimal display of pyrotechnics) and we are returning home with a collection of eight paintings having paid only the barest fraction of their true worth. Another hour and the ever-industrious Crane has found a buyer who possesses both the appropriate means and the necessary discretion. Two further hours and the business is transacted, the funds have been realised and Lowe and I have bid each other good evening, both in a mood of exultant self-congratulation.

"George!" I returned sharply from my passage into memory. "Haven't you been paying the least attention to what I've been saying?"

"I'm sorry," I said. "I suppose I'm rather tired. I'm listening now."

"I was saying," said she, irritably, "that you ought to ask him how he does it."

"Does what?"

"Does *it*! You know, with the ghosts and everything."

"Oh that — well, I've come to the conclusion that I don't suppose it really matters."

"Doesn't matter? Doesn't *matter*! But George, of course it matters! Don't you see?"

"Not really," said I. The fact of it was that I was quite content. It had been four weeks now since the affair in Battersea and circumstances were maturing nicely. Lowe and I had settled into a comfortable routine. Pitt's gratitude had secured us admission not only to a range of fashionable evening events — many of which had made the ball at Claridges pale into insignificance — but had also earned us membership of a prestigious gentleman's club close to Piccadilly. Here, more than anywhere else, we were able to make the acquaintance of London's most well-to-do gentlemen, and by and by, the wealthiest of these (though we were sparing in our distribution to avoid any hint of detection) would find themselves tormented by some supernatural presence. Several rehearsals and a fully-fledged performance later, we had usually been able to transform some impressive piece of capital into more portable property.

Of course, we were not always successful in our ventures. We were not faultless and with each new enterprise there was always the risk of familiarity and complacency. Things which had once terrified me and set my pulse racing no longer so much as elevated my heart rate and I found the effort required to establish a facade of dread quite tedious. On one occasion we came very close to disaster. We had visited the home of Rupert Walpole whom, we had suggested, was besieged by the spirit of a recently deceased aunt, who had objected to his speculating on gold interests in the colonies. We were, however, all too eager to lay our hands on the deeds to several extensive territories and

Walpole was instantly suspicious and would, I believe, have thrown us out onto the street and attempted to handle the ghost himself had we not expelled the creature at once and then refused, most virtuously, any offer of a reward. It was essential that word of these private transactions did not get out. If rumour spread that the vanquishing of a ghost was almost always accompanied by the changing hands of money, then business would certainly dry up.

"I still don't understand why it took you so long to tell me about all this — nearly a month and not a word about it," she was looking at me earnestly, now. "Don't you trust me?"

"It's not that," I said, but this was not strictly true. Molly's unusual and inquisitive nature was all part of what made her attractive, but there was something about her I could not bring myself to trust and even had I not been gagged to some extent by the clauses of the contract Crane had made me sign before entering into partnership with Lowe, I do not think I should have wished to share everything with her. There were simply too many unknowns. For instance, her employment at the Vaudeville under the Gatti brothers seemed extremely peculiar. She kept, apparently, no regular hours (for she was always willing to meet me at any time), could never answer me satisfactorily when I asked her precisely what she did, and never once permitted me to walk her back to that establishment when our liaisons were through.

But despite this and despite her infatuation with Lowe — for that seemed entirely immovable despite all my efforts to interpose myself betwixt her and hero — I felt that I was falling in love. I had scoffed many times at the wittering of romantics who insisted on the division of heart and head and who excused foolhardy actions by the assertion that the former had ruled the latter, but now I found myself in that precise scenario. The rational part of myself knew Molly to be dangerous and volatile. I had also some vague premonitory sense that she would somehow bring me into conflict with my employer — though I had no sure evidence of it, but my more vulnerable, emotional self was investing heavily in this woman and doing so with complete abandon.

"I just didn't want to talk about it," I said. "Not then — it didn't feel as if it were important."

"Not important?"

"No — not when we had succeeded in our venture."

She looked at me hard, scrutinising me as was her habit from time to time. "Do you ever think," said she, "that what you are doing may be — somehow — immoral?"

"We are helping people," I said, preparing to rehearse Lowe's arguments to me on this theme.

"Are you, though?" she said, the corners of her mouth lifting into a soft, rueful smile.

"What?" I asked, conscious that she had seen a connection that I had not. "What is it?"

"Well," she said cautiously, aiming her gaze down at the cloth of the table before us and smoothing it out with her hands, "don't you think it's rather a coincidence that every time you meet a person of means, they suddenly find themselves the object of a haunting?"

Of course I did. How could the question not have become the sole object of my thoughts for weeks on end — ever since Lowe had disappeared into his private room with the black door at the mention of Pitt's paintings? It was, however, another uncomfortable topic and I had pushed it forcibly into the darker recesses of my mind along with my other concerns. Talking about it, drawing the thing out so that the cold, hard light of day could pour judgement onto it would only make it worse. It could not be coincidence. I was certain of that. Lowe was doing it — by what means I did not know, but each time I thought about it I could not pull myself away from those horrible, shaken, sobbing sounds.

"George!" she exclaimed again, with a laugh. "I do believe you're beginning to find my company tedious! Aren't you going to answer my question?"

"I suppose," I said, with as much conviction as I could rally to the cause, "that such men are more likely to attract the attention of ghosts and spectres."

"Why so?"

"Well," said I, thinking very much on my feet. "I suppose that in obtaining great wealth these men have often had to do something that is dubious — something significant, that is."

"Oh tosh!" she cried, tossing her head and narrowing her eyes at me. "You're talking absolute rot, George, and you know you are! Dubious indeed! I never heard of something so absurd. What about Tommy, then? Do you really suppose that *he* was capable of doing something *significant* as you term it?"

She had bested me there — I had to concede it. I had met Tommy Bathurst at an evening party in Knightsbridge. Lowe had not been in attendance and it was my habit, on those occasions when I was not joined by my employer, to extend an invitation to Molly who was always more than happy to come along. It was she who had introduced me to the man — a charming fellow who was all meekness and humility. He was the sort of man whom one might have run through repeatedly with a sword only to have him apologise for the bloodstains on the carpet. His grandmother had left him a substantial bequest, and with almost sickening altruism, he was toying with the idea of establishing a school for

159

orphaned boys — all this, of course, I learned from Molly who was most useful at extracting these details. When Lowe had heard of the scale of the bequest and of Tommy's intentions for it, he had become almost apoplectic, denouncing the man as an irresponsible fool. Several days later, as was the usual sequence of these things, he fell victim to a curious occurrence during the night and sent for us to attend upon him.

We performed all the usual rituals on arrival using an assortment of props from our trunk (whose load of fantastical instruments grew heavier and heavier as the weeks passed and our ingenuity grew) and at length Lowe — who had not previously had opportunity to discover the idiosyncrasies of Tommy's character for himself — asked him whether he could think of any action he had undertaken which might have earned the wrath of his dear and departed. That gentle, humble individual had dissolved into floods of remorseful tears. He had, he confessed, been overly proud and overly selfish. He had conceived a scheme to found a school by which, he had realised, there was a very real chance that he himself might be glorified, indeed immortalised even, through the establishment. Lowe had chastised him roundly and had insisted that all such imaginings must be renounced at once before the exorcism could proceed. But here Tommy had surprised us — he had renounced his dream of founding a school and had, already, donated the entire sum of the bequest (not the half he had originally intended) to an existing institution in anonymity. It had only been with the greatest difficulty that I had persuaded Lowe to expel the spirit at all and his mood on our return journey that evening had been unspeakably foul.

"Perhaps there were darker things in Tommy's past than any of us knew," I replied. It was a weak response and we both knew it. But I could not accept that Lowe was fully in control of every haunting. On several occasions we had found ourselves in real and obvious danger, and no matter how good an actor he was, there was no disguising the fact that the terror Lowe felt whenever we were suddenly plunged into darkness without warning (which was something that happened with increasing frequency during our house calls) was a quite genuine one. I had no wish, however, to share this with Molly, for I had not even discussed it with Lowe himself.

"And another thing," she said, pressing on with her inquisition. "How is it that every haunting is precisely the same? Each new encounter you describe to me is exactly the same as the last."

"I don't think that's quite true — Lowe and I—"

"Oh, I'm not talking about what you and Lowe get up to, whatever novel performance you put on might well be different — but the ghost always appears in precisely the same way."

She was right, of course, and once again she had lifted a rock in my conscience and allowed all the dark and dubious things that lurked beneath to crawl out into clearer focus. It was always the same — the chill wind from nowhere, the crackling sound, the ice. It was all wonderfully predictable, but why shouldn't it be? After all humans and animals are creatures of habit — why should it be expected that the occupants of the spirit realm should be anything other? The insistence on the variety of spectres was surely nothing more than the product of fantasists and purveyors of substandard literature and must, I rationalised, represent a significant deviation from a more regular normality. This I expressed to Molly who seemed at least partially placated by it.

"Nonetheless," she said, "something seems wrong about it. I don't like to say it, George, but the whole thing has the feel of a scam of some kind."

"I find that rather offensive," I declared, bristling to hear my own disquiet so clearly voiced. "I'll admit that the rights and wrongs of the business are not as straightforward as in other industries and I'll freely confess that there is a degree of deception involved, but to suggest that Lowe is some sort of shyster or that what he does — what we do — is some sort of confidence trick is too much, Molly. It really is."

We were interrupted by the arrival of the afternoon tea — which neither of us now felt much like eating. We affected a brighter and more conciliatory demeanour for the benefit of the waiter but returned to the debate at the moment of his departure.

"What do you know about him?" she asked, defiantly.

"What do you mean?"

"What do you know about Percival Lowe — the man?"

"I know him to be a gentleman of good character, if that's what you mean?"

"It isn't! Ask yourself, George, what do you *really* know about who he is? Where has he come from? Who were his parents? Does he have brothers or sisters? Where was he educated?"

The questions went on and on peppering me with doubt as I heard them and I realised, with some distress, that she was quite right; I really had no idea in the slightest. I could, I suppose, have drawn some small clue to the composition of his identity from the personas he adopted whenever we were visiting clients — for on each occasion he was careful to present himself as an individual who could not only be trusted, but related to. The characters he assumed varied wildly but each was as convincing as the next — the little boy who had frolicked in the street outside Pitt's residence in Battersea was also the youth who had worked on his uncle's farm in the countryside or the young gentleman who had once managed a flour mill in Derbyshire. There were some commonalities between the stories — the early death of his parents, some time spent in the navy, a moment of near financial ruin — these I assumed had been drawn carefully from the concrete past. But Lowe's history was not a fixed thing; it was whatever the situation demanded of it, and curiously enough, until now, that had been enough for me.

"I don't know," I mumbled, distracted.

"No," said Molly, quietly, "you don't." She reached out and took my hand. "I'm not saying all of these things to upset you, George," she said. "It's just that I care about you — about us. You are hopeful that we can build a future together, you and I, are you not?"

The joy that unleashed itself at this prospect caused me to miss entirely the impertinence of the question, and all at once, I found that all the worries and concerns that had flooded my mind only seconds before were now mere memory. The past seemed as fictitious as one of Lowe's invented personas; all that mattered now was the future.

"Nothing would make me happier," I said.

"Then all I ask is that you exercise a little more caution," she said. "Be careful what you become embroiled in. You have found yourself suddenly elevated — you have money now. Don't be swept away by it, be careful!"

I nodded and a resolve began to form within me. She was right. It was foolish of me to proceed in this business without understanding more about it, no matter how comfortable I had become — and I was indeed comfortable. I could not say that I did not find great pleasure in reading the letters of astonished gratitude from my mother who was now in receipt of almost half my salary, nor that the periodic gifts, bonuses and allowances that Lowe bestowed upon me whenever he was of the mood had not given the feeling of being an entirely new man. This sensation was increased dramatically by the fact that my clothes had arrived and I now felt myself, in appearance, at least, the equal of men I would hitherto have considered well above my rank and station and to whom I would have feared to utter a word in my previous incarnation.

The chief joy to which I had turned my little fortune, thus far, was in the acquisition of a little square piano which had been delivered into my rooms. I had never played before but had engaged the services of the repetiteur from the Vaudeville whom the Gattis were only too pleased to release to me for an hour every week. I had assumed that he might raise some objections to taking on a pupil with only a single hand, but he was quite ambivalent about it. It was his belief, he said, that with the appropriate willpower I could achieve some degree of proficiency. The instrument proved an invaluable means of passing the time on those days when Lowe had either shut himself away or gone out on private business. I had also added considerably to the little library in my study and had taken great delight in impressing Molly with various quotations from authors and poets I considered erudite; my leisure time had, in fact, become quite blissful

Nonetheless, if I were to be responsible now not only for my own future, but also for Molly's I knew that she was quite right. I must ensure that it was founded on an entirely secure present.

"I think it's time I asked Lowe some questions," I said.

I had expected her to seem pleased or to be impressed by my maturity of approach, but she was neither, instead she looked suddenly tired — exhausted even. When I thought about it afterwards I realised that she had in fact worn upon her face that same fatigue that I had so often observed upon Lowe's. "I should go, George," she said. "I've got a lot to do and it's growing late." She rose from the table, the tea untouched, kissed me lightly on the cheek, took one last lingering look at me and then walked purposefully out into the street.

I decided to walk back to Victoria. I had been shy of taking cabs ever since that business on our return from Mrs Finn's, and though Lowe insisted on using them as our primary means of transport, I preferred my own two feet whenever I had my liberty. On this occasion, however, my decision proved a poor one. For the fine clothes that provided me with a camouflage by which I was permitted to interlope among the upper echelons of society, were not well suited to the paths I considered to be familiar in the city, in which I now looked to be an easy prospect. On two occasions, would be attackers were warded off with an admonitory glance, but when I was still a mile or more from home, I noticed that I had picked up another tail. This pursuer was not to be so easily shaken or surprised as those I had encountered before. I employed, of course, my usual tactic of lying in wait around blind corners, but whenever I did so, the man did not follow me and at length I was forced to continue with my journey.

Eventually, having become heartily sick of the fellow and having ascertained by inconspicuous backward glances that he was a slight man of more advanced years than myself, I decided on open confrontation. I slowed my pace, little by little, as I went which forced the distance between us to close up until it can have been no more than ten feet. Then, suddenly, I turned on the spot to face him.

"I assume you have something of importance to say to me,

sir," I said. "Since you have been trying to catch up to me for some time?"

The fellow reeled in shock and I do believe that for an instant at least he contemplated making a run for it, but it was at that moment I realised who he was.

"You are Mr Samuel Ivor," I said, in surprise.

The man said nothing, but only gave a slow nod. I surveyed him warily. There seemed to me to be nothing in him that presented a particular threat and I could not for a moment imagine why it was that Lowe was so resistant to his petitions for help. He was certainly not a wealthy man — that much was clear — but I could not believe that even Lowe would be so callous as to deny help to a fellow creature in such obvious distress.

"Can I be of any assistance to you, Mr Ivor," I asked amicably. Then added with a smile, "Or have you come back for the rest of our windows?"

"I'll pay for the damage," said Ivor, gruffly but earnestly.

"I'm sure there's no need to concern yourself with that," said I. Ivor's character was not at all what I had expected. The figure who had thrown stones at our window had appeared weak and deranged. This man was evidently in full possession of his right mind and there was a curious strength about him despite his insubstantial frame.

"I want your help, Mr Fairlea," he said, simply.

"In what sort of a matter?"

"The usual sort, Mr Fairlea, let's not play games with one another."

"Very well then — you must give me the particulars and I shall see what Mr Lowe and I may be able to do; though I must warn you that Mr Lowe..."

"Not Lowe," growled Fairlea. "I don't want him and I don't

want his other assistant neither — I want you; just you."

This caught me off guard. I was about to respond that Lowe and I operated in tandem (along with an explanation that Crane, to whom I assumed he was referring as 'the other assistant' certainly did not hold the same rank as myself) and that it would be quite impossible for me to attend to any business without his cooperation, but Ivor cut me off.

"I had a daughter, Mr Fairlea," he said. "Do you see?" He held up a small photographic portrait of a girl who could not have been more than eleven or twelve years old — possibly she was much younger. It grew suddenly cold, and from somewhere close at hand, I could hear — so subtly as to be almost not there at all (but my well-attuned ears were alert to it) — the slow, crackling creep of ice across stone.

"What was her name?"

"That's my Lizzie, there — Mr Fairlea. They took this photograph two days before she died."

"I'm sorry for your loss," I said, quickly, noting with some horror that Ivor's eyes were filled with tears. Those all-too familiar sounds grew louder and the temperature fell even lower.

"She never did any wrong, Mr Fairlea," said Ivor. "She was a good girl. She always said her prayers and always put others before herself. She was a good Christian girl, Mr Fairlea."

"How did she die, Mr Ivor," I asked, gently. Some impulse within me told me that the peculiar man needed to tell the story just as much as I needed to hear it.

"She never came down to breakfast that morning," he said. His eyes were glazed as he allowed the memory to run its course. "She'd always made the breakfast for me ever since she grew tall enough to see the stove. Her mother died when she was born."

"I'm sorry," I said, again, but the man did not hear me.

"I waited almost an hour and then I went to her room but found no sign of her. It was springtime and she sometimes used to take a walk by the brook at dawn. She loved nature, Mr Fairlea, she was a gentle soul like that." He paused for several seconds and I thought for a moment that he might be unable to go on. How long had he waited to tell this story?

"I found her in the end," he said, simply. "I found her floating under the ice of the brook with her face turned up to me — and with such a look upon it, Mr Fairlea! Such a look as would keep you awake every night for the rest of your life. They said she must have slipped in and drowned, but if she only slipped in, Mr Fairlea — you tell me why her bracelet was missing?"

"I'm sorry for your loss," I said again, dumbly.

"But she isn't lost, Mr Fairlea," said Ivor, his tone darkening, his face flooding with a sudden, terrible dread. He drew close to me and stared hard into my eyes. "She isn't lost at all! I wish to god she were! It's been ten years — she's still here."

At his last pronouncement, the ice, which had been lingering on the outside of my perception, creeping up the wall to my right and snaking a frosted tendril around the lamp post, suddenly burst into full view covering the pavement in a mirror sheen that reflected my astonished face as I looked down into it, reflecting back a truth that had now become so horrifyingly clear.

"I love her, Mr Fairlea," said Samuel Ivor, who was also staring down at the ice around his feet. "But she doesn't belong here any more. She can't stay here! You have to help me — help me send her on!"

CHAPTER TEN

I burst into Crane's office with such a clattering of the door that I thought half the street should have heard me, yet the old man remained as composed as ever. He looked up at me from his desk and smiled a thin, professional smile from behind those luxurious moustaches.

"Good evening, Mr Fairlea," he said, as if he were simply passing the time of day.

"Is it?" I shot back. "That remains to be seen. Where's Lowe?"

"Mr Lowe is in his quarters, sir," he said. "He asked me to tell you—"

I did not stop to hear the last part of the sentence but pushed past him and made way along the corridor and through the door that led into Lowe's rooms. My mind — already stirred up into rebellion by Molly's incitement — was now inflamed by what I suspected about Lowe's connection with Samuel Ivor and his daughter. I had left the latter person with no firm promise, other than that I should do what I could to persuade Mr Lowe to look into the matter, though I was already sure that this was a course of action he would stubbornly refuse. Having passed through the door, I half shouted Lowe's name into the gloom beyond, but found my attention arrested by something out of place. The great black door — the only differentiating feature between the layout of his rooms and my own — was not shut, bolted and chained as it had always been in my experience to date, but stood very slightly ajar. A soft light came from within, and curious, I drew a little closer.

"Come in, Fairlea," said Lowe in a tone that hung in a delicate balance. It reminded me of the way high-wire walkers move their feet — gentle, precise and laced with just that hint of fear but no less confident for that. For some reason I did not move — not even so much as a muscle. I simply stood there, silent. "Do come *in*, George," said he. He had never, as far as I could remember, called me by my Christian name before and the surprise of it brought me back to my senses. I pushed back the door and entered.

The chamber was striking in almost every regard. With the exception of a single small, flat section where the door was positioned, it was a perfect circle and the walls, by strong contrast to the others in Lowe's establishment (done out in uniform bottle-green) were a deep burgundy colour. There were no lamps or sconces and indeed the only source of illumination came from two silver candlesticks. These were set atop what I first took to be a table but then realised, with some surprise, to be an ancient stone altar of the sort found in old-fashioned country churches. Upon the top of it rested no altar cloth, but the stone had been intricately carved. How long ago this was done I could not tell, but the characters, though recognisable, looked strange and misshapen. Despite these deformities, I could make out that all the letters of the alphabet were arranged in a circle around a deep depression in the centre, acting as a stone bowl. In this bowl lay a good quantity of water which had fallen, I discovered upon looking upwards, through a small aperture in the ceiling which could be opened and closed by means of a length of stout rope. Lowe was in the process of opening the aperture as I arrived and the silence was periodically interrupted by a gentle splashing sound as the occasional droplet of rainwater made its way down that narrow chimney and into the small pool beneath.

"I feel it is high time," said Lowe, "that I took you a little further into my business, George."

I said nothing. What was I to say? The room was so completely overwhelming that all expression deserted me, and I hung there, dumb.

"You will have questions," he continued, "and by your loyalty and good service these past weeks you have earned yourself the right to some answers. Come nearer, George! Come and look at this." He gestured toward the altar in the middle of the room and invited me to step towards it. As I did so I noticed two things I had not observed when I had entered the room. The first of these was the dome of a miniature bell jar which stood on the altar so that the circle of its base covered the carving of the letter 'E' below it. The second was that the stone bowl was not empty of anything but water as I had first supposed, but contained a very small, simple silver bracelet. I realised at once that I had seen the slender silver chain before. It had been this trinket which had protruded so often from the closed fist of Lowe whenever we made our house calls.

"Is that what they call a Ouija board, sir," I asked, finally mastering my breath.

"I suppose it is similar," said Lowe, "but you shall see its function presently. It is time you understood how it is that these hauntings are brought about. Does it surprise you to learn that they are not random acts of chance?"

"I'm afraid I have suspected for some time, sir, that they are not."

"Quite right too, George," he said with a smile, but I noticed that all this while he never took his eyes off the bracelet. "You are no fool, else I would never have employed you. Yet for all your suspicions you have never mentioned your concern to me — we have never discussed it. Why is that?"

"I did not consider it my place to do so, sir," I said, perhaps too hastily.

"I wonder whether you might have felt your place to be rather different had I not offered you such a handsome salary?" It was not a question that required an answer and I chose not to respond to it. Nonetheless, the shame was written clearly on my face and trumpeted by my silence.

"Don't be dishonest with yourself, George," said Lowe, still keeping his eyes fixed upon the bracelet. "Lying to yourself is the first step along the road to ruin. Trust me, I know, I have been there."

At that moment the temperature in the room seemed to cool slightly and I saw Lowe's eyes glitter and his mouth widen into an expression of delight. "It is nearly time."

"Time for what, Mr Lowe?"

"Nearly twelve years ago, George, I went travelling. I won't bore you with the details — the experience was really quite tedious. I had been engaged to a young lady and she had died — no spare me your formulaic sympathies, George, I have no need of them. Such things happen. Such is the way of the world."

The temperature dropped further, I could now see my breath as a thin cloud of vapour in front of my face, but Lowe had eyes only for the bracelet and the little pool. "I took it into my head that I should like to see Capri. One reads about these places, but seldom has the opportunity to go. I took a room at the hotel in Sorrento and then arranged a passage for myself to the island with a group of fishermen who seemed eager for my custom. They were not, of course, eager for my custom at all, but as I discovered, to my dismay, eager instead for any items of property I might be carrying about my person. I was an Englishman in a foreign country travelling alone. I was, in short, easy prey."

Another raindrop fell from the ceiling, but this time it did not produce the regular pattern of ripples on the surface, instead it landed with a gentle tinkling sound as it collided with the thin sheet of ice that had now formed across the pool's surface.

"They rowed me out a mile or more from port," he went on impassively. "They stripped me naked and then they beat me bloody with the oars until I was completely insensible. Then, having taken from me all that they considered valuable, they threw me overboard and rowed away into the darkness."

He paused and seemed to stiffen and shudder slightly at the memory.

"I do not know how I survived," he said. "I do not recall how I was able to swim back to the shore and emerge panting onto the silent beach under the light of the moon. But I remember my first thought when I reached it and drew myself up onto the sand, still warm from the heat of the day. I thought to myself, George, I thought — I am *dead*! I have *died*! And the knowledge did not fill me with dread nor anguish. Instead I felt an extraordinary sensation of release."

"But," I dared interrupt, "you do not mean to tell me that you really did die?" I had seen and heard so much that seemed so unnatural in recent weeks that the extreme suggestion did not seem too bold.

"Of course not!" he laughed. "Don't be simple, George! In every medical respect I was very much alive, but the person who I was then — that name, that position, that rank, all gone. Washed away into the bay of Naples, never to return."

"I don't understand."

"There is no freedom in life, George! You must know that. We are endlessly obliged to our families, to our superiors, to our government and to our God — all because we live in fear of death. Yet I had *passed through* death! It could not touch me any longer and I found myself in a position to be able to cast off those strangling chains and start afresh — do you see?"

"You took a different name?"

"I took a different form!" he exclaimed. "All that existed in this vessel," he said gesturing to his body, "all that might have been considered a person was done away with in that undignified and unholy baptism. All evidence of him was left in two packing cases in a dingy hotel room. All love, all emotion, buried in an empty coffin beneath a headstone somewhere in the Home Countiesl, and *I* was born. *Percival Lowe* was born."

The bracelet was no longer visible beneath the ice, which had become so thick now that it stared up like a pupil-less eye, a white circle beneath the open sky. Lowe's tale seemed an extraordinary one, and at first, I could not bring myself to believe it. I had seen him apparently disclose his past to so many clients on so many different occasions that I wondered whether I might not now be falling victim to that same old routine. And yet the way he trembled as he spoke, the way that his anger and his delight and his pride at his own cleverness rolled themselves into the confidence of his tone left me in no doubt that this was, indeed, the truth.

"Where did you go?" I asked.

"To Rome," said he. "I recalled reading somewhere that all that is foul or profane flows into and converges at Rome and I was keen to taste all of it — don't look at me like that, with such disapproval! Yes! I indulged myself in every form of wickedness, I bathed myself in a world of licentiousness and I jumped at every

174

opportunity for corruption."

"Were you not ashamed, sir?" My question was genuine, though it was not a reproach. All men, I suspect, have at some stage or other dreamed of what it might be like to cut loose from the restraint of civilised society and simply do as one pleased — to live entirely for pleasure and for one's own selfish gain.

"Ashamed!" he laughed. "Ashamed? What had I to be ashamed of? I who was *dead*? I who was *reborn*! I who could not be touched by any petty rules or laws! No, I was not *ashamed* — I revelled in it — and I believe I was happy."

I confess that my mind was now beset by disgust and envy in equal measure. I recoiled at what Lowe had done, the things he had experienced and yet I wanted them for myself. Children are taught in schools and by good Christian parents too that pleasurable living is sinful and will yield the fate of the prodigal, nothing short of utter dejection and a complete absence of joy. Yet here was a prodigal now who seemed, apparently, resolute in his determination not to return to a more respectable plane; here was, of all things, a happy sinner!

"There was one thing, however," Lowe went on, "that irked me and chafed at me during that time and that was that I was perennially short on cash. I undertook the occasional scheme to earn a little, even did some casual labour from time to time, but my enjoyment of life's pleasures was always marred by the knowledge that I would soon have to work again to stay afloat."

He was drawing near the climax of his tale now, I could tell, and the time for me to understand the purpose of that great, foreboding altar was coming close at hand.

"I had fallen in with a group of highway thieves just outside the city," said he, as if it were the most natural thing in the world. "And we were making a modest living on the takings from various wealthy passers-by, but one night an armed guard came out from the city to hunt us down and we were forced to scatter into the neighbouring countryside. My fellows were quickly found and hanged," he went on without emotion. "But I was too clever for them. I had found, during my wanderings, the opening to some catacombs on the Appian road, and by night, I groped my way back to it and dropped inside. I knew myself to be safe then, you see, for even had the guards known of the place they would never have entered it — they are fearfully superstitious about the catacombs.

"Convinced that I have passed out of danger, I climb down a narrow passage that leads into an open chamber which must have been used as a prayer chapel in ancient times. I clamber down in there amongst the tombs with the intention of waiting for dawn, but to my surprise there is someone there already. At first, panic grips me — I fear I am discovered or betrayed, but closer inspection of the figure reveals that this is not the case. It is a priest — a young man, not so very much different in age from myself. He is sitting in one corner of that cavern, with his knees drawn up against his chest, and to my great astonishment, I find that he is sobbing uncontrollably."

The rain which was falling through the aperture more heavily now, had started to behave in a most curious fashion. The room now having become bitter cold and all the water in the pool having turned solid, the drops themselves were transformed into hard pellets of ice which shattered on impact. Lowe, however, noticed none of this and continued with his story.

"I had now no fear of discovery, and having taken a good look at the man, I calculate that I should emerge a convincing victor if it came to a fight, so I scramble down from my hiding place and stride over to him. At first, of course, he flies into a

176

mad panic — believing I have come with the intention of seeking him out — but when I reveal that I am a fugitive from the world above myself, he calms and is, I think, glad of my company."

Lowe's eyes remained fixed in front of him, seeing nothing. His vision was entirely consumed by the memory he was recalling.

"He was in a state of disgrace for he had loved a woman — something that is not permitted for any priest in Italy — and the girl had fallen pregnant and thus been immediately betrothed to an elderly and wealthy cousin to spare the family's shame. To renounce the church and to be with her was impossible — for in his shame was hers too. Thus, he had taken himself to the catacombs with the thought of drinking poison (which sat next to him in a pretty looking little vial) but had then found himself unequal to the task. I offer my condolences as you can imagine and then, when he asks for it, tell him my own story to which he listens with rapt attention, particularly to the parts at which I speak of being dead and yet alive."

I shifted my feet uneasily from side to side. Something was coming — some truth or action that would throw my world into disarray. But I was like a blindfolded man awaiting the fall of the axe, there was no knowing when it would happen, only that it would and that no force on earth could prevent it.

"When I had finished telling him all about my rebirth, he sat in silence for a long time. Then he told me that it was curious that I had told him such a story in such a place for there was a myth prevalent about the very catacombs in which we now sat. It was claimed that a certain old alchemist had discovered that, when an innocent soul is untimely detached from its body, it does not flee straight to heaven or hell as do those souls who meet their end at the appointed hour. It waits — it lingers just beyond our

177

understanding, still able, in some small way, to exert influence on this world. Nature abhors the perversion of it, you see, George. Nature *itself* will not permit the soul to depart."

I was excited in spite of myself, the prospect seemed extraordinary and I imagined Lowe's clever mind racing through the possibilities as he sat in that dank cavern hundreds of feet below Rome.

"This much he told me freely, but when he saw I was becoming more than casually interested in what he was saying, he refused to go on. He had already dismayed his church — he would not now profane it by going further. Fortunately, George — as you have already discovered, much to your discomfort — all men have their price and the priest finally relented to divulge the supposed secret of the craft in exchange for my rendering him a certain service to which I eagerly agreed."

"What was the secret," I whispered, my voice hoarse with anticipation. "Tell me!" Looking back now, I see that my thirst was his own thirst — my lust for that knowledge echoed the words he had spoken to that priest so many years before.

Lowe looked at me — as if he were weighing me up. I felt as if the knowledge, the secret he was about to impart, was something so momentous that he needed to be absolutely sure that I was quite worthy of it.

The room was cold now and almost perfectly still.

He seemed to make up his mind.

"For thousands of years — perhaps longer, man has contemplated his place in the universe," he said, slowly, returning his gaze to the altar. "And for just as long, we have wondered what lies for us beyond life — in the hereafter."

He lifted his head to look at that peculiar oculus in the ceiling. "But only I have come to *know*."

I did not speak. The tension in the air was so palpable I felt that if I made any sound it would shatter into fragments and the moment would be lost.

"The souls of the innocent are reborn in death," said Lowe, quietly. "This much has always been supposed and there is enough corroborating evidence to support it as proven fact — but there is a key a principle point that no one but I has fully grasped."

I was trembling — whether through cold or anticipation or through an overriding presentiment that what I was about to hear would define the course of the rest of my life.

"It isn't about *God*, you see," Lowe mused. "It isn't about some divine puppeteer pulling the strings and opening the hatches. But it isn't random either — there is a rhythm to it all. A pure and logical rhythm and if one can detect it..." Here he inclined his head slightly as if he were listening to music I could not hear, and clicked a pulse with his fingers. "One can control it."

He straightened himself again and turned his attention to the altar once more, his tone becoming crisp, business-like.

"But they do not pass into the other realm equipped with all their faculties, and when they come into being there, they are like babies — like children." He smiled, as if at a fond memory. "At first they tear about deranged and demented. But after a time — and it is a slow process that can take months, even years in some cases — they begin to understand their predicament better and they begin to decipher their surroundings and memory begins to return. All this, you must understand is pure supposition and theory — but I think it carries a certain rationality. After all, we emerge into this world as incapable infants, why should we expect our experience of the other to be any different?"

"But you are able to control them," I said boldly. "How is that possible?"

"Ah!" exclaimed Lowe, proudly. "This is where I must say that I have been rather clever — cleverer in fact than generations of mediums and spiritualists and all sorts of other tin-pot pretenders. For I — and I alone — have discovered the secret of the anchor."

"The anchor?"

"Indeed. You must perceive the realm of souls beyond our own as being akin to a tempestuous ocean," said Lowe as if he were a schoolmaster instructing a class. "The souls are blown and tossed around at random with no direction, no purpose. But if you have an anchor, you can keep a soul in a single place. You can also prevent it from going on into some other realm as all souls will in time."

The road forked before me here. I wanted to ask about the other realm — wanted to discover what he had learned about what lay beyond this life and I sensed that if I pushed him, he would tell me. Even now, I wonder how different things might have been had I taken that path. In the end, however, it was my desire for control that won out, as it will win out in all men when the moment of crisis is presented.

"But what *is* the anchor?"

Lowe looked at me with eyes that sparked with wild excitement, he knew now that I was the rabbit in the snare. Suddenly, he stretched out a fist, and bringing it down with a mighty crash into the very middle of the ice in the stone bowl, shattered it into fragments. Sweeping these aside, he drew out the bracelet and held it up for me to see.

"The anchor could be anything at all: a book, a scarf, a portrait or a piece of jewellery such as this, but it *must* be something in which the person has invested significant emotion and should you wish to take ownership of it, you must be present at the moment of their death."

I looked at him non-plussed, not understanding — not seeing what I should have seen.

"There are stories of sailors lost at sea," he said, "who navigate their way back to their home ports not by the stars or by maps or by charts but by instinct. The tendrils of connection with that place are so strong, that no matter the storm they can find their way home. That is why the anchor is so important — that is why *this* is so crucial." He brandished the silver trinket once more.

I stared at the bracelet and felt suddenly sick. "That bracelet belonged to Elizabeth Ivor," I said.

"Indeed," said Lowe, unblinking. Then he uttered the three words that I knew he would utter — indeed had known that he would utter from the moment I had set eyes on Samuel Ivor earlier that evening and read in his face the tragic grief of a father in mourning.

"It still does."

With that there came a noise like a great wind that thundered around the room and which seemed to originate through the aperture in the ceiling. Frost covered everything, including my own clothing, hand and face and the candles struggled to stay lit.

"And you'd dearly like to have it back," said Lowe, maliciously. "Wouldn't you Lizzie?"

Splinters of ice-glass hurled themselves across the room at Lowe, but they shattered harmlessly as they touched his skin.

"You see," said Lowe. "My fulfilment of the obligation I owed the priest made it impossible for me to remain in Italy and so, with my new scheme already forming in my mind, I decided

181

to return to England." Lowe had raised his voice to compete with the howling gale that now flew about us. When the noise became so loud that I was almost unable to discern the words, he threw down the locket into the stone bowl on the altar impatiently and then, taking up the bell jar dome, moved it across a number of the letters so quickly that I was unable to discern the word he spelled out. The noise abated at once — but even in the ensuing silence, I was conscious of a third presence in the room, watching us and waiting like a caged beast.

"That's better," said Lowe.

"What was that?" I asked, pointing at the altar.

"A sure recipe for peace and quiet, for a few moments," said he. "Now where was I — yes, I was recalling my return to England, I believe."

There was something horrifying about the surreal nature of the whole experience. Here was Lowe challenging my understanding of reality, but doing it in so casual a manner that he might have been relating a favourite anecdote at a dinner party.

"The trouble is," said Lowe, "that the innocent don't die nearly as often as you might think and it's remarkably difficult to position oneself to be there ready for the event. I trawled the gutters and the slums and the workhouses too, but while there were plenty there who were either dead or dying, there was not one whom I might have been able to describe as innocent. Such is the nature of those places that they corrupt even the brightest of souls.

"I had been out on just such a venture late one night. A child in an orphanage had promised to die from consumption, but by three in the morning it had become frustratingly clear that he was more than likely to survive. Irritated and dejected I decided to take a walk to clear my head — just as you sometimes do,

George, when things get on top of you or perhaps when Molly is nettling you too much about your ignorance."

It was a gentle reference but also, I knew, a clear reminder of just how much of a close eye Lowe kept on my comings and goings. He could not, I imagined, risk the revelation he was now making becoming common property.

"Anyway, so I took a walk. It doesn't much matter where. Suffice it to say that it was a cold January morning and I was walking just adjacent to a stream whose swollen waters had frozen over during the night. Well, there I am walking along, very much minding my own business, when I look up and I see, in the distance, a small figure venturing out onto the ice where the water runs a little deeper. As I draw a little nearer, I realise with a building sense of unease that it is a small child — no more than eleven or twelve, I suppose — a pretty little girl. She seems to have lost something in the water — but she has now strayed a long way from the bank, and though it has been a cold night, the ice on the surface is only thin. I pick up my pace and I shout to her — warning of the danger; but she is oblivious to my calls and only dances further out to where the brook is at its widest.

"I am almost near enough when it happens, but not quite. Having apparently found the object for which she was searching, she straightens herself and gives a little cry of elation. The sudden movement, however, is too much for the ice which gives way beneath her, plunging her into the waters below. With no thought for my own safety, I run to the spot where she has broken through and plunge my hands in, hoping to pull her free. But the floodwaters have made the current too strong and I see her little form beneath the ice, writhing against it, desperate for air, trying to break through. Once, twice, three times perhaps I smash my fist into the frozen surface, but on each occasion I am outwitted by the flow of the water which drags her struggling body away from me, until, at length, it comes to rest, silent and still against the bank, her wide eyes staring heavenwards, open and clear.

"I returned to the place where I had set down my pack and was just wondering in which direction I ought to head to inform the authorities of what had passed when I noticed something out on the ice, not a foot away from where the girl had plunged in. It was a bracelet. I went out to it and took it up in my hands and realised that, quite without meaning to, and in circumstances that I could never have wished or contrived, I had come upon the very object of my own search. So it was that I stowed it away carefully and brought it back here.

"These rooms, George, were not as you see them now when first I occupied them. No, indeed! This building had suffered destruction in a fire and I had taken it in hopes that my very modest means might, at some time, improve and allow me to do something a little finer with the place. Besides which, I had no wish to draw attention to myself, for at that time I was foolish enough to think that some acquaintance of my previous self might recognise me, but I was forgetting, of course, that once a person is dead a year, their memory fades almost entirely. Nonetheless, it was to this very spot that I brought back the bracelet. Now you may imagine that I spent days or weeks or months perhaps, experimenting and trying to bring the girl's spirit to me, but you would be quite mistaken. The moment I held the bracelet in my hand and instructed the child to come —she came! Imagine my elation! I could not see her of course, but the effect that she creates is not easily overlooked, I think you will concur.

"Frustratingly, I was unable to make much further progress. Being able to summon the spirit at will was useful, but to create

184

for myself the means of employment I sought, it was essential that I should have the capacity to send her to places at will without my presence being required. You have already noted, I am sure, that it seems a remarkable coincidence that people with whom I have contact are mysteriously haunted — a suspicious coincidence perhaps (but only to those who are looking upon it in such a way). Now imagine a situation in which hauntings do not begin until I enter a building? That, I fear, begins to look rather artful."

"You wanted to be able to send her to different places — so that she could cause a problem that you would then attend to and rectify?" I said, saying it out loud more for my own benefit, than his.

"Precisely," he said. "Only the ghost wouldn't go, would she?" he smiled wryly at the empty room. "So, I took to reading. Not books about haunting or witchcraft you understand, not those dusty, worthy academic tomes; they have nothing to recommend them and certainly contain nothing of value. No, I occupied myself chiefly with consideration of mythical stories — King Arthur and the like. For it dawned on me that I could not have been the first person in all of time to employ an anchor such as I had. There must have been others before me. I then recalled that in those old fashioned children's stories there are always magical charms and amulets and the idea of magic being associated around particular objects — do not fear George, I have no belief in magic — that is pure stuff and nonsense, or 'poppycock' if you like. But I began to wonder to myself whether the power of these strange objects might not have been magical at all, but rather drawn from some associated spirit. Do you follow?"

I nodded weakly. I knew I should leave. I should go home to my mother. I should devote the rest of my life to avoiding this thoroughly dangerous man, but ambition and greed, those twin forces of destruction drove me on. Looking upon myself now, my aged form cries in outrage against the impudent youth who risked everything through avarice. If Lowe really had the power to command spirits, then I wanted to see him do it, I wanted to know how it was achieved. Furthermore, I knew that if I brought my relationship with him to an end, I also necessarily drew to an end my relationship with three hundred pounds a year. Each man had their price — that had been made painfully clear, and Lowe had hit upon mine precisely even before I stepped through his door.

"Anyway," said Lowe, glorying once again in his genius, "I realised that the link between the two worlds is found through the investment of emotion, that is how I came to discover the anchor. The spirit stretches back from the netherworld to try and reach something in this world. So, I reasoned that to improve my link and to assert my dominance, I needed something that did precisely the same thing, but in reverse." He tapped his hand on the altar. "Here it is," he said, pleased with himself. "What better artefact than this? This, which has been the object of people's yearning for the otherworld for nearly a thousand years?"

"I don't understand?"

"When the anchor and the altar are united — the symbol of the spirit's desire for this world and the symbol of our desire for the other — the boundary becomes thinner and communication becomes far easier. I'm sure that the ancient men and women who carved this altar knew that, that's why the letters are here. Now it functions as a means of communicating, a crude one, but an effective one."

"How does it work?"

"As you so astutely observed," said Lowe over-brimming with enthusiasm, "the device is very similar to the Ouija board.

On that principle, the spirit exerts its effort on the glass and spells out a message — though usually it's nothing more than a scam. Here, the process is reversed. Here, I move the dome of the bell jar and the spirit is forced to see the letters, and such is the power of the altar, she must follow my instruction. Of course, as time has gone on and the spirit has matured — she has been nearly ten years now in my service — we have found other ways to communicate and she will respond to my voice as you will no doubt have observed at our house calls. But this remains the surest form of instruction."

He extended his arm and put it around my shoulders, drawing me right next to the altar. "Now," he said, "it has come to my attention that there is a very fine cheese seller operating out of Duke Street. I am persuaded in my mind that if we could show ourselves to be of use to him, then we may be assured of a constant supply of fresh produce — what do you say?"

"It is not right, sir," I said, shaking my head and backing away. "You cannot imprison the soul of a young girl to perform tasks such as these — nor indeed to perform any tasks at all! You must release her!"

"Oh come, George," said Lowe, with a laugh. "Don't be dramatic. They still put children down the mines, don't they? We still have lads sweeping our chimneys, don't we? Indeed — are there not trained lions and bears and monkeys in every circus in every city in every country of the world? In any case you must get it out of your head that this is a *girl* we are talking about! It is a remnant, a physical force and nothing more; she has no real idea of her own existence nor those things to which you believe she is entitled. It is no more repugnant than if we were to keep a dog and teach it to do tricks — besides which, who is going to stop us? On what charge will we be summoned into court? There is nothing illegal about what we are doing here."

"It is not a question of legality," I exploded, my anger and indignation boiling over within me. "It is a question of morality."

"Morality!" he scoffed back. "Don't come at me with morality, George! We are in a place so far beyond the conventional understanding of right and wrong that morality needn't ever enter into it."

"You can't incarcerate this poor girl's soul against her will — keep her here when she wants to go — to go on!" Samuel Ivor's phrase echoed in my own.

"But who's to say she wants to *go on* as you so delicately put it? Who's to say exactly what *on* might mean in this context? There is nothing to suggest, for example, that I am not saving her from some eternal torment. Don't arraign me on a charge of blasphemy, you know I am a godless wretch. If there really were a God and he disapproved of what I was doing, don't you think he'd have acted? Don't you think he'd have tried to stop me? At least, one would have imagined, he would have given me some sort of negative sign to indicate his displeasure? Yet what have I received instead? Nothing but what good Christian people will consider a 'multitude of blessings' — are we not fed and watered by His almighty hand?."

"I want no part in it," I said suddenly.

"But you already have a part in it," snapped Lowe. "You are already involved?"

"Then I shall terminate my association with you," said I, boldly. "And I shall continue to abide by the terms of my contract. I shall not disclose anything of what I have seen here to anyone, I shall not discuss it. I am of a mind to leave London. In fact, I think I shall leave England altogether. You will not hear from me again, sir." I had only thought all of this as I was saying it and my valiant defiance felt far less secure once it had emerged from the confines of my mind, still less so when it dashed itself against Lowe's self-satisfied smirk.

"Dear me, no," he said. "I don't think I could allow any of that."

"Allow it?"

"Indeed! You have a poor sick mother to whom you have a responsibility and who has, Crane tells me, become quite content with her generous allowance, basking daily in the pride she feels for her son who has done so well and risen so high. Do you really imagine that a veteran in your condition will easily find gainful employment here or abroad? Certainly you will not find it on anything like the terms I have offered you."

"I shall re-enlist," I said — and meant it too. "It's been done before."

"Will you go back to living on military pay? Scratching around for subsistence? I don't think so."

"The money doesn't matter," I lied.

"You wouldn't last five minutes back out there and you know it. A single Boer attacking you in your tent man-to-man is one thing, but on the frontlines? You'd be a hindrance to the men, and you know that as well as I do."

"Nonetheless, I feel I must go — you need fear nothing from me, Mr Lowe. I shall be utterly discreet."

"I do not doubt it," said Lowe. "But that really doesn't matter — not in the least. Let us imagine you were not a gentleman of your word and you took yourself off out into the city and proclaimed my story to all and sundry? What damage have you done me? Precisely none. For who would believe you? You, a serviceman in tatty uniform with a stump for a hand?"

"Then why not let me go," I asked. Even now there was a

sense of inevitability hanging in the air. I knew I could not leave. I wanted to believe that it was my sense of duty to my mother compelling me but it was not. It was the money. I had come in from the cold and the wet and an uncharitable world that made no allowances for persons such as myself. I had been welcomed with open arms and made acceptable — more than that I had been made desirable. At that moment I caught sight of my naked soul — not my soul as I imagined it, but as it truly was. For all my talk of morality and piety I was no better than Lowe. In fact I was a good deal worse. He had *done* these things, he had pioneered. What had I been but an accomplice?

"I cannot let you leave," said Lowe. "Not because of what you might tell others, but what you have the capacity to do yourself. You would go, I am sure, and be good to your word, I have no doubt. But one day — one morning — you will wake up and the thought of what I have told you will take root inside of you and you will begin to want what I have. You will begin to need it. There is a hunger inside you, George, as there is inside every man and once you have once sensed the possibility of power and control you cannot put it out of your mind until you have taken it for yourself. Then, you would return to me, not as my friend and colleague, but as a greedy fool. You would demand from me by force what I now offer willingly."

He was right. Lowe appeared always to be right. He had known all along how I would react — had known that there would come a time when I demanded to be allowed to leave. His argument was sound. There was no need for me to concede defeat to him, that had never been in doubt.

"May I ask one thing," said I. "Before we proceed?"

"Of course," said Lowe. It was as if my defiance to him had been nothing more troublesome than something in his eye.

"Where do I fit in?"

"What do you mean?"

"Why should you need me?"

"Well there is company for one thing," said he, with a bright smile.

"No," I said, insistent. "That's not it. You're too methodical for that. You'd never willingly bring someone in unless you had a reason. You keep Crane out there at arm's length — so what do you want from me?"

Lowe sighed and a great weight of sadness seemed to press down on him. "You are right, of course, George. The fact of the matter is that I am becoming fatigued by the whole business. I think you will agree that I want for very little and that those things for which I do want may now be easily acquired from the funds I have accrued these last ten years. Small niceties like the cheeses we shall later set our minds to are unnecessary fripperies in the grand scheme."

"Then why not stop?" I asked. "Why not end it?"

"I shall," said Lowe. "I fully intend to before the year is out. Ghosts grow and mature just as humans do and Lizzie is no exception. She was young when she died, so I have had good service from her, but she has become bolder, more disobedient — more creative too, you must have noticed that?"

I suddenly saw the truth of all those occasions upon which I had seen Lowe's confidence desert him: the accident with the cab, the darkness in the theatre, the chalk on the wall at Pitt's house in Battersea. It was obvious that he could no longer control the ghost of Lizzie Ivor as he had once been able to.

"Then why bring me in?"

"Because," said Lowe, "even though I shall soon retire from my occupation I am concerned that it should not fall into disuse.

I have gained much knowledge — much understanding not only of my particular and peculiar craft, but also of the human condition. I am eager that this should not be lost to memory and so I am inclined to train up an apprentice of sorts to take my place when I am done."

"You intend me to learn to control the ghost."

"Perhaps," said he — and here I noted that he would not meet my gaze. "But I doubt it will be as straightforward as all that. There will be much for you to learn first and she is not yet strong enough to overcome me."

A sense of the scale of the employment to which I had now fully committed myself began to unfurl in my mind. To become like Lowe held its attractions of course, but I shivered to think of myself as an older man, locked away behind black doors and sobbing as if my heart would break. He had not mentioned this aspect of his work and the part of me that was prone to deny anything that presaged discomfort reasoned dubiously that the weeping had nothing to do with the ghost of Lizzie Ivor.

"Anyway," said Lowe, clapping his hands together enthusiastically and turning once again to face the frozen altar. "Who's for some cheese?"

CHAPTER ELEVEN

The days after the night of Lowe's revelation ground slowly on into weeks and then into months and I found that the unerring capacity of the human spirit to render normal any circumstance that might otherwise have seemed quite out of the ordinary, was equal even to the business of the summoning and dispelling of ghosts.

To begin with, I will admit, I gleaned considerable enjoyment from the process, more from the planning and preparation of the business than the haunting itself. Cheeses became the tip of a culinary iceberg which expanded rapidly to include various articles of confectionary, meat and indeed as an addition welcomed more by Lowe than myself, tobacco. The trick was to ensure that the ghost was deployed to locations which were close enough to be convenient, but far away enough from each other that the proprietors of the establishments should not discern the similarities in their experience. I became adept at giving the spirit its instructions — the method was not a difficult one. The glass on the stone altar, I discovered, must be moved slowly and deliberately to allow the message to pass quickly and clearly, but the real skill lay in phrasing the instruction so as to be clear and concise — communicating the precise nature of the task in as few words as possible. I would be lying if I said that I had not greeted the effect of my first effort — the nightly tormenting of a local grocer — with a shameful sense of pride. This feeling of satisfaction was only increased when the instigation of the haunting was converted, by means of the exorcism itself, into a consumable commodity. There was something enormously pleasing about dining each evening on the fruits of my labours.

As time went on, I was also permitted to take the helm in the exorcisms. This process was every bit as easy as Lowe had described before our visit to Reginald Pitt and the trick was, indeed, to extend the procedure to give the customer the impression they were receiving a service worthy of remuneration. If the spirit of Lizzie Ivor was sluggish at comprehending the commands laid out on the altar, she was a veritable dunce in response to verbal imperatives. It was necessary, I discovered, to repeat the phrase over and over, and even then, one could not be sure of a result. Only the final instruction to depart from a building was guaranteed to yield instant action; other commands took time to take effect. In time, however, I grew more confident and more demanding in what I required of her and I flatter myself that, on occasion, I could fashion a spectacle far more dramatic and impressive than anything Lowe might have dreamt up. At all times, however, I was conscious that the girl was fighting me — pulling at me and resenting the control I exerted over her. When I discussed the matter with Lowe, he told me, simply, that such rebellion must be punished and that, whenever she proved truculent, I was to require her to undertake something quite trivial as a consequence. By degrees, like a trained dog, she grew comfortable with my position as her master, though I sensed, as Lowe did, that she was growing more powerful and that it would not be long before she would become a danger.

"What will you do when she does become too strong," I asked one day as we left the house of a milliner on the east side of town. "How will you make yourself safe?"

"Simple," said Lowe, confidently. "When the moment is right, I shall release her."

"Release her?"

"Her anger is driven by the fact that she wishes to move on to another place. When I release her she will do so immediately. She will present no further threat to us then."

Us. I realised in that moment that I was now fully embroiled in this affair. If Lizzie did grow stronger then there was every chance that she would direct the full force of her fury at me just as much as at Lowe.

"May I ask, sir," I ventured, hesitantly, "why you have not offered any aid to Samuel Ivor, her father?"

Lowe looked away, out of the cab window. Though there had been breaks in the weather, the clouds had proven thoroughly obdurate and the rain had continued to fall so that it was almost impossible to imagine the conditions being anything other than dreary.

"I should like to help him," he said. "But I cannot. It is my single greatest regret in this whole business that he must suffer discomfort for our endeavours to proceed."

"Could we not buy his house? Can't we place him somewhere where she could not find him?"

"She *would* find him. Besides, I have reason to believe that he would reject any such offer. I have had Crane send him a good deal of money over the years, but he has refused to accept so much as a farthing. Grief is a powerful force. He does not want comfort or relief so much as he wants his wife and daughter back."

"But when you release Lizzie, he too will be at peace."

"Naturally."

With this imperfect solution I satisfied myself for a time, but the conversation I had had with the man and the earnestness of his expression and the desperation in his eyes ate away at me at night. I suppose I might have eased my mind by discussing matters with Molly, but finding myself now in possession of such extraordinarily sensitive knowledge, I did not feel able to meet with her. She had a habit of drawing things out of me and I could not risk inadvertently revealing Lowe's secret and therefore contravening the terms of my contract. I therefore resolved to have no further contact with her until I could be sure of my defences. She, of course, was not to be put off quite so easily and left countless messages with Crane, even resorting — I noted — to frequenting the street in which Lowe's offices stood in the hope of catching me off guard. Crane, however, made an excellent watchdog. He seemed to have taken a particular interest in my relationship with Molly, or Miss Easton as he insisted on calling her. In other circumstances I might have considered this peculiar, indeed intrusive, but since my chief wish at present was to avoid the young lady and her skills of interrogation at all costs, his watchful eye proved quite useful and I was able to evade her attentions admirably.

Lowe was in strong spirits during these weeks — though there were still occasions upon which he would retreat into his rooms — sometimes even sending me out on the most mundane of errands so that he could do so in private. Once or twice, passing the door to his quarters I could hear again that sound of anguished sobbing from within. Still I dared not ask him. Still I did not wish to believe that his fragile emotional state could really be connected with his occupation. These periods of darkness aside, however, I continued, quite content, for nearly two months until something occurred to catapult me out of my

196

lethargy and into a state of disquiet from which I was unable to hide.

Lowe had taken a shine to a particular automobile which was expensive even by his own lavish standards. It being the sort of thing that he considered an unnecessary frivolity and something that did not touch upon what he liked to think of as the core business (property, land, deeds and so on and so forth) he offered me the opportunity to coordinate the whole event. This was no small operation. First of all, I must find a mark — someone in possession of the automobile (Lowe stipulated that it must be a careful driver — he did not want the prize in anything other than mint condition). This took some weeks of careful questioning at the club. None of the members owned such a vehicle, but three or four had acquaintances who did. Of these two were unsuitable — being the worst sort of rantipole youths who were more than likely to kill themselves on the road before any scheme could come to fruition. Of the other two, one was a very elderly gentleman and I could not bring myself to put such a kindly old man under such strain. The other and only remaining target was an American man of business who had, I discovered through a little careful research, plenty of disposable income with which he might replace the car once we had liberated it from him.

When I had selected the mark and had Lowe's approval on the matter I set to work on the construction of a story. It had to be something significant enough to finger the car as the cause of the haunting, but not so obvious as to make it look as if our acquisition of that item was the key objective. I sketched out various plans all of which Lowe read, scrutinised and ultimately screwed up his face at with exclamations of 'too obvious' or 'too risky' or 'too fantastical' and I had more or less come to the conclusion that the thing could not be done when I finally hit upon an idea that seemed perfect.

Mr Carlton, for that was the name of the gentleman, had no children of his own but doted upon his niece (a girl of four or five years and his sister's daughter) who made frequent visits to the house and who was often taken out in the car as a treat. The plan I conceived and which Lowe approved of (congratulating me for my creativity of thought) was to make the niece, rather than Carlton himself, the object of the haunting. The ghost was commanded, quite clearly, to enter the house at around midnight and to rouse the little girl by a light fall of snow. Through this enchanting display, Lizzie was to lure the child down to the garage where the car was kept at which point she was to present herself at her most terrifying so that the child would associate the blind terror with the vehicle. Her uncle, I surmised, unable to persuade the child to ride in the vehicle with him, would be keen to part with the car as quickly as possible and therefore at the most reasonable price. To avoid other parties having access to the item at the same value, Crane was instructed to pay a visit to Carlton several days before the haunting and indicate that should he ever wish to sell the car, he had a patron who would be most interested in the purchase. When the old man reported back that Carlton had laughed at the offer and said that he couldn't sell the car even if he wanted to on account of his niece's affection for it, I was sure that we were upon the right road.

On the second day after the haunting, just as expected, a message came to Crane; he was indeed interested in selling the car and for any price should we be willing to collect it that afternoon. I was pleased, if not a little surprised, by the instant and complete success of the plan, and having reported our victory to Lowe, I sat down to read the paper and pass the hours until we were afforded the opportunity to collect our prize. My feeling of euphoria evaporated, however, as soon as I glanced at the front page which held a picture of Carlton. The story that followed detailed how, in the middle of the night, Carlton had awoken to hear a disturbance in his house. Assuming thieves had broken into the premises, he had followed the noises to the garage taking with him a weighty fire-iron. There, sensing a movement in the darkness, he had set upon the supposed intruder with vigorous force.

The child had, of course, been taken to Great Ormond Street and was receiving expert attention, but even the sanitised report had made it clear that the damage was catastrophic and irreparable. The girl had lost an eye and an arm and had not yet regained consciousness. I jumped up at once upon reading of this and burst through into Lowe's rooms. He had been in the circular chamber with the altar, but upon hearing my approach exited that room swiftly and shut the door fast behind him. He did not look pleased to have been disturbed, but nonetheless, gestured for me to follow him through to the study area. I showed him the newspaper which he read in silence. At length he gave a grunt of irritation.

"We should go to the hospital," he said.

This startled me rather — for though I felt great remorse for what had happened I was not inclined to take responsibility for the crime. Indeed, I rather thought that attempting to explain matters to the parties in question might very well make the situation far worse.

"Do you think that will really help the girl?"

"Pah!" snorted Lowe. "I've not the slightest interest in helping her!"

"Then why go?"

"You truly are barbarically ignorant sometimes, Fairlea! We

should *go* because this may be the very opportunity we have been looking for."

"Opportunity?" I said, the sting of Lowe's remark biting hard into me. "I'm sorry sir, I don't follow — we have already acquired the automobile?"

"The automobile is nothing to *this*," he snapped. "Don't you see? If we hurry, we may yet be present for the death of an innocent. Don't you understand what that means?"

I wanted to be sick; I wished that some terrible force would emerge from within me and shatter everything that was breakable in that room. But even such a force, I knew, could not wrest me from the grip of my ambition and Lowe's money. I was bound to him now. There was no end to be had.

Ultimately, however, the discussion was nothing more than academic. Before the hansom drew up in front of the hospital the infant had already expired and the whole place was bedecked with what Lowe dubbed, 'the usual festivity of mourning'. We returned to Victoria empty handed and with Lowe in a blacker mood than I had ever seen him. His spirits rose modestly when the car was delivered and we took our first outing in it, but after that day he slumped into a thoughtful depression from which it was almost impossible to rouse him.

He became absent-minded and forgetful and spent more and more time in his chambers so that sometimes I did not see him for three or four days at a stretch. His past and his present seemed to be mingling in his head so that when we occasionally did meet, he would ask me for progress with cases of which I had never heard and then, when I expressed my ignorance, he wafted me away with irritation and impatience, declaring only, 'that was years ago' or, 'I'm sure I told you about that.'. Conversation with Crane was even less fulfilling than normal. Despite the fact that business had slowed — we sometimes went weeks without an outing — his desk seemed fuller than ever with documents, and whenever I asked whether I could be of assistance, he waved me off politely. In hindsight, of course, the signs of what was to come were all so obvious, yet I was entirely blinkered to them.

The months rolled on and Advent was soon upon us. My mother's illness had worsened — not drastically — but Lowe did not permit that I should visit her and informed me curtly that I must content myself with the writing of letters, which I did, daily. Looking back upon it I imagine he supposed that my resolve to leave might harden in proportion to my distance from his person, that the special world we two inhabited, with its own laws and moral code, would be stretched impossibly thin by my departure. He was almost certainly right, of course. Thus, I retreated further into my rooms and occupied myself in reading and in my study of the piano.

Of this I must say a little more here, for my simple hobby had taken a peculiar turn. I had been forced to discontinue my lessons, not because I had any argument with the approach or disposition of my teacher, nor because I had been making poor progress (it was slow, but consistent) but because I would have been unable to conceal that where there ought to have been one solitary hand playing there were now, with increasing regularity, two. Whenever I sat down to the instrument and began my plodding exercises with the left hand, I found that they were pleasantly, if sometimes clumsily, accompanied by a light touch on the right. There could be no means of explaining to my generous teacher that this was the work of a young girl, dead some ten years, nor indeed was such an explanation permissible under the terms of my contract with Lowe, and so it was that I was forced to let him go, claiming that my funds had run short.

This was, of course, a complete fabrication. My solitary lifestyle meant that the regular payments of my salary (in addition to whatever bonuses might be accrued from time to time) went largely unspent.

At first I found Lizzie's presence at the keyboard an intolerable abhorrence and for some days it was my practice, whenever her hands touched the keys, to take up the bracelet at the altar and send her off on some meaningless errand to buy myself a few moments' peace. But as even the memory of my meetings with Molly began to fade, I became, by degrees, tolerant and then glad of her company and there were times, in those long, winter evenings, when I confess I wished for her to come and duet with me. On those occasions I would take the bracelet in my hand and call her gently and as a request, not an order. I said nothing to Lowe about this of course — for I was sure he would disapprove of such a thing.

His disapproval would hardly have been diminished by the fact that Lizzie had become thoroughly rebellious in her duties of late. She was resistant now, even to the commands issued from the altar and would seldom respond to anything verbal when we were with a client, preferring instead either to remain sullenly inactive — so that Lowe was forced to expel her without the contingent fuss and theatrics which usually turned the best profits — or to prove so energetic in her destruction that our obligation to a pretence of fear and confusion was entirely mitigated. On these latter occasions she became adept at finding and destroying the very object for which we had established the operation. Cases of wine at merchants' shops and hotels became a speciality and she did a particularly impressive job on a small townhouse on which Lowe had been keeping a speculative eye. While these incidents drew Lowe deeper into his depression, causing him to spend virtually all his time in his private quarters in contemplation of what he now referred to as 'our problem', I began to find Lizzie's outbursts impressive. In fact, if such a thing can be believed, I found them almost endearing. I saw in her the sort of defiance of which I knew I could never be capable; she fought us with whatever strength she possessed when to have simply relented and acquiesced to our demands would have bought her an easy existence. Through her I was a vicarious revolutionary and during our moments at the piano together I spoke to her softly of my admiration and explained, as best I could, why I could not bring myself to help her directly. I had no idea whether she heard or understood these thoughts at the time, but it did me good to express them.

The festive season ought to have cheered me, but it did not. Where before I had delighted in the anticipation of the coming of the Christmas festival, I now found that I saw only the darkness. While the carollers sang of the joy of the coming of the Christ child and the warmth of the stable, I found myself hearing only those lines which concerned the frost edge of the wind and the iron coldness of the earth. Lowe had said that we two were above common beliefs and superstitions and eschewed any Yuletide celebration save the occasional party that might prove beneficial to his business, but I saw us as not above them, but outside of them. We were cut off, ostracised from the general feeling of seasonal goodwill; We could only watch on hungrily from the beggars' squint.

I was feeling particularly downhearted on Christmas Eve. A letter had arrived from my mother's physician to say that, although there had been a slight improvement, her position remained a precarious one. I had written back to him at once and also to her with messages of love and empty promises of an

203

imminent visit and had then gone to soothe my guilt at the piano. But my hand would only move slowly and sadly and Lizzie's improvisations provoked anguished and disjointed harmonies that only served to stir up my emotions further. I knew that I needed human company (and within that descriptor I included neither Lowe nor Crane, both of whom seemed to miss some crucial ingredient in that regard) and I resolved that I must seek out Molly. I sent an errand boy to enquire for her at the Vaudeville and to invite her to lunch at one of our old haunts and then dressed myself in expectation of a prompt and enthusiastic response. The very prospect of a meeting with her was enough to raise my spirits and I even found myself humming as I shaved. My euphoria was short-lived, however, because the boy soon returned and with a polite missive from the Gatti brothers to say that they were sure I had communicated with them in error — for they had no knowledge of any person matching Molly's description working on their staff. The note went on to extend their felicitations and to hope that I might attend the theatre again soon. Then there was some flamboyant reiteration of their gratitude for the service Lowe and I had done them and so on and so forth, but I had long since stopped reading.

Somehow, I was not surprised by this news — Molly had been coy about her arrangement with the theatre and I had long suspected that something was amiss. I would have pondered the topic further had I not been distracted from the note by a sudden and loud hammering at the door, which announced the arrival of Mr Samuel Ivor.

Crane continued at his desk, of course, as if he could not hear the perpetual thud of the man's fist. Having observed the identity of Mr Ivor through the window, he had no intention of risking Lowe's ire by acknowledging him. He only stirred, in fact, when he saw that I had crossed the room with the obvious intent of letting the man in.

"I am not sure Mr Lowe would approve," said he, still not looking up.

"I am not sure I care," said I. Something about that morning — perhaps the special nature of the day, perhaps the news of my mother or the discovery of Molly's deception or a combination of all of these had put fire into my spirit and I found myself suddenly and confidently defiant. Crane looked up at me and then, quite unexpectedly, smiled broadly.

"Just so, sir," he said. Then he returned to his work. The smile was gone — but it had been there.

I had half expected Ivor to have returned with the level of aggression and fury that had caused him to break our windows so many months before, but when I opened the door the look on the man's face was one of contrition. It had been snowing outside and the ash-grey flakes had settled themselves on his shoulders. He had not, I supposed, expected the door to open at all, let alone so quickly and stepped back a few paces, fumbling for his words.

"May I come in, Mr Fairlea," he said, quite calmly.

"Of course, Mr Ivor," said I. My boldness was strengthened by the knowledge that Lowe, who had not emerged from his rooms for two days, was unlikely to choose this moment to break his social fast. I stepped out of the way and allowed Samuel Ivor to enter the premises from which he had been debarred for so long.

"I'm very sorry to bother you, sir," said he, striding at once to the fireplace and allowing the warmth to begin the restoration of his limbs. He kept his face to the ground as he talked as if he feared that this were all a dream and that by looking up he might cause himself to wake. "I wondered if you or Mr Lowe had made any progress with my problem?" There was a long pause during which the only audible sound was the scratching of Crane's pen.

"I am afraid we have been exceptionally busy with other clients," I said, a deep guilt settling itself in the pit of my stomach. Then I added, by way of pre-emptive mollification, "These things do take time, Mr Ivor."

"Time," said he, nodding at the fire. "Time," he repeated.

Again, the scratching noise of the pen.

"I wonder if you might tell me," said Ivor, "what insult I have done Mr Lowe that he refuses to assist me in this matter?"

"I am certain that you have caused no offence, sir — other than the breaking of the windows which I am sure Mr Lowe deems quite understandable given your particular circumstance with which I fully sympathise."

"You!" exclaimed Ivor. "You? Sympathise with my 'particular circumstance'? Ten years I've lived like this. Ten years, Mr Fairlea! Have you children of your own sir?"

I confessed I had not.

"Nor even a wife, sir?"

I shook my head.

"Then tell me how — as man who has not known the love of child or wife — you can possibly sympathise with my 'particular circumstance'?"

I was lost for words and simply shook my head slowly.

"So I ask you again, Mr Fairlea," he went on. "And I'd request that you note that I am asking in restrained tones with my anger well contained. What insult have I done to your good self or to Mr Lowe that prevents you from rendering me assistance in this matter?"

"I am quite sure, sir," said I, "that you have done no insult or injury at all. It is simply the truth that we have been busy with other clients."

"*Other* clients, you say," he spat. "Richer ones, you mean?"

"Mr Ivor you must surely know that we do not make a charge for our services!"

"Oh I dare say there's no charge," he went on, bitingly. "I dare say it's all very above board — but you can't help it if someone gives you a little trinket or two from time to time, now can you? You can't help it if you accidentally come into possession of the occasional house or piece of land?"

"Our clients are often keen to express their gratitude," I began.

"Money!" he shouted — so loud, in fact, that I feared that Lowe might be roused. "Money makes the world spin. Well if that's what you want, Mr Fairlea, that's what you shall have." With that, he withdrew from his belt a large money purse and flung it at the hard, wooden floor where it burst, sending notes and coins across the boards.

"We do not want your money, Mr Ivor," I said, distressed at the scene unfolding before me. "I promise you that we are working on your problem and that we shall have a solution very soon; you must be patient."

I stooped down and began to collect the coins up and place them back in the bag. He watched me, his eyes bulging. I had almost finished when the silence was broken by the distant sound of the piano playing in my rooms. It was a childish melody, played falteringly but accurately. I stood up and held out the purse to Ivor, but he was transfixed by the sound.

"She is here," he said, in a fragile whisper. "I know that music." Then he grasped my wrist and drew me in close to him. "Why have you called her here?"

I was faced at this moment with an impossible choice.

Telling the truth was inconceivable (and to do so in Crane's presence would have been to immediately end my employment) and to concoct a plausible lie required a creative faculty of which, at the present moment, I was not possessed. Instead, I opted to play dumb.

"What music, sir?" I asked, pretending to listen hard. I could feel Crane's eyes boring into the back of my head from across the room.

"You surely hear it?"

"I fear I do not."

"The piano — she is playing the piano — listen, man!" He was becoming increasingly agitated.

"You have had a hard journey, sir, and it is cold outside. If you will sit a while, I will bring you some brandy and something to eat to restore you."

"You do not hear the music?"

"There is no music, Mr Ivor."

Crane was watching me intently now — the personification of my conscience as I dug my feet hard into the lie. Ivor released my hand and then made as if to sink into a chair, but as soon as I was a pace or two away from him, he suddenly leapt past me and into the corridor, following in the direction of the music. I did not pursue him. I knew that there was now only one route open to me. I darted down the corridor and flung open the door to Lowe's quarters not caring whether I disturbed him. I made straight for the black door and threw it open too, plunging inside and taking up the bracelet from the little pool. I placed it flat against my lips and cried, "Home! Lizzie, go home!"

The success of my ploy was immediately evident; the piano stopped playing abruptly and did so before the wrenching sound of wood indicated that Ivor had successfully forced my room open. A few moments later I heard him retrace his footsteps through the passage and depart through the office slamming the door behind him.

None of this, however, was of any significance.

In my haste to find the bracelet and expel the spirit of Lizzie Ivor, I had not noticed that the altar room was already occupied. There was Lowe, of course, looking at my intruding person in frank astonishment, wide eyed and open mouthed from his position opposite me, but there was another figure behind him. At first, in the shadow of that gloomy room it was impossible to see who it was until she stepped forward. Though unfamiliar for her unkempt hair and state of semi-undress, there was no mistaking the identity of Lowe's guest.

It was Molly.

CHAPTER TWELVE

I turned instantly on my heel and ran from the room back out into the office, slamming both doors behind me. Crane was standing by his desk, twitching in alarm.

"Ivor," I said. "Where is he?"

"I saw him take a cab, sir," said he. "A few moments ago."

"Get me his address," said I. The fuel of purpose was spreading through me and I knew now what must be done, what should have been done months ago. I still held the bracelet in my hand, and I tightened my grip upon it as I heard Lowe calling my name from the corridor.

"Faster, Crane," I said. "I do not have much time."

"Here it is, sir," he said, holding out a small card. "Would you like me to call you a cab?"

"Yes," I said and then thought better of it. "No — no, I'll walk." I took out my wallet and thrust it at the old clerk. "Take this," I said. "I won't have any need of it now." There was a light in Crane's eyes as I performed this action and I realised that in my rebellion I had become to him what Lizzie had been to me these last few weeks.

"Goodbye, Mr Crane," I said, extending my hand, but he only looked at me — too stunned to move a muscle. Lowe was drawing closer. I ran to the corner now, took my old coat and hat which I had hung there for posterity and then bolted through the door without so much as a glance behind me. It being Christmas Eve the street outside was alive with carts and horses and street sellers and people and once in that throng I was confident that Lowe would have no hope of finding me nor, since I was in possession of the bracelet, could he employ Lizzie's help to so do.

It felt good to be out of that suffocating atmosphere and to have finally broken my attachment to Lowe. A release filled me and all the petty concerns of my subsistence were eclipsed in my euphoria and by the task that I knew lay ahead of me. I strode on for it was now long past one o'clock and I wanted to make Finchley before nightfall. It will perhaps seem surprising to imagine me as having a fear of the darkness given all I had experienced in the last year, but in truth I worried that I might not have the strength to do what must be done under the blanket of the night.

The snow had stopped now, but it still lay in a thick coating on the pavement, trammelled and marred by footprints and wheel marks. In the knowledge that I was doing — perhaps for the first time in months — something that was right, the warmth of the season began to seep slowly back into my soul. The shop fronts and the windows of the houses misted from the warmth of the hearths within and the children barricaded against the cold by layer upon layer of fussy woollen wear filled me now with hope and lightness where before they had only darkened my despair.

How it should be managed I had no idea, but this was the chief occupation of my thoughts. A simple expulsion in the manner that Lowe and I had rehearsed so many times before in so many different places would obviously not suffice, for its effect was only local and in any case I doubted that such an injunction would be possible in the child's own home. The destruction of the anchor seemed to me the most logical thing — but how should that be achieved? Would it serve simply to pull it to pieces? Must it be melted down to its base components? Could it be flung in a river?

By whatever means, Lizzie Ivor must be set free and allowed to journey on to whatever place lay in store for her. This had, of course, been Lowe's intention — but not until he had found a replacement for her and such a thing might take years as it had done the last time he searched. Even then, he had only happened upon the scene of Lizzie's death by chance. Such a delay could not be tolerated — to keep her captive in this world was no longer justifiable by any moral code — Lowe's or otherwise. I tried to remember every conversation I had held with Lowe on this subject in the hope of recalling some key fact, but it was all in vain. I had asked him once what would happen when she was set free but he had said nothing of the method only that when given her freedom Lizzie would be able to choose whether to go onward or to remain in this world.

"*Could* she choose to stay?" I had asked.

"It is impossible to imagine that she would," Lowe had replied, batting the query away as if it were utterly meaningless. "There is nothing here for her now and in any case she would need to make herself a new anchor and there is no object in this world to which she has formed anything like a strong enough attachment."

Though I could remember nothing else of use, I was firmly convinced that, when the time came, I would know what to do; or that Lizzie herself would show me. The miles passed quickly, and I barely noticed them as I trudged on, lost in contemplation. It was just nearing half past three when I finally found myself standing before a narrow but tall terraced house that looked out across the fields of Dollis Brook. On the horizon I could dimly make out the silhouette of the railway viaduct against the pale

212

evening sky.

I stood at the door and knocked. For what seemed like an eternity there was nothing but silence, then there was a rustling sound from behind the green painted wood and the rattle of a bolt being drawn back. The door opened a fraction and I could just about make out the eyes of Samuel Ivor, peering at me from the darkness within. When he realised who I was, he pulled back the door and stepped out over the threshold with an expression of startled and utter disbelief.

"Mr Ivor," I said, for he was at that moment quite incapable of speech. "I hope you can forgive my conduct earlier. I was not — that is to say, I have not been for some time now — in my right mind."

He nodded, though it was evident he did not comprehend. In many ways this did not matter. It was for my benefit that the words of confession were uttered.

"May I come in?"

He nodded mutely and stepped back, gesturing for me to follow him inside. The house was oddly capacious given its outward appearance, but this impression, I decided, was given by the absence of any furniture of note. There was a rough sort of a table in the dining room with two plain chairs either side of it. The living room — or what I glimpsed of it as we passed — was entirely empty save for one battered, green leather chair and a forlorn and moth-eaten standard lamp.

"Are you moving out, Mr Ivor?" I asked as he led me through into the dining room and gestured for me to have a seat at the table.

"What would give you that idea?"

"You seem to have very little furniture."

The man grunted, almost in amusement. "What use have I

213

for furniture?" he said. "This is a house, not a home. It's shelter and warmth and it's a place to sleep."

There was real truth in his words, and I was deeply saddened to think of the change that must have been wrought in this man when first his wife and then his daughter were snatched from him.

"Do you work nearby?" I asked, hoping to kindle some conversation out of the ugly silence.

He shrugged. "Now and again — whenever there's work needs doing. There's not many things I've not turned a hand to in my time."

There was a very long pause which must have lasted several minutes.

"I suppose you'll want some food," he said, gruffly.

"Not at all," said I, mindful of the accusations he had levelled against Lowe in the office. "I want nothing from you, Mr Ivor."

"Nonetheless," he said, "a man can't go hungry on Christmas Eve. I'll fetch us something."

If truth be told I was glad of the offer — both because the long walk from Victoria had furnished me with a painful appetite and because his absence as he prepared the food gave me time to think. The confidence that had overflowed in me when I had first departed from the company of Lowe was now diminishing rapidly and I was deeply concerned that I should not be able to release Lizzie after all. Furthermore, another thought had now occurred to me: Lowe would surely know where I had gone and with what purpose. How long would it be before he arrived to prevent me? Indeed, the more I thought about it, the more puzzled I was that he was not already here.

From Lowe, my thoughts drifted to Molly. I cursed myself

for having been so blind — so stupid. She had never been my friend, still less had she ever intended to be anything more. He had set her on me as a watch. It was a clever stratagem, I had to concede that, for from her Lowe would come to hear of opinions and thoughts that I should never have dared share with him. Fool! Fool not to have wondered how it was that she was always available to see me at a moment's notice or that she was so often out in the street in front of Lowe's office. My head had been turned by her beauty and wit and I had been happy to overlook these inconsistencies as trifles.

I was arrested in this self-reprimand by the return of Ivor with the meal. Despite all his protestations to the contrary, it was in fact a good and hearty spread. It was what my mother would have called 'honest food' and it tasted all the better for it; the wholesomeness of the bread and cheese and ham unmarred by the frivolous eloquences of the fare I had endured at Lowe's. The supper was restorative and I was now once more certain of what must be accomplished, though I made a poor dinner guest and we ate in silence. I cursed myself for not having Lowe's wit and social graces and then cursed myself further for allowing his memory so much esteem, but it was no good. He was never far from my thoughts. His eventual coming (which I counted a certainty) brought me both fear and reassurance in equal measure. Occasionally I would be suddenly alarmed by the noise of a passing carriage and stiffen — listening intently to see whether it might stop outside of our door, but none did. Ivor noted this peculiarity in my behaviour, and at the third instance, broke the silence.

"I assume Mr Lowe does not know you are here?"

"He does not."

For several minutes there was nothing further and then,

suddenly Ivor asked me a most direct question.

"Can you tell me, Mr Fairlea, why Mr Lowe is so set against me in this matter?"

This placed me in a quandary. I did not wish the man to know what had become of Lizzie's spirit — nor to implicate myself in the business, but I must offer some response, not to do so would have lost me all credibility.

"I suspect that Mr Lowe does not see this as a task worthy of his dignity," I uttered the phrase with deep contempt so as to make it clear that this was not at all my position.

"And yet he came here once before," said Ivor, not looking at me, but clearing the plates and cutlery from the table and fetching from the sideboard an unusually large Christmas pudding and placing it on the table before us alongside a jug of cream and two glasses of brandy.

"My sister," he said, with a lazy gesture at the pudding. "She worries about me."

I smiled, but he had piqued my interest. "You said Mr Lowe *did* come to assist you in the past?"

"Not to assist me," said Ivor. "Never that. In fact I never knew the man, never heard of him nor had cause to at that time. It was just after—" he paused and looked towards the window which gave a mournful prospect over the meadows.

"Yes," I said. "I understand."

"And it was well before all the trouble began."

"And Lowe came to you?" This seemed quite extraordinary. Why should Lowe, who had been so concrete in his resolve not to come to this of all places have returned so soon after Lizzie's death?

"He didn't say much," said Ivor, answering the question framed by my face. "Just stood in the doorway and looked at me

— but it was like he was looking through me — as if I wasn't really there. I asked him what he wanted, but he didn't reply at first, just stood there, staring. Then he said he had something to tell me. I waited, but still he said nothing."

"Are you sure this was Lowe," I asked. I could not imagine the man behaving in such a way and less still could I imagine what he might have wanted to impart to Samuel Ivor.

"I could draw you his picture," said Ivor confidently. "Though I didn't come to learn his name until some years later when I saw him going into his offices, but that night I didn't know him from Adam."

"And he just stared at you?"

"For at least two or three minutes. Then he suddenly seemed to come to himself. He apologised for wasting my time and then said he'd made a terrible mistake and begged my leave."

"And that was it?" said I, astonished. "He just left?"

Ivor nodded, but then caught himself. "Not quite — just before he turned to go he put his hand in his pocket and said he had something he wanted to give me, but then he changed his mind and walked away again muttering how much of a mistake it had been."

A chill passed through me. I had a strong suspicion that the item Lowe had wanted to hand back to Ivor was, even now, resting in my own pocket. The man was human after all then. The acquisition of the girl's soul had not been without the sort of moral confusion against which he had so often chided me.

"And you have no thought as to the intended purpose of his visit?"

Ivor shrugged. "None," he said. "At the time I thought it might be someone who had witnessed Lizzie's death, who had something to say about the business, but that was wishful thinking."

"And what do you think now?"

"Perhaps he came to warn me? Perhaps to prevent her from returning?"

I smiled weakly; despite the appalling treatment he had received at Lowe's hands, Ivor still looked for goodness in the man. I was about to reassure him that I would do everything in my power to ease his suffering when we were suddenly plunged into utter darkness. The three candles that had illuminated the table and the gaslamp on the dresser were extinguished simultaneously and there was nothing in that silence but the gentle, creeping crackle of ice forming a thin coating of frost on every surface of the room.

"She is here now," said Ivor in a terrified whisper. "I shall leave you to your work."

This was quite unexpected. I had anticipated that Ivor would be as keen as I to see the business through to its conclusion. The prospect of facing the spectre alone was terrifying. "You're not leaving?" I asked, desperately.

"I shall go to my room," said he. "Wake me when it is over."

"Mr Ivor," I said as composedly as I could. "It may very well be that I need assistance with the process. I am on uncharted ground here and I should rather not be left alone. Surely you wish to help me release your daughter?"

I heard him breathing in the blackness, slow and measured breaths; breaths that indicated he had given this subject a good degree of thought.

"And what if I don't want her to go, Mr Fairlea?" he said, a tinge of shame creeping into the edges of his voice. "What if, when it comes to it, I can't let her?"

I did not reply, but I understood the point he was trying to

218

make. The form of Lizzie Ivor who now resided in his house when not employed by Lowe and myself might well have been a torment to him for a decade, but she was still an imprint of the daughter he had loved.

"I know she must go onward," he said, mournfully. "I know that it is right, but I don't have to like it, Mr Fairlea. I hope you can understand that?"

"I can," said I. "I do"

"Then you will also understand that I cannot be present when it is done — I would be a danger to both you and to her if I did so."

I set my teeth. What he said made sense, there was no denying it. Then he bid me goodnight, rose from the table, crossed the room and ascended the stairs in the hallway. I was alone with Lizzie now. I brought all my resolve to bear on not permitting myself to wish for the easy confidence of Lowe's company and instead concentrated on what I knew must be done.

"Lizzie," I said, feeling strangely foolish to mutter her name into the darkness at large. "I have come here to help you."

There was no response. Had she left? Did Lowe have some other means of summoning her back? Was this the reason he had not followed me? But I was worrying in vain. A noise arose out of the darkness, a peculiar scraping sort of a sound. I reached into my inside pocket where it had become my habit to keep several books of matches. I struck one and then leaned forward in the direction of the sound. It came from the surface of the table which Lizzie had already covered in a sheet of ice that must have been near to an inch thick. Into this, clutched in a hand that I could not see, she was driving the cheese knife so that it scratched out characters on the table. The movement went on slowly and deliberately for several minutes until, finally, it stopped. I blew away the shavings of ice and read the inscription.

"WAIT."

I sat back. Wait? Wait for what? Wait for Lowe? For Ivor? For how long should I wait? I had not expected this. I had imagined her making all sorts of impossible and grotesque requests, but I had not prepared myself to endure darkness and inaction for some unspecified length of time.

"How long, Lizzie?" I asked, impatiently. But by way of an answer she only picked up the knife once more and underlined the word. Then I felt something so terrifying that it stopped my breath; I felt the light touch of a tiny frozen hand upon my arm. I dared not look, but screwed up my eyes tight. I did not wish to see who or what was now clasping my elbow and gently tugging at me. In closing my eyes, of course, I neglected the match which quickly burned down to my fingers causing me to throw it down onto the table where it immediately extinguished with a hiss. The tugging was becoming more insistent now and I felt compelled to obey it. I opened my eyes — though it was so dark that it made no difference at all when I did so — and rose from the chair, allowing myself to be guided by that absent hand on my arm. We moved slowly across the room, I stumbling several times as we did so and knocking first into a chair and then the edge of the dresser and then finally into the corner of the dining table. Now I felt the hand pull my arm upwards and away from me and change the grip so that it rested on my own fist. This it placed upon the cold brass of a doorknob, and lightly tapped upon it to indicate that I should open the aperture to which it belonged. Having done so and the hand having relinquished its hold upon me, I felt brave enough to risk another match.

I stood now in a room that might have served as a slightly oversized study. Its current purpose was not entirely clear, for the

220

illumination given by the match was very poor indeed and I was forced to strike two or three more before I had my bearings. As with the rest of the house, there was little furniture in the chamber and what little there was had a thick coating of dust upon it such that it could not have been used for many years. There was a large window which again gave a prospect on the brook meadows and a clearer one this time for there were no trees to obscure it. The sun had long since set, but a defiant crisp, blue remnant hung in the western sky and by it I could just make out the meander of the river and the arches of the viaduct. I had moved closer to better observe the view — supposing that it was this that I had been brought into the room to see, when a sudden sharp noise rang out like a gunshot. I spun around with the match and saw by it that a flap on what I had supposed to have been a little wooden cabinet on the wall of the room opposite the window had raised itself, and there lay beneath it a little piano keyboard not dissimilar from my own.

I knew what she wanted.

I don't know how long we played for — she and I together. Time seemed to hold as little importance for me as it did for her. We began with the pieces we had rehearsed in my rooms, but soon the structure and form of the music was lost and my fingers traced patterns on the fractured wooden keys that were unfamiliar to me and yet somehow poignant and beautiful and she caught up those gentle rumblings in the bass and flung them high and echoing into the upper registers, fluttering and pirouetting around the melody with poise and expert flourishes. After a while I closed my eyes, for somehow I no longer needed them and the music continued and I felt the pair of us, who ought by rights to have been separated by an intractable veil, to be closer to each other than ever before, almost as if I could see her sitting beside

221

me, her chill fingers resting on the keyboard.

Then the music stopped, as if by common consent. Three gentle but distinctly final chords rang out into the shadowy corners of that room and I opened my eyes. To my surprise I found that the chamber was no longer dark, but illuminated by the brilliant light of a full moon which had now risen over the meadows. I looked at its brightness with some strange sense of achievement — as if by our music we had somehow summoned it, called it from wherever it had been before.

Her touch was at my arm once again, but its pull was not the gentle suggestion of before but rather an insistent, urgent tugging that left me no choice other than to follow its lead. She pulled me out of the music room (for that, I now saw clearly by the moon's illumination, was the function of the place) back through the dining room, along the hall and then out. Out through the front door into the frozen chill of that Christmas Eve; out through the wrought iron gate at the foot of the garden which slid silently open on its hinge as if it were party to some great secret and then out, out, out across the road and into the silent meadows of Dollis Brook.

The moon shone down so brightly here that it was as if it were some twisted inversion of the day, for I could make out every detail — every blade of grass, every edge of every stone on the gravel path. The colours were false, brooding, as if everything vibrant and living were asleep and only the core essence of each thing remained. A rabbit skittered just a few yards ahead, and from somewhere nearby I heard the gentle call of an owl. The touch left my arm, and foolish as it will sound, I found myself filled with a terrifying abandonment. I could only then have been some thirty or forty feet from the house of Samuel Ivor and from his aid should I have needed it, but something about that place felt horribly wrong. I cast about me for some sign of the familiar spirit, for I had come to take some comfort in her presence, but found nothing. Something moved in the copse to my right, but the light of the great silver disc, so obliging in the open, recoiled from the wooded places as if even it feared to enter there.

There was another movement to my left and I took a step back. Had it been a bat or a movement of the branches in the breeze? But the night was uncommonly still. I began to lose my reason; some premonitory sense in my mind, perhaps, tearing at my obstinate legs and insisting on a retreat. Another movement, but it was nothing, a small bird, disturbed by my presence, broke free of the strangling boughs and soared out into the open and disappeared into the heights. How I envied its freedom. I allowed myself the relief of knowing the source of the movements, and chastising myself for my childish fears, I resolved to trudge on, for I considered that having brought me to this place, it was Lizzie's intent that I should go onwards onto the meadow itself.

There was then a curious sensation on the back of my neck, something cold and wet and small. I put a hand there and found that a point near the base of my nape had a damp spot upon it. Even as my hand rested there I felt another spot fall and another and another. Withdrawing my hand to examine them I discovered, to my enormous surprise, that they were snowflakes. Beautiful and cold and crisp they sat upon my hand staring innocently up at me. There would have been nothing strange in this, of course, save the fact that the snow appeared to have fallen from a cloudless sky. The grim grey covering that had been so much a feature of my time in London seemed at last to have been drawn back and the moon, which still shone out grandly from its place above the horizon, was feted royally by a night over-brimming with stars. From where, then, had these flakes fallen?

I knew the answer, of course, but I dare not allow myself to think it. Instead, I moved on a few paces — at times whistling or humming and attempting, by degrees, to comfort myself with the idea that the snow cloud must be so high and so small that its presence could not be detected by my feeble eyes. Yet my neck continued to register that chill sensation and the flurry seemed to be growing in strength — as if it sought my attention. But I stoutly refused to turn, for I knew what I should see. I knew now what Lizzie Ivor wanted to show me and I could not bear it. For in the horror of that deed lay the truth — the proof that I had been a willing accessory to something monstrous and beyond redemption.

At length I came out along the side of the brook — its banks long since subdued by the floodwaters so that the flow languished expansively across the centre of the meadow; a dormant malice. I stopped when I saw it and could not shake from my mind the memory of the story Lowe had told me. How he had happened across Lizzie here too late.

Then I saw her.

The breath caught in my throat and a sudden paralysis passed through me so that I thought I had been turned to stone on the spot, for there she was, or rather, there she was not. The snow flurry had moved suddenly on ahead of me and it was now directly before me, a thick fall that seemed to come from nowhere but to occupy space some eight or nine feet high and several yards wide. So freely and so busily did the flakes fall that they formed a white curtain, shimmering and glistening by the moon's light. In the centre of that curtain was a perfect silhouette of a girl, every detail of her thin little form picked out by the descending flakes. Every so often a rogue particle of snow would

224

alight in the place where her face ought to have been and in doing so would describe, for a moment, the shape of her nose or the curve of her lower lip. For some moments she stood still and waited for me to come to myself.

At length my heartbeat slowed and the torpor that had held my ribcage relaxed a little and a reassuring cloud of vapour before my face indicated that I was, once again, able to breathe. Then she nodded at me and turned away so that the outline of her hair became visible. She moved off a few paces and I was not a little relieved until she turned, and with a slow and deliberate gesture, indicated that I must follow.

CHAPTER THIRTEEN

I had followed her for nearly a quarter of a mile at a safe distance, she pausing at intervals to be sure that I was still in pursuit. We came to a place where the waters of the brook were at their widest and where the strength of the current was clear even through the thin sheet of ice that lay above. Here she stopped and waited for me to draw close. The light of the moon reflecting off the surface of the water made the place even brighter yet somehow, darker and more dangerous. I fixed my eyes on the figure of the girl, waiting. She stood facing me and then, slowly, raised her arm and pointed to a place on the further shore. At first I dared not take my eyes from the spirit. it was not that I feared that she might do me any harm, yet there was, somehow, safety in keeping her in view; but the finger that was not there gestured urgently at the place and I reluctantly turned to look.

A dozen yards off, or perhaps slightly more, there was another miniature flurry by which was depicted a curious scene. There was a solitary figure in shadow walking slowly along the edge of the water. She (for it was, on closer inspection, the familiar figure of the girl herself) strolled along easily and lightly and I marked in her step the gaiety and carelessness that had been so absent in the sombre procession we had made to this place. I became conscious then that the spirit was illustrating for me something that had happened in the past, something I knew she wanted me to see, and in my heart of hearts I knew I had already imagined. The figure continued its progress along the edge of the river, turning and skipping every few steps, and once or twice, spinning on the spot with arms outstretched. Although I observed the spectacle in dead silence, I felt sure that if only I could hear her, the child would be singing. At the third pirouette, however, I saw something fly from the girl's outstretched wrist and tumble onto the frozen river where it slid gently across the surface and came to rest somewhere near the middle. The girl clutched her arm close to herself and I caught my breath, for this, I knew was the moment at which she had made the fateful decision to step out onto the ice. She looked first backward and then forward for any sign of someone who might assist her and then gingerly placed one foot onto the surface. Finding that it supported her weight she moved another step forward and then another. By slow degrees she crossed to the point where lay the bracelet and stooped to pick it up. Then she began to retreat to the bank.

I was confused. I had expected, at any moment, to see the frail form sink through the ice, though another part of me knew with unblinking certainty why she had not.

Then she was before me again. Right close to me so that the falling snow picked out every detail of her face which was screwed up into an agony of indignant fury from which I recoiled. Her hand flung itself out to her left and she indicated a further snowfall and a further figure. It was the likeness of a man, not much taller than myself, with a confident bearing; he was watching the girl intently from the bank and waiting for her to return to it with her prize clutched safely in her hands.

It was the likeness of Percival Lowe.

I would have known that silhouette anywhere. His precise face and strong stance would have been recognisable to me the world over, but if he had not come to aid the girl then why regard her so closely? I knew, of course. I suppose I had always known.

The girl made the bank, and elated by her good fortune in retrieving the bracelet, began to skip once again, although this time she kept the precious ornament clutched tightly in her fist. The figure of Lowe began to follow her and a sudden stop by the girl indicated that he had offered her some word of greeting. She turned to face him, and they seemed to exchange some words, Lowe pointed at the river several times and she nodded and shook her head in earnest. I assumed that he was admonishing her and illuminating the foolishness of stepping out onto the ice. She, in reply, was explaining her purpose, indeed she held out the bracelet to him as if by way of explanation.

As soon as the figure of Lowe caught sight of the bracelet, his whole body seemed to change shape; he seemed to grow suddenly larger and more formidable and he instantly drew closer to the girl. She, sensing his changed attitude, trotted backwards a few paces, but in doing so seemed to catch her foot on a stone and tumbled down so that she lay flat on her back on the bank. Lowe advanced now and stood over her. He extended his hand to help her up and she took it, but once she was righted he did not release her, but instead pulled her in closer to him and caught up her other arm in a tight grip. Then he began to work his way along the bank, staring at the surface, scanning it carefully. A few moments later he seemed to find what he sought and she, all the while struggling against him, pulled back with all her strength — eyes wide in terror.

The falling snow illuminated an aperture in the ice where the frozen surface had been fractured. I knew what must happen next and I turned away, but no sooner had I done so than the terrible figure of Lizzie Ivor appeared before me once more and demanded, by a gesture of her hand, that I watch the tragedy unfold. I saw Lowe lift Lizzie in the air and turn her upside down

228

so that her head was now perilously close to the water. She struggled against him, but her frail strength was no match for the heavy purpose that had filled his limbs. Slowly, dreadfully slowly, he lowered her into the water until her head was completely submerged. The struggling took on a terrifying urgency, her legs and arms which had so few moments before been flung out carelessly in the innocence of youth, now kicked and flailed wildly against the vice-like arms of her captor.

Then, quite suddenly, the scene became quite still.

The struggling had stopped abruptly, and the form of the girl was now limp and inert against his. It seemed as if her limpness was a contagion, for it seemed now to flood Lowe's own limbs and he collapsed back onto the bank, his torso heaving and his arms shaking. The body of Lizzie Ivor lay next to him, the head still resting in the water.

I should have been surprised or disgusted, but I was not. I had known the truth with certainty ever since Lowe had told me his version of the story all those months ago. It had been impossible to imagine that, once in possession of that extraordinary piece of knowledge, he would have waited for a child to die of natural causes before acting. No doubt he had observed Lizzie on the brook before, had planned this whole episode with his usual care. Indeed, I had no difficulty in believing that it had been he who had fractured the ice in that spot so that the murder might be more efficiently done.

Murder. That was what he had done.

Lowe would no doubt dress it up in some other form, would excuse it on the grounds of a superior code of morality or would reason his way out of the guilt. But the facts were stark and irrefutable. He had done murder.

It had taken its toll on him, though — he had not fully

maintained that aggressive confidence and dignity that had characterised the public face of Percival Lowe this last decade. The figure on the bank still lay there panting, but now sobbing too — sobbing with the same fierce passion that had emanated so often from behind the locked doors of his rooms. His hands had risen to his face, and when they fell away from his eyes and he looked down at the result of his industry, it reviled him and he slid himself up the muddy bank away from the corpse. Now I understood the days and hours he had spent in solitude, for by snaring the spirit of Lizzie Ivor he had perpetuated not only a memory of her, but a vivid recollection of what *he* had done; the atrocity *he* had committed. The agony of the guilt lay, always, just beneath the surface ready to lunge upward at him through the ice and drag him down into the depths.

The figure seemed, at length, to master itself. The heavy movements of the torso became more regular and at last its back straightened. He rose to his feet and dusted off some of the mud from his trousers. Then, as if it were the most ordinary thing in the world, he strode forward, and prizing open the dead girl's fist, removed the bracelet from it and placed it in a pocket within his waistcoat. Next, having first surveyed his surroundings to make quite sure that he was not observed, he placed a foot on the small of the girl's back and with one smooth, fluid motion, nudged the body forwards so that it slid easily through the hole in the ice and disappeared from view.

There the vision ended and the silence and cold of the brook returned to me. I looked about for any sign of the girl but there was none. There was no snow to be seen except for the odd little piles in the places where she had picked out the horror of her death.

"What must I do?" I whispered to the empty air. "Show me

how to release you."

Then I became aware of a curious sensation at the top of my left leg. Something in the pocket of my trousers on that side had become suddenly cold, so cold that it almost burned the skin of my thigh. Hurriedly I thrust in my hand and withdrew from it the bracelet. I could barely hold it for the sting of its frozen surface and was obliged to wrap it in a handkerchief to protect my hand. Looking ahead of me, I saw that a frosty footprint had appeared on the ground before me and was quickly followed by another. I walked on and the prints soon turned into a trail that led me onwards faster and faster until we came at last in sight of the viaduct. Lizzie was moving so rapidly that it was all I could do to keep up with her. There was a peculiarity to her movements too, for though she would sprint forwards for a sudden burst, she would then seem to pause a few moments before she went on, and when I caught up to her at these places I saw that the footprints were turned backwards to face the way she had come.

My first conclusion was that she must be turning to check that I was following her, but the logic of this rang hollow in my mind. If she were so concerned for me to follow, then why continue at such an alarming pace? Why not simply walk a few steps in front as she had done when she led me out from the house? I darted after her as best I could and for a few minutes I could devote the power of my mind to nothing but scouring the darkness in search of her footprints. When we reached the structure of the viaduct, however, she slowed to mount the embankment which led the scrub and earth up to the brickwork and when she paused to look back I did too and saw, to my horror, that we were no longer alone.

It was Lowe.

It will seem, no doubt, absurd to report that I, who was in the

231

company of the dead should have felt such a shudder of fear at the presence of a fellow living, breathing human, but the sight of him turned my blood cold. He did not run, nor was his walking pace especially fast; he simply came on — his strides measured with the rhythmic precision of a metronome. Lizzie, I realised, ran in fear of him. In a terrifying moment of lucidity I realised that her fate rested entirely with me; if Lowe were to reclaim the bracelet there was no knowing what tasks he would put her to, what punishments he might inflict for her betrayal of the secret that bound them. I pushed on and half-scrambled, half-climbed the last few feet of masonry to pull myself up onto the top of the viaduct. There I stood, panting, looking back at the man whom I had been so long content to call my mentor. Lizzie had stopped too, a solitary pair of footprints loitered only a handful of feet away from me.

As I looked back, however, I saw that Lowe had suddenly put on a burst of speed. He was moving now with athletic agility couched in an attitude of sudden desperation. This change in him vexed me — what had provoked it? I felt, once again, the touch of a snowflake on the back of my neck, and turning, I saw Lizzie Ivor far more clearly than ever before; the blizzard she had invoked around her bringing such dazzling definition to her features that I was able not only to regard her in her childish beauty — for there was no doubt she had been a pretty girl — but also even to see that from her eyes there flowed a steady thread of tears which followed down the curves of her cheeks and traced the edges of a mouth that was forming over and over the single word: 'please'. This solitary syllable she accompanied with a desperate gesture of imprecation, clasping her hands at me and shuddering in her desire.

I was so lost in the vision that I did not notice a further

232

shuddering that ran, now, through me too, nor did I sense, in anything but the vaguest terms, that Lowe had almost reached the balustrade of the viaduct and that he was hailing me loudly. I was drawn now to nothing but the girl; by the brightness of the snow. The rest of the surrounding world fell away into a shroud of darkness. A profound silence descended upon me and so clear now was the outline of her lips as she implored me to do... I knew not what, that I felt I could almost hear her pleading. For what was she asking me? What must I do? Then, some part of my mind awoke, and I recalled that I still held the bracelet, that slim chain by which her captivity was assured, in my hand. I looked down at it and her eyes suddenly seemed to sparkle; she unclasped her hands and held them out — must I give the thing to her?

I extended my hand slowly, allowing the bracelet to dangle in that strange snowfall, but though she continued to hold out her hand as if she desired to receive it, she took a step back. I followed, but the process was repeated again — I offering the bracelet, she appearing to desire it more than anything, and yet retreating from me. Four times we proceeded in this manner, but finally, on the fifth occasion of my offering she put her hands out and made a cup with them and indicated by a gesture of her eyes that I was to drop the bracelet into it. This I did with great relief, for it had grown so cold now that even the shroud of my handkerchief offered little relief from its frozen surface. I stretched out my hand and released my grip, but to my dismay the object fell straight through the place where her hands ought to have been and landed on the ground at her feet. My dismay, however, was not matched in her, for when I brought my eyes up to regard her face once again I saw there an expression of serene joy mingled with gratitude. Though her features were sculpted from the falling snow, they seemed to grow suddenly warmer, as if illuminated by a lantern. She took a step towards me and pursed her lips as if she would kiss me. Hardly knowing why I did so I bent down and offered her my forehead which she touched lightly with her frozen lips.

In that instant everything changed.

Whatever enchantment or other nefarious art had, up until then, shielded me from the reality of my predicament vanished with the girl and the silence and mystery was replaced with a deafening roaring, squealing noise and a fierce, blinding light that seemed to be bearing down upon me with impossible speed, its power causing the whole world around me to shudder violently in anticipation of impending destruction. I stood, rooted to the spot as the locomotive tore towards me out of the darkness, with a raw power no force on earth could prevent.

Suddenly I felt arms close around me from behind; a strong, uncompromising grip that crushed what little breath remained out of my lungs and raised me up several feet into the air. Time seemed to come almost to a halt and my senses to sharpen intensely so that I became instantly aware of everything: the golden showers of sparks flying out from those terrible wheels as we rolled through the air; the acrid scent of coal and smoke and steam; the blazing heat on my face; and the thunderous tread of the wheels as the train rattled harmlessly past and away from us into silence. And yet in the midst of all this confusion and violence one small detail did not escape me. The bracelet which had fallen directly onto a rail was swallowed up beneath the wheels and shattered into countless fragments which exploded into the night until, at length, all was peaceful and still.

The moon continued to shine down unperturbed from the heavens, as if what it had just witnessed was nothing out of the ordinary. As if the severance of an unnatural connection between this world and the hereafter were not in the least unusual and I believe in that moment I felt, more than I had at any other time in my life, how small and insignificant are the lives of men in the grander scheme. By the silvery light I took a moment to survey my surroundings and found that I had been flung clear against the wall of the viaduct, but that I was completely unharmed. Turning to my left I saw my rescuer, also apparently uninjured, reclining against the brickwork and attempting, as I was, to reclaim his breath.

"She is gone," I said. I did not know whether I intended it as a question or a statement, my certainty of the truth unhinged by my habit of deference.

Lowe said nothing, only nodded.

"You should have left me," I said flatly. It was true. Lowe must have known what Lizzie would show me on the bank of the brook. Indeed, had I been destroyed in the same instant as the bracelet then matters would surely have turned out exactly as he would have preferred.

Again, Lowe said nothing,, but with a significant effort he rose to his feet and brushed himself down. Then taking a few uncertain steps towards me, he extended his hand. I looked at it for a few seconds and then took it. He heaved me up.

"We must hurry," he said in an empty tone. "Another train will be along in a few minutes."

We crossed the tracks and found the place at which the bank joined the bridge and slowly began to descend once more. As we did so, I tried to bring some small sense of order to the jumble of half-thoughts and memories that flooded my mind. Had Lizzie tried to kill me? Had she intended to punish me for my part in Lowe's crime? Or had it been an accident? Had she been so delighted in the promise of her imminent release that she had forgotten the frailty of flesh and blood? Or had she known Lowe would save me? Had she waited for the precise moment to ensure not that I should die, but that I should be safe? Reasoning was futile. She was gone and I should never know her intentions.

The descent accomplished, we began our walk back across the common. For several minutes we continued in silence until I could bear it no longer.

"You killed her," I blurted out, suddenly.

Lowe did not respond, but only quickened his pace so that he drew a little in front of me.

"She was a child, Lowe!"

Still nothing.

"You *killed* a child!" I insisted.

"Do you think it was easy?" he said in a sudden explosion of fury. "Do you think I revelled in it? Do you think I enjoyed it? Do you think it has not cost me?" He had caught me up by the shoulders and shook me with each question, his eyes burning into mine with the light of hell behind them.

"Cost you?" I spat in disbelief. "What did it cost her?"

"I am a pioneer!" he raged. "I am the first to do what I have done! What moment in human history, what invention, what accomplishment can hold a candle to what *I* have done? You tell me which great scion of our age has done more to explain or understand the human condition than I?"

He released his grip on me and turned away into the night.

"You don't understand it at all," I said quietly. "What understanding have you gained? You dabble, Lowe; you have no more idea than I where Lizzie Ivor is now."

"I've a damn sight more idea than anyone else on this planet," Lowe raged, turning back to face me.

"And what have you achieved?" I persisted. "Have you

shared your discoveries with eminent philosophers and scientists?"

"Of course not," he exclaimed.

"Of course not," I echoed. "You have put yourself at the centre of the universe and you have bent its most intimate laws to adhere to your will." The thought of that great moon, hanging silently over us, untouched by the drama of the night filled me once again with that pressing sense of our insignificance. "You think you exercise control, Lowe, but you do not! You are meddling with forces that are not meant for human hands."

"Spare me the Sunday school lecture, Fairlea," he scoffed. "Don't you see that you are limited by your crude understanding of the world? You are no more than a child who thinks that thunder is the noise of giants traipsing about the clouds. You have no idea of the potential we have — no idea of what we could accomplish."

"And what have you accomplished?" I said. "Fraud? Deceit? Has it brought you happiness?"

I do not know from whence I drew this sudden strength and boldness. Days or perhaps even hours before I should not have dared to speak to Lowe in such a manner.

But Lowe's anger seemed to leave him then; the fight seemed to evaporate from him as if none of it mattered any more.

"We should get back," said he quietly. We had drawn towards the road now and I saw that the cab was waiting for us a little distance from the house of Samuel Ivor. "Crane insisted on awaiting our return."

I knew I must go with him though I could not say why. We began to walk towards the cab, but a sudden thought turned my feet back toward the house.

"Where are you going?" asked Lowe, though I could tell he

237

knew the answer, just as he knew what the outcome of my enquiry would be.

I lit the candles in the dining room, and taking one of them, mounted the stairs in the direction in which I had last seen Samuel Ivor departing. I called out his name as I ascended but there was no response. Some sense of what awaited me slowed my feet just as it drew me, inexplicably to the door behind which I knew I should find him.

I could tell by looking at him that he had been dead more than an hour. The hastily tied rough noose by which he hung suspended in the centre of the room, creaked slightly as the draught spun the body gently round.

I said nothing to Lowe when I returned to the cab, but the look he gave me told me that he already knew. "He could not bear to lose her again," he said, drily. Then, without so much as a pause he raised a hand to the roof of the cab and rapped sharply upon it. "Drive on."

CHAPTER FOURTEEN

I could not decide whether it was a comfort or a disappointment to me that all I possessed in the world was packed with relative ease into a small case that Crane had procured. On the one hand it made my imminent descent into poverty loom all the more forebodingly before me, but on the other it gave me some solace to see that I was able to extricate myself so easily from at least the material fabric of Lowe's world. The packing done, I sat upon my bed and surveyed the room by the dismal light of that overcast Christmas morning. The piano sat alone and unattended in the corner. I knew I should never play again, for the memory of Lizzie Ivor would, I was convinced, remain a vivid one right up until the day of my own death. The books too, I had decided to discard, for these had been purchased with the funds realised by our abuse of her spirit and I would have none of it.

Lowe entered the room without knocking and looked about him. "I see you are resolved to leave," said he. "I will not stop you."

"I do not see that I have any other choice," I replied.

There was a long, frozen pause between us as each fumbled for something to say. At length we both spoke at once, but he fell silent at my words. "You need not worry that I should go to the police, sir," I said.

He gave a quiet little laugh that reminded me suddenly of my former impression of him, when I had almost idolised him for his easy manner and confidence. "That is kind of you," he said.

"But I had no cause to worry on that account. After all, what evidence have you at your disposal? Would you tell the police that you came by the truth by the revelation of a ghost? I think not, Mr Fairlea."

He was right, of course. I should just as well take myself off to Bedlam as try to implicate him in Lizzie Ivor's murder.

"There is nothing I can do or say, then," he said, taking on a more serious tone, "that will convince you to remain here?"

I shook my head. "I cannot stay, Mr Lowe."

He took a step closer to me and extended his hand. "Shall we then at least part as friends?"

I eyed the hand, and for a second, I considered taking it, but then I remembered the cruel uncompromising grip of those fingers around the frail form of Lizzie Ivor. After a few moments he withdrew it. "So be it," he said, crisply. "Crane has hailed a cab and instructed the driver to take you wherever you desire."

"I shall go home, sir," said I. "Directly. I have been away too long — I think I have forgotten who I am."

"As you wish."

I rose and picked up the trunk by its handle and moved to the door.

"Do you have any message for Molly," he said. There was the slightest hint of cruelty in his voice as his spoke and I resented this last twist of the knife. I turned to face him again.

"You may tell her that I wish her every happiness," I said. I had intended that to be my parting shot to him, but I still felt the bite of curiosity.

"How did you know?" I said.

"Know what?"

"How did you know that she would go?"

"Who?" Lowe was becoming impatient.

240

"Lizzie — how did you know she wouldn't stay even after the anchor had been broken?"

He gave a rough, contemptuous snort. "Don't be ridiculous," he said. "After all that time yearning to get away, why would she stay?"

"For revenge, perhaps," I said, darkly. I saw him stiffen and was pleased at the effect my words had had upon him.

"Impossible," he said, more for his own assurance than for mine. "She would have had to have found a new anchor — without it she would be entirely lost."

I nodded, solemnly, picked up my case and walked past him out of the room, all the while feeling his eyes boring into the back of my neck. Crane was waiting for me in the office when I had passed though the corridor, but the usual impassiveness of his manner was strangely absent and his features were, in fact, peculiarly animate. As soon as he saw me he darted forward and took me by the arm.

"You *must* stay," he insisted in a hoarse whisper. "You *must not* leave, Mr Fairlea." I wondered at the transformation in Crane's character. I could have sworn that, on the previous day, he had been exultant at my departure.

"I cannot, Mr Crane," I said resolutely. How much did the old man know? Would he stay if he knew what Lowe had done? The old man looked me up and down once again and an expression of resignation passed across his brow. He stepped back to allow me to pass, but then seemed to think better of it.

"Mr Fairlea," he said, again, his moustaches dancing madly. He stooped down to his desk and picked up an envelope from atop a small pile of unopened correspondence. "This arrived for you this morning."

I knew it must concern my mother, for I received no

241

correspondence on any other subject. I took the letter up quickly and read the words that I had expected now for some months. She had succumbed at last to the illness and my presence was required to attend to the business of the funeral and the disposal of her small estate.

Crane must have noticed the change of expression in my face, for he put an arm out to my shoulder at once and stiffly offered me his sympathies. I did not pause to accept them, but picking up my case, strode instead out into the street and hailed a cab to the station, the old man watching me, his open mouth forming the first syllable of words he was unable to speak.

I remember very little now of that journey which seemed to pass under grey and sombre skies and which was dominated by a war in my mind between the potent forces of remorse, relief and guilt. The remorse, of course was only natural. But the relief which came from knowing that my mother's passing lessened my burdens and also that her meagre estate would provide a temporary roof over my head if nothing else, quickly spiralled into guilt at these selfish thoughts which, in turn, perpetuated the remorse. I was, thus, barely conscious of a familiar figure on the road, at the station, on the train and indeed in the tiny cobbled streets of my little village.

I confess to having experienced a sudden surge of emotion upon seeing my home again — produced no doubt by my bereavement, and of course, by exhaustion. Nonetheless, in the light of all I had experienced in my time with Lowe, there seemed something about the place that was earthy — grounded even. These people, I reflected, would not even dare to contemplate a life beyond the tasks and offices of the daily machine; their only notion of God derived from stained glass or the lofty and incomprehensible ramblings of an ageing priest. Several of them recognised me as I went, but my injury prevented some from approaching. Though I knew that they recoiled only from my physical deformity, I could not help but worry that they pulled back, also, from some spiritual mutilation in me; perhaps my soul had been more damaged by my encounters than I knew.

Though I had intended to, I could not bring myself to stay in my mother's house that night; the sense of her presence in it was too overwhelming. I thus took what little money I had readily about me and impressed my predicament upon the caring nature of the wife of the innkeeper at The Hound, who reluctantly obliged me. I slept deeply — though my thoughts were constantly ravaged by mangled images of Lizzie and my mother and the terror-stricken faces of others that Lowe and I had prayed upon. I woke in the early hours of the morning, drenched in sweat and breathing heavily. After some minutes I returned to sleep but this time only to dream of the war, disturbing flashes of recollection and a searing pain in my arm. When I finally opened my eyes it was still not yet light — though it felt to me as if this night had gone on an eternity. I had begun to dress myself when I heard a noise that stopped me on the spot.

It was the gentle crackling sound of ice. I didn't move; I dared not. That noise — that noise that had been once so familiar to me and almost a comfort became now something that was beyond terrifying. It was small, but insistent and then it stopped.

There came a sudden rap at the door. I opened it at once and found that it was the innkeeper's wife with a tray of breakfast. She looked at my dishevelled appearance in astonishment.

"Is everything all right, sir?" she asked.

"The ice," I said, before I had the sense to think better of it. "The ice on the windows!"

"Yes," she said, sensing my confusion and employing the kind tone one might use with a child. "There's been a mighty frost this night, sir." She looked at me curiously; my uneasiness puzzled, and I think, amused her.

"The noise," I said hoarsely.

"Yes, sir," she said. "The glass cracks in the cold sometimes. I could try to find you another room tonight, sir, if it please you, but I dare say they'll all be the same. The windows is old, sir, you see?"

I exhaled slowly, watching my breath plume upwards before my face in the cold room.

"That won't be necessary," I said. "I shall not be staying here tonight."

She bobbed a polite curtsey and deposited my breakfast. She had produced, for reasons that I could not fathom, two plates of breakfast: one large and one small. As she placed them on the table she gave me a small smile and a wink.

"I don't mind, sir," she said, with a half smile. "Only don't let my husband catch you."

"Catch me?" But she did not respond to the question, only put a finger to her lips, smiled that warm smile once more and then retreated out into the corridor, closing the door behind her. Had I not been so preoccupied I might have meditated more thoroughly on this peculiar exchange, but as it was, I was too much consumed with the tasks that lay ahead of me.

Despite my recent scare, the coming of morning and the two breakfasts had restored some strength in me and I was resolved that I should spend that night in my mother's house after all. I finished my breakfast, made the bed and then, once I had descended the stairs, settled up affairs with the landlord. He seemed unduly out of sorts as I forked over the price of my stay and bestowed upon me several hard stares. In fact, so dour was his attitude in general that I found myself compelled to ask him if there was something the matter.

"Oh there's something," he said. "A *little* something."

I stared back at him in incomprehension.

"Don't play dumb with me," he said, slamming the ledger shut and sweeping the assortment of coins into a drawer which he then carefully locked. "I've met your sort before. Up the drainpipe was it? Or did you bring a ladder suited to the purpose."

"I assure you, sir," I said, too confused to be offended by his tone. "I have no idea to what you are referring."

"No," he said, narrowing his eyes at me. "No, I dare say you don't."

"If I have given any offence," I began, but he cut me off before I could continue.

"Get out!" he exclaimed thumping his fist down on the bar. "Be off with you now and don't come back. If it weren't Christmas and if my wife didn't have a heart of fool's gold, I'd have flung you out of here in the small hours, do you hear me?"

I felt that to protest further would have got me nowhere so, in a state of some confusion, I picked up my case and set out into the frozen morning. It was a still day and the snow clouds were clearing now so that the brilliant blue of the sky was unfurling across the white landscape. I had several small matters to attend to before the funeral and I went about the tasks without relish. Principally my time was absorbed in conversation with the solicitor who was a remarkably tedious man. He insisted upon reading the entire testament in full and in pausing every other word to provide explanations and definitions that were more than unnecessary. To my surprise, I discovered that my mother' natural thrift and caution had grown her little fortune quite considerably over the years, for other than the doctor's fees, she had not touched any of the salary that I had sent her from my time with Lowe. I should perhaps have thought twice about taking possession of these funds, were it not for the fact that my mother had intended them to come to me as a gift. The goodness and selflessness of this gesture, to my mind, purged the money of its iniquitous past.

"It will no doubt prove useful to you and your good wife," said Olman, the solicitor when he detailed the final amount.

"I am not married, sir," I said.

He looked oddly taken aback at this and I assumed that my mother must somehow have confused him in her remembrances of me. He stood and walked to the window, gazing down into the street below.

"You are quite sure of that?" he said, in the same reproachful sort of tone that the innkeeper had used less than an hour before.

"Quite sure, sir," I said.

"And no children?"

"No, sir," I said, rather indignantly.

"Forgive me, Mr Fairlea," he said, evidently sensing my discomfort. "Forgive me — but I had gotten a different impression."

"From whom?" I asked, determined to establish the source of these rumours, but my luck was clearly out for the man simply brushed the matter away with a laugh.

"Oh, it is of no consequence, Mr Fairlea," he said, jovially. "Just a simple misunderstanding."

The matter was not raised again as we proceeded to discuss various other small bequests to members of the village, all of which I undertook to execute within the week. I was glad to be out of his office, for the man himself had reminded me of Crane and the whole atmosphere of the place was reminiscent of my former home in Victoria. I had intended to go straight to the house after that and spend some time there before the funeral, but something in me refused to tread that path until it was absolutely necessary and so I passed two idle hours wandering the backroads of the village and reacquainting myself with long-forgotten childhood memories.

My mother, being an efficient sort of a woman, had made all the necessary arrangements long before her death so that by the time I arrived at the church that afternoon and watched the undertakers carrying in her casket, I began to feel more a distant relation than I did her son. As the priest droned on with the mechanical process of the funeral service, I recalled, with no small degree of sadness, how little I had known about her. She had been my mother — and yet she had also been her own person. Of the first of these I knew something, of the second, nothing at all. The service was mercifully short, but still tedious. The vicar, whose proficiencies lay rather in the arts of conversion than in the comforting of the bereaved, made no secret of the fact that this irritating last rite was a sombre interruption in an otherwise joyful day. My only solace, as he rattled through the liturgy, was that mother had always considered him a fool and viewed attendance at his services as a personal act of penance.

The whole thing felt fully infantile or perhaps even primitive. I, who had experienced so much of a world beyond our own, listened to the clumsy fumblings of this cleric with deep scepticism and contempt. In fact, it was my rising anger at the confidence with which he made pronouncements about something of which, I was convinced, he knew nothing, that caused me to notice that I was not — as I had thought — the sole mourner. There was a woman, veiled and dressed all in black, but extravagantly so, as if she were a character in a melodrama. The particulars of her appearance were not easily appreciable, but I judged from her bearing that she was younger than myself — though not by a great margin. I had not seen her at first because she had positioned herself right at the back of the church and then, when we had proceeded to the graveside, she stood a way off from me, as if she didn't wish to be seen.

At length, the business was over and the priest had hurried off to some happier duty, leaving the gravediggers to the more earthly labours of the day. I stood and watched them for some time in quiet contemplation. The winter sun had now sunk low against the horizon and the cold of the air began to sting my cheeks as several pinpricks of starlight became visible overhead. I turned away from the grave then and began the slow walk home. I had hoped to catch up with the woman, to ask her how she had known my mother and perhaps even to share a drink with me and a reminiscence if she could spare the time, but when I looked for her I found that she was long gone.

My feet led me, almost of their own accord, to the house of my mother. I stood at the gate for a moment, wondering how it would feel to enter the house without her powerful presence. She had not been an overbearing woman, my mother, not the sort of dragon that I'd heard my companions talk about in my army days. She had had a quiet, calm authority about her. I took out the old black key from my pocket, and having slid it into the lock, pushed open the door amid squeals of protest from the cold hinges. The whole place was bereft of light and heat and it seemed, if possible, colder inside than it had been on the street a few moments before. Everything was quite the same inside as it always had been and yet all was different. There were the pictures and the portraits hanging in the hall and the coats and hats on the stand. It was as if the place had frozen itself in time at the moment of her passing.

I went further in, leaving the door open behind me. I did not wish, you see, to be trapped in the place should I wish to leave. I had a horror — and one I knew to be quite irrational — that the door would close on me and I should be incarcerated amid the memories. I went into the sitting room and saw the chair where she used to sit and my father's photograph on the mantelpiece. This I took up in my hands and looked upon it as I had often done when I had been younger. I studied his face for a likeness — but aside from a slight curve at the end of the nose, I could find nothing to bind me to him.

I was just placing the picture back upon the shelf when I saw a movement in the glass, a swift and sudden movement that was as silent as it was deadly. By some instinct I swung around and ducked to the left and the hand bearing the knife swung down harmlessly into the stone of the mantelpiece unleashing a spurt of sparks into the room. It was too dark to see my assailant clearly, but I knew without further investigation that it was the woman from the funeral.

I had no time to collect my thoughts, before I had regained my footing she struck out at me again and the blade grazed my cheek. This time, however, I was alert to her strike and able to capitalise upon it. Reaching up with my hand I took hold of the arm that held the knife and dragged her down as hard as I could so that she lost her footing and fell headlong against the chair. Pressing my advantage, I maintained my grip on her forearm and drew it up hard behind her back so that with a further twist I might break it.

"Stop," she cried, panting. "Stop, I beg you."

I knew the voice; it was a voice I had longed for at one time.

It was the voice of a woman I had loved.

"Molly?"

"Stop, please, George," she cried, the agony spilling into her voice. "You're hurting me!"

"Drop the knife," I said, without emotion. "Drop it."

The knife dropped onto the wooden boards with a heavy thud and I kicked it away with my foot. "I'm going to light the lamp," I said. "Don't move."

She said nothing, but she did not struggle when I released her, and after a few moments, I had lit the lamp and she had pulled back her veil.

"It was Lowe," she cowered.

"Lowe?"

"He made me follow you, told me to kill you!"

This made no sense to me at all. Lowe had been supremely confident when I had left him. There was no question of my going to the police, he knew that — he knew I was too ashamed of my share in all we had done to discuss it with anyone else.

"Why would Lowe want me dead?"

"He doesn't believe you'll keep the secret," she panted. There was something desperate in her — something dangerous that I could not bring myself to trust.

"And what do you know about the secret?" I asked. "How much has he told you?"

Her face flickered for a moment and I saw something etched there for a fraction of a second, something that looked like conceit, but then she affected the demeanour of the poor misused woman once more.

"Oh, I don't know, I don't know, George," she said. "He says a lot of strange things — he's mad — he's dangerous, he threatens me." The desperation was growing in her and I was sure I could see her beginning to tense up — though to what end I could not fathom.

"Why send you to kill me?" I asked. "He's not shy of doing that sort of thing himself — indeed he might have done it in London! But why send you?"

The mask finally fell from her face — she could maintain the pretence no longer. Suddenly the whole thing became abundantly and terrifyingly clear.

"But he didn't send you," I said, slowly. "Did he?"

"I don't need him," she spat.

"You came here to kill me — to bind me to you — to use me like Lowe has used Lizzie!" It was all so obvious now that I cursed myself for not having seen it sooner. She had not only been Lowe's lover, she had been his pupil. Of course he had taken on two of us — of course he had! Why would he not — he wasn't the sort of fellow who believed in taking chances. I had disappointed him, but she had not. We had been in competition from the outset. Whichever of us turned out the stronger would be worked upon to dispose of the weaker and in doing so create a replacement for Lizzie. It was a perfect scheme, and though I hated myself for it, I could not help but feel admiration for the man's foresight.

"He's using you," I said. "Don't you see?"

She stared at me for a few seconds, unblinking.

"He'll have you kill me and then he'll make you use me for his own ends — you mark my words! You think you'll be free of him, but you won't. He's too strong for you."

She continued to stare at me blankly. I moved close to her and extended my hand to help her to her feet. She did not take it, but just sat there, breathing heavily.

"He would have had me kill you if I had stayed," I said. "You

251

know that."

Her pride, her resolve — her confidence. All of it seemed, in this moment, to crumple and fade and I recalled that moment at the ball when she had first laid her head upon my chest.

"Oh George," she said, feebly. "Oh George, I'm so lost."

In that instant I forgave her everything, her deception, the attempt on my life — everything. Here was a young woman in need of nurture and care. Here was a young woman for whom I — even I in my disfigurement — could provide. I offered her my good hand again and she took it, rising to her feet. I cupped her face with it and tried to pour all the kindness and goodness of my soul into her eyes. Then, drawing her close to me, I embraced her. It was an embrace that held the promise of a future. In my mind I saw us limping on together; we two who had been so wounded by Lowe. We would find solace in each other's understanding of the experience; we would be bound by our loathing of the very man who had sought to separate us.

The second blade swung through the air so fast and so silently that it was almost the end of me. As it was, I caught it almost too late and it plunged deep into my shoulder.

"So unbearably predictable," she cried in triumph. "Can't resist a damsel in distress, can you George?" She pulled the knife from the wound and drew it back for a second strike.

I do not remember clearly what followed — though I have tried many times to understand it and wished with all my heart to undo it. The memories I have are blurred and indistinct. The knife falls once again but its flight is arrested as I grab hold of her wrist. Then we are both of us sprawling on the floor, rolling back and forward with that lethal blade pointed always against my neck. Then she throws me upon my back — for she has the advantage of both her arms. Then the knife is coming nearer to my neck:

252

nearer and nearer. But then in my recollection, something strange happens. A strength, from I know not where, seems to rise though me, and by each painful fraction of an inch the knife is turned back upon my assailant. I can recall her eyes widening and her lips parting in a scream that echoes throughout the house and is taken up through the village by shouts and the sounds of running feet. Then there is a hammering on the door — hard and fast — and I do not respond. Then it comes again, harder and harder until there is an ear-shattering splintering of wood and a tinkling of glass and the room is suddenly alive and alight and I am being dragged to my feet and there are more screams and questions are being fired at me and I cannot hear them.

I cannot hear them because I am looking down at a body, a pathetic lifeless corpse.

I cannot hear them because it is only now that I have understood the true genius of Percival Lowe.

CHAPTER FIFTEEN

It took him a shorter time to come to me than I had imagined.

I knew he would, of course; the pattern of his behaviour after Lizzie's murder told me that if nothing else. There was a need in him — a deep-seated, urgent requirement — to revisit the crime in its immediate aftermath. That was why he had called upon Samuel Ivor at the time of the funeral and that was why I knew he should come to me now. I had thought, however, that the security of the place in which I now found myself and the complications of my constant surveillance might in some way impede his progress, but when I saw that familiar figure striding confidently down the gantry toward my cell, I smiled at my own foolishness. Where was the prison in England into which Percival Lowe might not easily enter? Where was the prison guard whose mother or sister or daughter or niece had not been salvaged from the terrors of some unthinkable demon by the services of his establishment? How splendid was the architecture of this scheme! How naive its victim!

"George," he nodded to me as he entered. The guard shut the door behind him and then dropped away into the shadows, evidently by prior arrangement. Lowe pulled up a rough wooden stool that I had placed beneath the meagre window in the hopes of standing upon it to look out. He dusted it off and then sat down upon it. "George, George, George!" he said, shaking his head and chuckling to himself. It was not a conversation. He looked at me now not as colleague or friend, but as if I were some sort of specimen in a glass tank. I said nothing.

Leaning back on the stool, Lowe reached a hand down into the breast pocket of his coat and removed from it an envelope. It looked worn and tired — as if it had been studied many times. From within it he drew an equally fatigued piece of paper. Unfolding it delicately, he held it out to me.

"This," he said, with smug pride as he shook the letter aloft. "This is, I believe, the source of all your woes!"

Though it would be a lie to say my curiosity was not piqued by this pronouncement, I refused to give him the satisfaction of seeing it. Fixing my gaze firmly on the floor, I said nothing. Whether he was deflated by this or not I could not ascertain for, with a flourish he held the piece of paper out before his face and began at once to read.

"Dear Mr Lowe," it began. *"I write to you regarding your correspondence of the January in this year which, I must tell you, I considered to be of a most unusual nature. I had, for some months, put any consideration of your request quite out of my mind, finding it impossible to believe that you were quite serious in what you were asking or indeed that I should chance across any such individual. Nonetheless, this last fortnight I have made the acquaintance of a fellow who fits your description precisely and who may prove to be of use to you for whatever purposes you have in mind.*

"He is seriously wounded — he has lost a hand — but not so seriously as to be entirely dependent. It is doubtful that they will find a use for him again on the frontline and I understand from him that he is likely to face destitution if they cannot do so. Thus, your first two criteria — that the man should be wounded and desperate — are easily answered. Your requirement that he

255

should be without living relative is perhaps not so easily settled — for though he has no father, brother or sister surviving, his mother lives (though I am given to suspect that she is long into her dotage and may perhaps have deceased at the time of your reading this letter).

"The final condition that you laid down — that though being a 'man of extraordinary valour he must also be capable of acts of extreme violence' was my stumbling block until just these two nights past. Our camp is now no great distance from the frontier and a party of Boers came raiding just after midnight. One of them came at him in his tent and he woke to find the barbarian seizing him by the throat. It being that he only had one hand, you might have thought him at a fatal disadvantage — but you would have been quite wrong (as was I). For he wrestled the demon off him single-handed and it started to beat a hasty retreat. Then the most curious thing happened. A haze of sorts seems to have descended upon our man and instead of letting go, he held on to its leg and dragged it back. Then, throwing it onto the ground he climbed upon its chest, and with his one good hand, tore the life from the creature's throat with his very fingers.

"As soon as I saw it I knew I must write to you and inform you of what had transpired. In Mr George Fairlea, I think you have a man who will fit your purposes magnificently well. For a small consideration I would be delighted to send him to you.

Yours faithfully, Doctor Henry Stubbs."

"I got you at a bargain price, as it happens," said Lowe, folding up the paper and putting it away again in the envelope which he tucked back into his breast pocket. "Twenty pounds was all he asked — and twenty pounds was all I sent him."

I eyed him fiercely, but he was immune to any sense of

betrayal. I was a commodity, purchased for the function I was soon to fulfil.

"There never were two pupils, you see," he went on. "In fact, there was never really one."

I looked up from the floor and fixed him with a glare. "It was only ever about you, wasn't it?"

"Naturally," said Lowe. He looked puzzled as if my incomprehension of what he had done was illogical or foolish. "Though I won't say that it wasn't useful for a time to have you about, George — and I won't say that there didn't come a moment — just a *moment*, mind — when I considered a change of plans. That business with the car and the young girl — I saw for a moment a possible fruitful deviation — but it all came to nothing and Lizzie was growing too strong, George — far too strong!" He stretched a hand idly back above his head and began to pick at the loose plaster of the wall. "And there was so much already in place — it would have been so tedious to unravel it all."

"So my life is to be the price of your idleness?"

"Not your life, George," he said, with a smirk. "I think we know it goes well beyond that."

"And Molly?"

"Oh, she was never a serious prospect, George — have some sense! She was useful as a watcher on your tail for certain, but a woman? In this line of work? She'd never have had the nerve!"

"She had nerve enough when I last saw her," I said, bitterly.

"Oh, but that's not the same thing," said Lowe in tones of conciliation. "Anyone can kill a man — or try to. But to do what I do, Fairlea — what we do — it takes a different sort of courage; you know that."

"And what if she had killed me?"

Lowe tapped the pocket wherein lay the letter. "There was never any real possibility of that, not knowing what I knew."

"But you couldn't have been completely sure?"

"It would have made very little difference."

"Very little difference?" I could no longer keep my anger in check. "It would have been the difference between her life and her death!"

"You misunderstand me," he said. "I mean to say that it would have made very little difference to my scheme — for you see, had she killed you, she would have done so at *my* provocation! On the strength of *my* suggestion and instruction! By all the laws that govern these circumstances I would have been responsible for your death and your spirit would have passed into my custody just as it will now."

"But what about Molly?"

"You forget that only the innocent linger," said Lowe, quietly. "Molly was hardly that, besides which I had not taken pains to discover an anchor for her."

"Neither do you have one for me!"

He smiled at me in pity and shook his head. "I have purchased your mother's house, George," he said. "Within that place any number of items will suffice for the purpose — especially with your grief being quite so fresh."

"And am I then, innocent?"

Lowe cocked his head at me. "It remains to be seen," he said, thoughtfully. "It is my contention that you have committed no act that has not been the result of provocation or self-defence. Indeed, your decision to leave my service in spite of the attractions of the remuneration with which I had plied you, despite my pleading with you, provides suitable evidence that you stand a good chance."

258

He had discoursed on the matter as if it were some intriguing philosophical nugget.

There was a long silence. The other prisoners must have gone to the yard for exercise for there was a strange tranquillity about the prison in that moment that was somehow at-odds with its function.

"Are they treating you well, George?" Lowe asked — and I believe he meant it. On my arrival the governor had given me to understand that a benefactor had arranged for me to enjoy one of the less disgusting cells and for my food to be brought in from a local kitchen at a quality inexpressibly higher than the traditional prison fodder.

"They tell me," he said, when I gave no response, "that the *event* is scheduled for Friday. Is that correct?"

I nodded. He already knew. He would have been the first to know.

"From what I can glean," he said in a tone of reassurance, "the passing itself is relatively painless."

This was not what I had been given to believe. Other inmates had taken every opportunity to taunt me with talk of my imminent execution. Delighting in spinning me tails of hangings that had gone wrong or been unduly elongated or simply to list for me the catastrophic effects my body could expect to experience when it happened.

"I will fight you," I said, in a low voice. "I will fight you in everything."

Again, that pitying smile slid across that self-satisfied face. "Oh George," he said. "You will not remember, and even if you should remember something of your death your anger will be directed against your executioners — I will not feature. That, you see, George, is the beauty of this scheme! It is for that very reason that I have gone to such extraordinary lengths."

"I couldn't die by your hand," I said, voicing the conclusion I had reached on the night of Molly's death. "You had to be responsible for my death — but not actually carry out my murder."

"Correct," he said, in agreement. "That was the problem with Giovanni — oh don't tell me you hadn't fathomed out I killed that Italian Casanova; he was my first. He didn't remember anything about his life, but he remembered his death and he fought me — my goodness he fought me — almost flung me from the ship when I was returning to England. I resolved to get rid of him and find a younger substitute. I cast his anchor — a little bible given him by his lover — from the docks at Southampton and set about my quest to discover a child."

"Lizzie remembered you, too," I said.

"Alas, yes," he said forlornly. "I reasoned out the truth of the matter too late. For three or four years she obeyed me meekly and without question. But as time went on she formed a clearer and clearer memory and it became apparent to me that I must find a new specimen — and this time I must let the business of killing be conducted by someone other than myself."

"And who better than the public executioner," I said, drily.

"Who indeed?" said he, absorbing my statement as a compliment. "I had been too close — you see. Too close to Giovanni, too close to the girl. Even had Molly succeeded in killing you it would have been only a matter of time before your spirit charted its way back to me. That would have been a most undesirable outcome. Wouldn't you agree?"

"Why are you here, Lowe?" I asked him, suddenly and directly. "What do you want?"

"Nothing," he said, throwing his palms out wide. "Only to

say that I am sorry that matters have come to such a pass between us."

"I don't believe you," I said simply.

"I beg your pardon?"

"I said: I don't believe you."

He seemed to stiffen, troubled by my new-found confidence.

"Well if you must know," he blustered, after a slight pause. "I came here by way of celebrating my success; to see the plan to fruition, as it were."

"You are lying, Percival."

"I'm not sure I comprehend you, George," he said with a patronising smile. "Perhaps the prison air has addled your mind."

"I am quite in my right mind," I declared, calmly. "You have come here for the same reason you returned to the house of Samuel Ivor."

"And what reason was that?"

"Remorse. Guilt. Anguish. Call it what you will, but you cannot escape your own feelings on the matter."

"What utter rot!" he spat. "You hold all too lofty an opinion of yourself, George! You think I'd come here out of sympathy for a man like you — a man whose passing will be mourned by no one? A man who shall be missed by no single person on this pitiable planet?"

"And yet you are still here."

The ice of my tone hung in the air between us for several moments and I fixed my eyes upon his until the intensity of my gaze caused him to turn away.

"I should be going," he said, brusquely. He rose and turned to leave.

"Your confidence in your own reasoning is absolute then?" I asked, innocently enough. He turned back towards me, puzzled, but then gave a single stiff nod.

"What a pity," I murmured.

"What's that?" He was rattled now, I could tell. He took a step back towards me.

"It's only that I think in all your planning you have overlooked one small yet fundamental detail."

"Which is what?"

I stood. "Goodbye, Mr Lowe."

For a moment incredulity flitted across his face, but it was soon replaced by an expression of unutterable horror. For, at the moment of my rising the room had been filled with an all-too familiar sound of the crackling of ice and within a very few moments, the floor and walls were covered in a bright white frost. Lowe backed towards the door, terror in his eyes.

"That's not possible," he stammered.

"I'm afraid it is all quite possible," said I, advancing upon him. "I realised it some weeks ago, the night I spent in the inn when I dared not return to my mother's house. I didn't understand it at first, but then it all began to make sense. Lizzie Ivor is very much still with us, Mr Lowe."

"But," he declared, his voice now coloured by outrage as much as fear. "The anchor was destroyed! I saw it go under the wheels of that train — you saw it!"

"Indeed I did," I agreed. "Lizzie's bracelet can no longer be used to command her, that much is clear."

"Then — how?"

"Simple logic, Mr Lowe," I declared with a smile. In spite of what I knew must now unfold I couldn't help but enjoy this moment of denunciation. "Simple logic dictates that she made a new one — did she not?"

"But that is not possible — there was no object to which she could have become attached."

"Indeed there was not."

"Then how?"

"Did it never trouble you, Mr Lowe," I said, "that a man of my limitations," and here I raised up the stump of my hand, "should become so accomplished at the piano so very quickly?"

Lowe was in a lather of panic — he thrust around in his mind for a logical release from the position in which he now found himself. "Then," his eyes widened suddenly in great alarm.

"Yes," I said, advancing so that I looked him full in the face. "I am the anchor."

"That's not possible," he repeated over and over again until he became almost insensible in his babbling. I took a step back as the frost crept up the iron bars of the prison wall behind him. The ice seemed to pull at the metal and distort it until suddenly, with an alarming, wrenching, clanging rattle, two of the bars fell from their place and clattered to the stone floor.

"Goodbye, Mr Lowe," I said again to the man who stood before me, immobile. "I trust you will have a speedy journey on."

I stepped past him, out of the cell and into the corridor beyond. Then, as an afterthought, I turned. "From what I can glean," I said. "The passing itself is relatively painless."

I did not stay to look upon him, to see the death-frost slide quickly up his legs and over his knees, his waist, his chest until at last it touched his face and fixed that horrifying expression of shock permanently upon it. But I did hear a sound like the tinkling of glass as his frozen body shattered into a million meaningless fragments on the hard stone floor.

Printed in Great Britain
by Amazon